VIOLENCE

BOOKS BY RICHARD BAUSCH

Real Presence, 1980

Take Me Back, 1981

The Last Good Time, 1984

Spirits and Other Stories, 1987

Mr. Field's Daughter, 1989

*The Fireman's Wife
and Other Stories*, 1990

Violence, 1992

VIOLENCE

Richard Bausch

HOUGHTON MIFFLIN / SEYMOUR LAWRENCE

Boston • New York • London 1992

Copyright © 1992 by Richard Bausch

ALL RIGHTS RESERVED

For information about permission to reproduce selections
from this book, write to Permissions, Houghton Mifflin Company,
215 Park Avenue South, New York, New York 10003.

Library of Congress Cataloging-in-Publication Data

Bausch, Richard, date.
Violence / Richard Bausch.
p.   cm.
ISBN 0-395-59509-6
I. Title.
PS3552.A846V5   1992   91-31419
813'.54 — dc20   CIP

Printed in the United States of America

The author is grateful for permission to reprint lines from
"In a Dark Time," copyright © 1960 by Beatrice Roethke,
Administratrix of the Estate of Theodore Roethke, from *The
Collected Poems of Theodore Roethke* by Theodore Roethke.
Used by permission of Doubleday, a division of Bantam
Doubleday Dell Publishing Group, Inc.

Always, for Karen

What's madness but nobility of soul
At odds with circumstance? The day's on fire!
I know the purity of pure despair,
My shadow pinned against a sweating wall.
That place among the rocks — is it a cave
Or winding path? The edge is what I have.

A steady storm of correspondences! —
A night flowing with birds, a ragged moon,
And in broad day the midnight come again!
A man goes far to find out what he is —

— Theodore Roethke,
In a Dark Time

VIOLENCE

THE DAY after Christmas, they set out for Chicago to visit his mother. It had snowed off and on all week, but the roads were dry. The small plowed ash-colored banks on either side were crusted over, and some of the cars that passed them still had snow on the roofs. Now and again as a car went by, feathery clods of the dry snow blew into the air, exploding onto the surface of the road, looking like stones breaking up.

There wasn't much traffic. They drove all day, toward a lowering wall of clouds, into a fine mist, and they did not exchange more than a few words — talk of the weather, the slow trucks on the curves in the mountains, the occasional panorama of fog-patched Appalachian range, a view of farms with their snow-dusted shade trees and their silos and paint-peeling barns. Beyond this mild remarking of what was out the windows of the little car, their conversation was marred by long silences, and Connally knew this trip was only a form of running away.

Now and then he glanced at his wife, who sat with her hands in her lap, gazing out at the far shapes of hills and houses. She seemed content. At one point, she turned the dial of the radio, looking for something to listen to. He watched the road, aware of the miles rolling away in the distances behind them, like a series of irretrievable actions, with consequences.

They stopped for gas, and something to eat, and then went on, past sundown, into the hours of the night.

He had been the one worried about money.

To begin with, they were going to have to stay in a motel, because his mother had no room for them in the small one-bedroom apartment where she lived — a retirement complex on Lake Shore Drive called Leisure Village. Since they couldn't afford any of the hotels closer in, they would have to remain outside the city. The whole thing was absurd, and yet they had departed Virginia this morning in a bone-cold, predawn wind, like people compelled by powerful circumstance — refugees, or fugitives.

"I guess we ought to check in at a motel before we go see her," he said, now.

"Whatever."

"It's late," he said. "We'd just have to turn around and come back."

"We pick up an hour, remember."

"It's still late, Carol."

"I'm willing to stop."

Since her discovery that she was pregnant he'd been thinking about the journey, dismissing it as impossible — yet feeling the need of time in his mother's society (the residue of a childhood preoccupation, since for long periods of that childhood she had been in some distance or other, always about to arrive). In a way, he was like a kid in trouble wanting to run to the texture and smell of an apron — he was aware of this, and vaguely ashamed of it. He tried not to show it to Carol. But his restlessness was apparent, and at last she had suggested that they make the journey. Out of the blue, she had expressed the wish to meet his mother. "We should've got out there before now," she said. "We could drive out between Christmas and New Year's. I think it would be nice if I met her." Meaning, of course, that since Carol was carrying Tina Connally's grandchild, it was about time the two women got to know each other.

Connally realized that he might've taken any reason, the thinnest pretext, wanting to get out of the house, out of his present life with its daily helping of confusion and worry, and the continual, disheartening feeling that everything had been called into question. He had started college late — this was his junior year — and time was running out. The job market only worsened every day; even with the degree, he knew he would have trouble finding work. They had been living on the meager salary she made as a dental hygienist and on several student loans through the GI Bill.

Finding out she was pregnant had made Carol happy, and at the beginning he had been happy, too, had felt surprise and then pride; he'd thought it was a good thing. But then as she began to talk about what was coming — the changes, and all the work and the shifting of schedules and his school taking a back seat to this new responsibility — he'd grown agitated and uncertain. They'd found themselves close to quarreling in circumstances that had once been easy and comforting, and it seemed that each gesture, each passage in the day, required complex negotiations.

They'd bickered and snapped at each other in the morning, trying to decide what to pack for the trip, and it had put them in this mood, barely speaking, riding on in a tolerant and careful disregard of each other — like an old, bored couple.

Now, he pulled into a motel parking lot.

She said, "Looks deserted. Is this close enough?"

"It looks cheap and clean."

"How can you tell it's clean?"

"I guess I can't," he said.

It was a small private establishment — a single row of rooms, each with a little stoop and with white numbers on the doors, which were painted some indeterminate dark shade; the doors looked black in the lamplight. The office was in a low-roofed building, not much bigger than one of those street-vending trucks one finds on city streets. There were red candles in the window, and a wreath. Connally got out of the car, feeling the shock of cold air and mist on his face, and hearing the whoosh and rush of traffic on the interstate. Beyond the motel parking lot was a shopping center with an apartment complex rising behind it like a monolith. There was a faint scattered sparkle in the big shape of the building: Christmas lights. To the right of the motel, down a long hill defined by a ragged hedge and wild grass, a service station and a convenience store, perhaps a hundred yards apart, made two shimmering islands of light in the mist; another apartment building rose out of the cupped shape of the light emanating from the convenience store. Connally took a deep breath, straightening, feeling the stiffness in his legs; the pleasure of stretching them. Some part of his mind reached for the simple tactile comfort of being able to walk, and he thought of going on, past the motel office, into the falling mist beyond the huge shadow of the apartment building. He could hitch a ride and head south, out of the complicated mess of things. *I love my wife,* he thought, as if he were invoking a name in a prayer; and then he was thinking how it was true: he did love her, and in the moment of realizing this, he was sorry about everything, vaguely angry with himself.

Carol opened the window on her side of the car as he walked away from it. "I don't like the look of this place."

"I don't either. But it's as good as we can afford." He crossed the lot and entered the motel office. A little bell dinged above the door. The room was small, neatly arranged — two chairs on one side, opposite a coffee table with magazines stacked on it. There was a chest-high counter along the back, beyond which a doorway led to another room — clothes piled on the table, stacks of newspapers in a corner. Connally stood at the counter, which apparently had recently been polished or laminated, its surface a wine-dark red with lighter places showing through, like stains. On the counter was a pen and a small pad of forms, next to a plaster Nativity scene in sprigs of pine; it looked like something lying in a nest. Connally began to fill out one of the forms, hearing the faint strains of music from a radio. Presently, a teenage-looking boy appeared in the doorway of the next room and squinted at him. "Are you Wilson?"

"We wanted a room," said Connally.

"You're not Wilson."

"No."

"Well shit."

"Do you have a vacancy or not?" Connally said.

The boy approached him. "We were waiting for somebody."

Connally was filling out the form. In the other room someone coughed, a heavy glottal sound, and now an old man stood in the doorway, one hand up to scratch across a dark gray shock of hair. "Is it Wilson?"

"No," the boy said.

"Shit." The man was wearing brown slacks and suspenders over a sleeveless undershirt. The skin of his neck looked as though it had bunched and gathered there through some catastrophe in the face. He walked over to look at Connally, his hooded eyes narrowing. "Good evening, sir. This is my nephew Eddie."

Connally nodded at them both. He did not want introductions.

"Go back to sleep, Uncle Arlen," the boy said.

"Want anything done around here . . ." the man said, turning, shuffling back out of view.

"Twelve dollars for a single," the boy said.

"How far is it into the city?" Connally asked.

"Eleven miles more on the interstate. But the prices go up quick."

"How much for a double?"

"Sixteen dollars."

"Do you have a weekly rate?"

The boy called out. "Uncle Arlen. What about weekly?"

"Give it to him," came the answer. "You don't know the goddam rates by now?"

"You said you wanted to handle any weekly rentals."

From the other room came the cough again, apparently a dismissal by the old man.

"Sixty dollars single, eighty double."

"I'll take a single."

"We're supposed to have TV in the rooms," the boy said. "Something's wrong with the dish, I guess." His hair was matted and curled around the borders of his face, and he looked almost angelic, smiling apologetically, leaning his elbows on the counter and gazing at Connally.

"Are the telephones working?" Connally wanted to know.

"Far as I can tell."

He paid in cash.

"Our television reception's screwed," the boy said, handing him a room key. "We thought maybe you were the guy to fix it."

"I can't fix anything," said Connally.

Outside, he saw Carol framed in the window of the car, watching him. The expression on her face of concern, of unhappy attention, made him heartsick. He got in behind the wheel and handed her the key. "A week of bargain-basement luxury," he said, then leaned over and kissed her on the cheek.

"How much?"

He told her.

She held the key up and squinted at it. "Room five."

He backed the car around and turned, went slowly down the row to the door with a white 5 fixed to it. She was quiet, holding the key in her small fist. When he cut the ignition she sighed. "Okay?" he said.

"Tired."

He chose to accept this, though he'd heard the note of sufferance in it: she did not like what she saw; the dark motel room door with the number 5 hanging crooked on it. He let her go in first, stood for a moment in the entrance as she turned a light on and regarded the place. It had the look of something that had wilted under dry, bright lights. There was a bed, one nightstand, a bureau with a television bolted to it. The walls were decorated with a pattern that had faded, and looked like smudges. The heavy drapes over the window were perhaps a foot too long; they seemed to express somehow the room's dilapidated, slovenly appearance, like someone in a suit three sizes too big.

"What's that smell?" Carol said. "It smells like gas. Isn't that gas?"

He went in and closed the door, breathed, watching her move around the room as if looking for something. "I don't smell anything," he said. "Maybe a little cleanser."

"No. It's gas. Don't light anything."

"It's not gas, Carol. Here, I'm opening the window."

But the window wouldn't open; it was sealed shut.

"I don't smell it in here," she said from the bathroom. He dialed his mother's number.

"Yes?"

"Tina Connally, please."

"It's me, Charles. I've been waiting for you to call. Where are you?"

He told her.

"That's a little ways out, isn't it?" The deep rasping sound of her voice surprised him.

"We're fine," he said.

"All right. You're the one who has to drive it."

"Should we come ahead tonight?" he wanted to know.

"Oh, Charles — I don't have the energy I used to."

"We'll come out in the morning."

"It's almost midnight, sweetie."

"We'll see you in the morning," he said.

A moment later, he opened the room door and let the cold air come rushing at him from the dark, from all the noise of the highway. The mist was turning into drizzle; you could see it in the lights of the motel sign. Across the way, in the electric candle–lighted window of the office, he saw the boy leaning on the counter, being talked to by the old man. The old man was waving his arms and being emphatic about something.

"The gas smell's not as strong now," Carol said behind him. She had come from the bathroom, was leaning over the heating unit. He thought he could see the swelling in her hips and thighs, though it was still too early for her to be showing. When she straightened, she seemed to totter a moment. "I guess it's all right."

"We don't have the money for anyplace else," he said, closing the door. "We don't really even have the money for this." He had meant it as a joke.

"We'll make it." She smiled. "I wonder how old this place is," she said. "Now it smells musty."

"Why don't you stop thinking about what everything smells like. Why don't you turn your nose off for a while."

She stared at him.

"A little joke," he said. "I'm sorry."

She made as if to shrug her irritation aside.

Together, they pulled the spread and blanket back on the bed. The sheets looked faintly gray, and there was a sewn patch on what would be his side.

"God," she said. "Certainly clean-looking."

"Well," he told her, "it *is* clean. These are old and thin, and the mattress shows through a little, that's all. It's only a few nights, right?"

She got out of her coat, began unbuttoning her blouse. Her demeanor was dismissive now, as if she meant to forget he was in the room with her. He undressed, went into the bathroom, and drank from the tap. The water tasted of rust.

"Something's wrong with the television," she said when he came to his side of the bed.

"I'm going to sleep," he told her.

"Are we paying the full rate for the room?"

"Carol," he said. "For Christ's sake."

"Did they charge us the full rate?"

"I don't know whether they did or not. I guess they didn't. If you're so worried about it go ask them."

She said nothing for a few minutes. He was lying there in the dark, listening to the sound of her breathing — the subtle agitation in it of her worry and her unhappiness. "Charles?" she said. "What's wrong with us?"

"Oh, please," he said.

Again, she was quiet. In the next moment, she touched his shoulder. He did not move, found that he could not bring himself to move.

"Honey?"

"I just want to sleep," he said.

She moved, turned so that her back was to him. He felt the slightest movement of her shoulders.

"Carol," he said. "Are you cold?"

"No."

"What's wrong? You're shivering."

"Nothing." It dawned on him that she was crying.

"Carol, I've been driving for fourteen hours cooped up in that Honda like a sardine. I mean — what is it?"

"Just go to sleep," she said.

He arranged himself, tried to get comfortable. This was not going to do any good, coming to Chicago; it wouldn't help at all. And perhaps whatever he had thought might make him recognize her again was far from this room or any room. In the dark, hearing her muffled sobs, he remembered that her moods were subject to sharp swings; it was all a part of the new situation. But he was exhausted now, and irritable, and he had to resist the urge to wrench himself out of proximity with her.

"Carol," he said, "I'm nervous about everything too, you know."

She said nothing.

"It makes us short with each other, okay?"

"I don't want to talk now."

He lay quite still, feeling the heat of anger in his face and neck. It seemed to him now that this had been her reaction whenever he tried to introduce the subject of what was troubling him. They had both talked about the lack of money, about the worsening job market, the difficulty moving a family, of looking for another place to live — and even so, she had kept this carapace of imperceptiveness, protecting herself.

Yet part of his frustration now was that he had been so far unable to state simply that he didn't want the baby. He had been unable to admit it to himself, in fact. The thought caused a fluttering in his stomach.

"I can't relax," she said.

He waited.

"Charles?"

He breathed slowly, feigning sleep. A moment later, with

an abrupt little sigh of abdication, she left the bed and went into the bathroom. He sat up, looked at the thin line of light under the door, hearing water running in the tub, and then he was up, too — pacing. When he peered out the window, he saw that there was sleet in the mist now.

"Carol," he said, hurrying to the bathroom door. "Carol."

The water stopped running. "What."

"It's sleeting, honey. I don't want to get snowed in here. We can't get snowed in here."

"I'm not going anywhere," she said. "Go to sleep."

"Did you hear me?" he said. "It's going to snow. We have to get closer in to the city."

"I don't want to drive at night when you haven't had any sleep."

"I'm not sleepy," he said.

She didn't answer. He heard the little plashing sound of her bathing, and tried to open the door. It was locked.

"Carol," he said.

"Please go back to sleep, Charles."

"Open the door," he told her.

"Charles, I'm not going anywhere."

He moved across the room, feeling an unreasonable surge of anger, his whole body tensed, as if to resist some force traveling toward him out of the dark. This was not right, this feeling of wanting to hit something. He sat on the bed and put his hands to his face, ran them through his hair. It was impossible to sit still. Finally he opened the room door again and stood in that cold column of air, trying to calm himself. But the sleet was rattling on the pavement and he felt all the more the need to get out of the motel and closer to the city, perhaps within walking distance of the subway, before everything turned to ice and snow.

He returned to the bathroom door. "Carol," he said, "I'm leaving in five minutes. Come on now, really. We have to."

Nothing, not even the sound of the water now.

"I'm serious," he said.

"Charles, stop it. Go to bed."

"I'm telling you I'm leaving in five minutes. Less than five minutes now."

She said something he couldn't understand.

"I can't hear you."

"I said, 'You go ahead if that's what you want.' "

"You don't think I will?"

Again he couldn't understand her answer. "Will you open the fucking door?"

"I'm in the tub. I'm taking a bath. I'm not going to be ready to go in five minutes. I *couldn't* be. So I guess you've got your mind made up to leave me here, Charles."

Now he could hear that she was crying again.

"Jesus Christ," he said. "Just get ready and let's go."

Nothing.

"Carol," he said.

"All *right*," she said. "I'm getting out now. But I'm not going anywhere."

He put his clothes on, looked at the room, the bed with its sewn sheet, the dull pastels on the wall — of horses in a pasture, birds on a branch, elk on the bluffs of a painted mountain. He looked at the clutter of clothes and the overnight bag on the bureau, and the bureau itself with its marks in the fake-wood surface, and the wide, dull continents of stain in the rug, and something under his heart moved as if to cause him to begin tearing the place apart. At that moment, he might have blithely watched any human catastrophe.

•

These two had been married almost three years, and had been living in a small frame house on Grandville Avenue just north of the Old Town section of Point Royal, Virginia. The windows of the house looked out on the street, one of the busiest in the area, and though they had worried about having to make their home in such a small, run-down place so close to a main thoroughfare (the house was really built around what had once been an outpost for hunters, back in the days when that part of Virginia was all woods and wildlife), the constant soughing rush of traffic had turned out to be soothing to them both, like the rhythmic, tidal music of a shoreline. And there were other things they liked about it: the large flagstone fireplace in the living room (neither of them had ever lived in a house with a fireplace before); the tall, graceful oaks and black locusts in the back yard; and the screened side porch, with its pleasant view of the soft blue peaks of the mountains west, its peaceful-feeling, verdurous twilights, full of the singing of birds in the high branches of the trees, the drowsy susurration of breezes in the leaves. The rent was low, and while the roof leaked when it rained hard enough, they could think of the place as being cozy and warm, the right place for their loving. They had fallen into a pattern of life there: she driving to work at Dr. Wilder's office each morning, and Connally walking the short mile to school. He had entertained the hope that he might one day teach history, perhaps on the college level. He'd thought they might manage this mild poverty long enough for him to get the advanced degree. Carol had insisted that he finish the undergraduate program at least, and after that, they could see. They both wanted children. Neither of them wanted to wait too long. Connally had lost the years in the Air Force, and she had spent three years avoiding most contact with men, after having suffered through a bad youthful marriage to a heavy-handed, clumsy, casually brutal young man who had mostly troubled and frightened her. The young man, whose name was Martin, was living in

San Diego now, at the big naval base there, and occasionally he sent cards to Carol or called her on the phone: he wanted to keep in touch, he told her, out of friendship.

Last year when he was in town seeing his father, he insisted on taking Connally and Carol out to dinner. It seemed important that Carol know he was happy, that the divorce hadn't left any lasting marks on him. He picked them up in his new Cherokee, and took them for a spin through the mountains to the west, then brought them to a newly opened supper club in Arlington, within sight of the bronze travail of the Iwo Jima Memorial with its lighted flag and its backdrop of the temples of democracy making their double image in the glassy smoothness of the Potomac. Everything was friendly and boisterous. He talked and joked, and told stories about having joined the Marines, ordering the drinks and insisting loudly on paying for everything. Clearly he was the sort of person who thought himself funnier than he ever truly was, and whose own voice provided him with a source of continual satisfaction. He had a way of saying very familiar things and then laughing hard, slapping his knees and staring, as if to gaze upon the reaction about which he had apparently never been brought to the point of doubt: people laughed out of sheer discomfort, and he interpreted this as the result of his charm and wit.

"Well," he said, "marriage is a great institution for some people. But then so's prison." This was given with great portentous noddings and nudgings, and the laugh broke forth again, the knee-slapping.

"I didn't know what to do with my face," Connally said later. "He was looking right at me laughing like that and slapping his knees. Jesus — where does he get that?"

"It's new," Carol said. "I swear."

The whole evening was an embarrassment. Connally faked laughter, faked interest, keeping a smile pasted on his lips and wondering about his wife, unable to imagine her married to someone like that. If he hadn't been aware of her unease and embarrassment, he might've teased her about it. In any case, he could not imagine what she might have seen in Martin. She had told Connally that what had attracted her to him, Connally, was his gentle manner, his tentativeness with her, and his humor. He hadn't even minded that she was at first unable to think of him as being attractive or magnetic, but just a nice young man with a good healthy self-deprecating sense of the ridiculous and a shy way of looking off when he spoke.

"Well," he said to her after the interminable evening with Martin, "at least I don't slap my knees when I laugh."

"No," she said. "And you don't hit me."

"He hit you?"

"I was always afraid he would."

"Did he hit you?"

"A couple of times. He was always contrite afterwards."

"Goddam," Connally said. "What the hell were we doing having dinner with him?"

"He's a boy, that's all. He's just a big rough boy. And it was so important for him to have me see that he's happy."

"The poor guy," Connally said. "How about giving him a Western Union gift certificate. He could send you telegrams: Carol, I'm happy. Martin."

She put her arms around him. "My love. My sweet, gentle man. Make love to me."

"I can't believe I actually laughed at his jokes. Where the hell does he get them — can you *imagine* the person he gets them from?"

"My tender friend," she said, kissing his neck. "I took care of myself."

"Somebody ought to knock *him* around once," Connally

said. But the words sounded hollow, and he thought of the bravado of a little dog barking at a bigger one.

She kissed the lobe of his ear. "You don't need to fight him," she murmured. "You've got what he couldn't have. And he might as well be five thousand miles away."

Oh, such a sweet girl, to lure him out of his unhappy knowledge; she was moving to the rhythms of their wonderful intimacy now, unbuckling his belt, pulling him toward her, as if to say the Marine was already forgotten.

"Love me?" she whispered.

"Oh, baby," he said.

•

In the musty motel bed, they slept with their backs to each other. Her hair was tied in a towel, and smelled of shampoo; she could not go out into the icy night air with her hair wet. The smell of the shampoo kept him awake; it reminded him of the fact that they were stuck here. The sleet and snow rattled against the window, and the heater fan whirred. Somewhere a radio was playing. He listened to it through the walls. Now and again she turned or sighed or moved, and he kept himself to his side of the bed. When he looked over at her, at the soft, virginal shape of her in the dark, he had to resist the urge to make enough noise to wake her — to cough, or fake a nightmare. Something. Finally he lay with his hands clasped across his chest and decided that in the morning he would simply tell her, straight out, honestly and calmly, that he didn't want the baby. He went through the whole scenario in his mind, playing it out — her objections and his own rational and inescapable conclusions. It was almost peaceful, thinking about it. After all, they loved each other. It was because he loved her and wanted the best for her that he was against having the baby now. The pregnancy was an accident; one didn't have to live with accidents anymore. There would be a time for having children — when they were older and more settled and could better afford it. It was important to plan for such a thing, not just walk into it blindly.

As usual, he was too restless to sleep. But now he felt bright with purpose, with the truth. Quietly he got himself dressed, then put his coat on and let himself out of the room. He thought he would look for a place to have a drink, or eat a sandwich. For a while he stood in the lee of the little stoop and looked out at the Christmas-bright colors of the mall shining through the sleet and snow. Across the way, in the office window, the old man and the boy were facing each other and talking. They looked animated in the light. Connally made his way to the door and pushed it open, leaned in to look at them.

"What," the old man said. His suspenders were down, and he was shirtless.

"I was wondering if there was a place around here where I could get something to drink."

"Coke machine," said the boy, pointing out the window.

"He doesn't want Coke," the old man said, shuffling into the other room.

Connally started to close the door.

"Wait," said the boy. "Come on in."

He did so. The wind blew at his back; he was covered with a dust of snow. The old man returned with two cans of beer. He'd put on a shirt. He handed one of the beers to Connally, then sat in the vinyl chair on the other side of the counter. The boy had lighted a cigarette, and climbed up on the counter, and he sat with his legs crossed, elbows resting on knees. He smoked the cigarette, watching Connally sip the beer.

"Where you headed?" the old man wanted to know.

"We've arrived."

"Here? Oh, that's right. You're a weekly."

Connally nodded.

"Don't get many weeklies who have all their teeth, these days, you know what I mean?"

"I wonder," Connally said. "What's the price of a room when the television works?"

"Two dollars more on each."

"Two dollars a night?"

"You hit the nail on the head. That seem fair?"

"Fair enough," Connally said.

"Well, that's good," said the old man. "It's nice to have a definite feeling about some things."

"To definite feeling," Connally said, drinking. For a moment, no one spoke. The old man reached up inside the undershirt he wore and scratched himself at the chest.

"My wife's pregnant," Connally said abruptly. He hadn't known he would say it. Yet now he felt a sort of necessity moving in him, and it was with some effort that he refrained from saying more. He took a swallow of the beer.

"Congratulations," the boy said.

The old man held up his beer as if to toast him, then drank it down and crushed the can. "Want another?"

Connally said he did. And then he and the boy were waiting while the old man went to get it.

"I don't drink," the boy said, blowing smoke. This seemed to be offered as a kind of gambit; Connally nodded at him and tried to appear receptive to whatever else he might say. But the boy just took another drag on the cigarette, and occupied himself with one of the magazines on the counter.

"So," the old man said, coming back with two more cans of beer. "Your wife's pregnant."

"Right," Connally said.

"A happy occasion," said the old man. "Only I never thought of it as all that happy."

"Jesus, Uncle Arlen."

"Who said anybody was happy?" Connally told him, only mildly surprised at himself now, feeling as though he were acceding to something deep inside. He took a long pull of the beer while the old man turned to settle into the vinyl chair again.

"Well, now — I believe we're looking at a desperate man, Eddie."

"A *des*perate man," said the boy.

"I was looking for a place to kill myself," Connally said. They laughed.

"Everything has to have a goddam consequence," Uncle Arlen said.

"You married?" Connally asked him.

"Wants to know if I'm married."

"I was," the boy said, laughing. "Yes, sir. I was."

"I ain't never been married," Uncle Arlen said. "This boy never should've been."

"You like being married?" the boy wanted to know.

"Yes," Connally said quickly. It was true, and now he felt an odd need to defend it. "I sure do."

"Sounds like a desperate man," said Uncle Arlen, and the nephew laughed. "Sounds like somebody that needs another drink of something cool."

The nephew put out his cigarette and lighted another, and the old man stood, cleared his throat, turning to Connally. "Might as well not drink alone, son."

"I was hoping I wouldn't have to," Connally said.

He drank three beers and listened to them talk about failed marriages. He was more than a little light-headed by the time he got up to make his way back to the room. The cold and blowing snow seemed beautiful, so silent. He crossed the lot unsteadily. With elaborate care, trying for quiet, he turned the key in the door and felt the latch give. He stumbled slightly as he entered. Everything was shifting, and he couldn't find the light.

"Close the door," Carol said, a curled shape in the bed.

He said her name, murmured the drunken syllables of his love. He was certain she would see reason about the baby if he explained it all to her calmly enough.

"Hey," he whispered. "Guy that owns this place —"

"Charles, please."

He got out of his clothes, crawled in next to her. The room was spinning. "Nice people. Old guy and his nephew."

"You smell like a distillery."

"I had some beer."

"Well — and you smell like a distillery."

"For your information," he said, "they make beer in a brewery."

"Brewery, distillery — what difference does it make?"

"You don't distill beer."

"Oh, please," she said. "I was asleep."

He lay quiet, only dimly aware of himself as having been uncharacteristically literal with her. Her misapplication of terms felt unseemly to him, like the declaration of an importunate thought; in the pleasing glow of intoxication, he considered that such carelessness about language indicated something, and for a drowsy moment he was suffused in the nebulous sense of the whole affair as being a trait of her family: it seemed to him now that they had often enough shown themselves to be nervous, imprecise people with no eye for details.

He was thinking of her father, with his weird energy and his multiple episodes of mental trouble, and then he was trying to put his mind on something else, feeling wrong, feeling petty and mean. *Everyone's been so kind*, he thought, and then wondered at the randomness of the words. *There is nothing wrong with anyone*, he thought. It seemed to him that in the next instant Carol was pushing at his shoulder.

"Charles."

"What?"

"Lay on your side."

"I am."

"You're lying on your back and you're snoring."

"I'm sorry," he said. "I can't help it."

They were quiet. There was the sound of the sleet on the windows, and the slow ebb and surge of traffic; the heater whirred, and something clicked in the fan. For a long time they lay there, awake, listening to everything, aware of each other, saying nothing.

•

She woke to the sound of her husband's snoring — the thing he did whenever he was overtired, or had drunk too much. He lay on his back, his hands folded over his chest in that arranged way of corpses in coffins. In the poor light from the window curtains he looked stricken, his mouth open, his face drained of color. She got out of bed carefully, not wanting to wake him just yet.

In the bathroom she stood in front of the mirror and gazed at herself, holding the top of her pajamas up to see her abdomen, which was still merely itself. This had become a habit of her mornings, and how strange to think what had started here, under the skin and muscle. She touched the smooth place below her navel, pressed lightly, finding it impossible to imagine how much it would change. Then she washed her face, cleaned her teeth. The toothpaste always made her feel a little nauseous, and she drank water from the tap, trying to concentrate on swallowing. Her mother had told her that she might not have much sickness in the mornings. But this morning she was sick, and she sat on the edge of the bathtub, waiting for it to happen. There wasn't anything else to think about for a few minutes but the demands of her body. She coughed, spit. Nothing happened.

But she was very woozy. Perhaps ten minutes passed before she felt strong enough to stand.

She washed her face again and dried it with a bath towel, feeling curiously as though she were hiding her face in the cloth. Then she went out and began putting her clothes on. She would warm the car up while he slept. For a while as she dressed, she felt strong and certain of herself. She wasn't even twenty-five yet and she had already been through a lot. She'd learned that she could handle herself in trouble. Toward the end of her marriage to Martin, she'd gone to school and started training as a dental hygienist; she had done it on her own, with her own money for working as a temporary secretary at a travel agency during his absences — hunting trips with his father and various temporary duty assignments with the Marines. She had done it all without his approval, and, for a while, without his knowledge, too.

Outside, the sleet had indeed turned to snow — a powdery layer of it, which kicked up like sand when the wind stirred. The snow was not deep: along the border of the motel parking lot, the grass stood up out of it like hair out of a scalp, looking darker and somehow more brittle than grass. The air felt too cold to breathe, though the sun had broken through the clouds and was blazing in the whiteness all around.

She started the engine, put the heater on high, then went back into the room and lay down next to her husband, snuggling against him, still wearing her coat. He stirred, but slept on. She looked at his face, at the whiskers starting on his chin and along the line of his jaw. His skin was so fair; he had tried to grow a beard last summer, and nothing would grow just under his lips. The mustache had come in patchy and uneven, so that from a distance it looked like a dirty stain above his mouth. He had used one of her mascara brushes to darken it, but then that was immediately notice-able as makeup. It had made her laugh, and he had wiped quickly at his lips, trying to get the mascara off, an embar-rassed little boy.

Now she touched his cheek. "Charles."

He opened his eyes and looked at her. "I'm not awake."

"Wake up," she sang, trying for the old ease with him. "It's the wicked witch of alarm clocks."

His hand came from the blankets and touched her nose. "Is this her snooze button?"

"It's getting late," she said. "Come on, love."

He groaned, stretched, put his arms over her shoulders. For a moment they were light-hearted and glad of each other. She kissed him and smiled into his mouth. "The car's warming up."

"Oh," he said, moving to get up. "Right." His motions were tentative now, drowsy and somehow discouraged. He stood, put his arms into his shirt, turning his back to her.

"Charles?"

"Yeah."

"You're not still mad at me?"

"I'm not mad at you." He sat on the bed, began getting into his jeans, and on an impulse, out of the once familiar pleasantry of their life together, she put one knee in the middle of the bed, reaching across, and pulled him by the shoulders until he fell back. Now she was looking into his face upside down, her hands on his chest.

"Hey," he said.

"Tell me you're not mad at me."

"I'm not mad at you."

"Say you're madly desperately totally in love with me," she said.

"I'm madly desperately in love with you."

"Not totally?"

"Totally. Did I leave out totally?"

"You're forgiven," she said. But his face had begun to take on a different configuration. She let go, stood back, watched him finish getting dressed. He said nothing until he was in his jacket and facing her. "I just woke up. You know I'm groggy when I wake up."

"Just in that one second, I didn't recognize you," she said.

"Don't be silly."

"I feel sick," she said. And a moment later she was in the bathroom, alone, in the bright light, washing her face, with that feeling of having to contend with things, of her young life complicating itself around her. From her late teens, it seemed, she'd often felt jostled by her own experience of things, as if living were a pitched battle, a test requiring the very limits of her energy and resourcefulness. "You wanted to grow up so fast," her mother had told her. "You were so sure. You were in such a hurry."

True.

She had married Martin two weeks after her eighteenth birthday. He'd been working at a bank in Washington, and she met him while working there the summer she was seventeen. The fact was, there seemed something forlorn about it all: her parents were in the process of divorcing, and while the divorce was amicable it was also quite sad; her father had gone into another one of his long spells of confusion, and whenever Carol stepped out of the house to go to work that summer she felt as though she were being set free from a tether. She'd dated Martin off and on over the fall and winter months, and by the end of her senior year, after he'd joined the Marines and was gone to his basic training at Parris Island (a period of slow time during which she felt herself to be sick with longing for him, like one of those sad women in the war films, keeping the home fires burning and worrying about the mail), they had become engaged.

She had been living with her mother in an apartment in Point Royal, her parents having separated that spring. She went with him to a little cove near Wilde Lake, where other parked cars faced the shimmering column of moonlight on the water, and he gave her a ring he'd bought with per diem money (that was what he told her). They made love there in the car. That first time he proved to be clumsy and too rough; he was in a tremendous hurry, and the low, guttural sounds he made frightened her.

"Jesus," he said when it was finished, "I'm sorry." He had been in his uniform, and he was putting it back on, rattling the metal belt buckle and fumbling with the buttons of his pants. He now seemed in a great rush to leave what they had done behind them.

"Wait," she said when he started the car.

"What."

"Let's look at the moon over the lake."

"I don't feel good," he said. "I think I should take you home."

That night she sat propped with pillows in her bed, thinking about how it was done now and there was no calling it back. She wondered if she and Martin would really marry. She had said she would, had cried and kissed him and they had agreed on June as the time; and yet there seemed something vaguely fabricated about everything, as if the ring were something he had borrowed and the engagement nothing more than a fraudulent game, like children pretending.

The night of her senior prom they drove to Maryland's Eastern Shore, and were married by a justice of the peace. After the ceremony, they accepted the kindly offer of champagne from the justice and his wife, and spent a pleasant few hours in their company — two gentle old people married fifty years, responsible for thousands of marriages and proud of it, still in love, still happy, with their little cottage by the Chesapeake and their many grandchildren in the pictures on the walls. They were people with a long story, their wonderful history together and their deep affection for each other, like old pals, they said. It showed in the way they looked at each other, and in the casual patting and caressing they did, talking and laughing, pouring champagne. Everyone got a little tipsy, and toward the end of the night, the old couple began talking about breakfast. They fixed what they called eggs Benedict — the old woman's own special recipe, using a crepe-like one-egg omelet with cheddar cheese, and orange juice instead of lemon for the hollandaise — and then Carol and her new husband settled into the car and drove the two hours to Chincoteague Island, Virginia, where they sat out on the cool sand to watch the sun come up over the vast agitation of the sea. All her young life, she had never been so happy.

With Martin, she was never to come near such happiness again.

He quickly showed himself to be inclined to spells of rough treatment of her — would jostle her, bump her, manhandle her like a big playful bear — and it seemed that he didn't know his own strength. When he was angry with her — and he was angry a lot after the first few weeks, as the differences between what he expected from her and what she was capable of giving him became apparent — his lips whitened, and she had the frightful suspicion that he was on the edge of a destructive fit. The muscles of his jaw moved, and his whole upper body seemed to expand. On one occasion he did cuff her around, and though he was contrite afterward, she knew she was going to have to find a way to leave him: the facts of the matter were that even when he was in the sunniest of moods she felt fearful around him. His casual, stupid brutality made her shudder inside whenever he was near, and when he was sent away, on tours of temporary duty, she found that she could move more freely, with more energy, through the hours of the day. She slept better. The mornings were luxurious and wonderful.

It had all been more complicated — and more difficult — than this, but she liked to say that one afternoon shortly after her second anniversary, she packed a few things in an overnight bag and simply made her way out of the Marine sergeant's house forever. And she had come to think, during the three years she was alone, that she would never be married again. It was not, at the time, an unpleasant thought.

She'd met Connally at a gathering of old high school friends, one of whom had spent time in the Air Force with him, and was providing him with a place to stay while he looked for work in Washington. Because Connally had been in the military, she was wary of him at first; but very quickly she found that she could be comfortable with him. She liked his face, the open expression of it, as if he could never be devious. The eyes were wide, the brow crooked to make him look almost sad when he was excited. He had the kind of face that grew in attraction as one knew him better: there were facets of it that hid until certain emotions, certain aspects of laughter or interest, crossed his mind. She liked staring at him, waiting for these changes.

As their friendship grew, she discovered elements of a kind of simple modesty in him, a marvelous deference to others — even those who had not shown themselves to be worthy of such consideration. He had kindness. And when he was relaxed he could be quite entertaining and funny. Moreover, he seemed to know how to be serious; there was something focused about him, a steady light in his gaze, the aura of ambition: he wanted more from life than good times and diversion, and she liked his confidence in himself. He was a man you could build a family with.

They were married in a church. She had met a female

minister during her time of leaving Martin, and the minister, a thin, energetic woman named Nancy Halstead, performed the ceremony. Ms. Halstead was earnest and very devout, and she seemed about to break into song as she recited the somber phrases of the rite. When it was over she surprised them by producing, from the black folds of her ministerial robe, a small bottle of champagne. "This is for verve and nerve," she said, smiling. She kissed Connally on the cheek, and hugged Carol. She was a friend; the whole occasion was suffused with cheerfulness. The new couple went into Washington and stayed at the Hilton, and spent nights lying awake in the dark, whispering to each other, telling dreams, planning the future. With Martin, everything had been separated out from the lovemaking; she had felt as if the rest of the marriage were somehow excluded from the few moments she lay beneath his struggling body. In the first days with Charles, she had a sense that everything was one thing; she could be aroused by talk, by a silence, by the feel of him in the room, by his hand lightly caressing her shoulder in passing.

"You turn me on just pouring orange juice," she told him one morning.

He laughed. He sat down across from her and offered a toast: "To orange juice."

She did not consciously wish to compare, and yet she could not resist the rather curious — and ironic — realization that one of the superficial differences between the two men extended all the way to lovemaking: Connally had a gentler, more subtle sense of humor, and in fact his lovemaking took time, was friendly and tender and so leisurely as to provide a sense of their intimacy as an extension of everything else between them — the smallest, most trivial pleasantry, the pitted interest, the talk, the games and the nibbling kisses, the whispered endearments. It was all one.

Even the laughter (and how this surprised her! this sense of play in him, this willingness to be goofy and to clown for her, even as they were deepening together, in each other's arms). Martin, for all his loud jokes and big talk, had been incapable of laughter in the bedroom. Everything had been too serious, too intent.

How lovely, then, how luxurious it was to be alone with someone so likably unhurried, so relaxed. She had never, not even living at home as an only child, felt so much the center of attention. He would say he really meant to spoil her, and while his voice and demeanor were full of the humor of such a remark, she saw a wonderful intentness in his eyes, too — a kind of resolve that thrilled her. And so when she urged him to start college, she thought of it as something she could give him. There had been times when she allowed herself to consider that her own difficulty with a job in which she was quite unhappy — it hadn't taken long to discover that, for her, working in people's mouths was too close for any sense of comfort or confidence; all the blood discouraged her — was just a part of what she had decided to do for him, for their future together.

•

When she came out of the bathroom, she saw that he had dressed and gone out. He was sitting in the car, a hunched shape behind the clouds of exhaust and condensation. She closed the door to the room and began making her way to the passenger side. The sidewalk was slippery, and she had to lean against the motel wall for a moment. He opened the door.

"You need help?"

"I'm okay," she said. She got to the front fender of the car and used it to steady herself. On the interstate, traffic sped by, trucks rumbling and bouncing over the uneven places in the road surface. She got in next to him and pulled the door shut. The inside of the car was warm — felt airless, in fact. She struggled out of her coat. He was sitting there staring at her.

"What?"

"I didn't know you had the car running."

"I told you."

"I don't think you did," he said.

"I thought I did." A moment later she said, "What is it, Charles? I'm sure I told you."

He backed the car out of the space. The tires spun a little, then caught.

"Do you have the room key?" he said.

"Somewhere."

"Shouldn't we ask for maid service?"

"They'll come make the bed."

"Do you want to eat? Are you hungry?"

"I was just sick."

"I'm hungry."

"You can stop and get something if you want. I'll wait in the car."

"You'll make that sacrifice."

"Charles, will you tell me what's the matter, please?"

"Nothing," he said. "That was a joke. I guess it didn't sound like one particularly."

"Well, I can take jokes that don't have some other purpose."

He had pulled onto the entrance ramp to the interstate. They were behind a big truck with a battered, dirt-smeared door on which someone had painted the word "kiss."

"What purpose?" he said. "What does that mean?"

"I don't know," she said. "You seem to want to dig at me lately for everything I do."

"Oh, now don't get *mad,*" he said. "There's nothing to

get mad about. I mean, aren't you being just a little touchy?"

"Maybe we're both touchy."

The surface of the interstate was thinly snow-covered, with two dark tracks where traffic had worn the snow down to the pavement. Connally got the car into the tracks and picked up speed. They passed over several places where cars had spun out; the concentric whorls in the snow were still visible. In the distance, up a gradual incline between two high, rocky banks, they could see a long line of trucks and cars beginning to stop.

"What's this?" Carol said, wanting him to see it and slow down.

"Probably a wreck," he said. "Damn."

They came to the end of the line, and were at a standstill. She tried the radio, but couldn't find anything she wanted to hear — it was mostly news and static — and when she turned it off he looked at her.

"Did you hear something you wanted to listen to?" she said.

"Carol," he said. "Honey, I'm scared about the baby."

She waited.

"I mean — maybe we should think about this a little more."

So this was what he had been working himself up to, and now that it was out, she felt as if she had known it all along. She sat forward slightly, thinking, *Of course, of fucking course,* looking out at the snow-encrusted bumper of the truck in front of them. Illinois license plates. Some facet of her mind merely read the numbers. The numbers went through her like an idiotic refrain while she gathered herself to speak. "Okay. What do you want to do?" she heard herself say.

This made him shift in the seat. He grabbed the steering

wheel and gave forth a sigh of frustration. "Jesus, I don't know. What kind of question is that?"

"I'm asking what you want to do."

"I want to finish school."

"I'm not talking about school, now."

"But don't you see?" he said, his face taking on that boyish exasperated expression, a look that had often charmed her out of disagreements with him. It only made her more angry now.

"I don't see," she told him. "What do you want me to see?"

The traffic had started to move. He stared out at the road, his hands tight on the wheel. They inched forward, then had to stop again.

"Just say it," she told him.

Again, the traffic moved. They rode in silence for a time. To the right, the high bank gave way to a view of smokestacks and unbelievably tangled-looking aggregates of pipes and tubes and metal sheeting; it all looked connected. She remembered climbing through the mountains near Wheeling, along a precipice punctuated by the tops of trees, overlooking an expanding vista of snowy fields — the vision of a wide valley in the center of which some village lay nestled, with its one white steeple and its snow-coated roofs, a wisp of smoke lifting from each chimney like a feather in a cap. A scene of tranquil beauty and grace, and she had found it difficult to imagine that lives were being lived in that placid winter scene, in the rooms of the white cottages, which from that distance looked like the artificial houses of the electric train sets, arranged in the fake snow of Christmas decorations — those impossibly enchanted towns in their miniature valleys that had lain in such gorgeous and silent perfection under all the Christmas trees of her girlhood.

Now, oddly, looking at the remembered image of this

dawn-lighted prettiness in her mind, she caught herself thinking of arguments, of the bustle and uproar of television sets; and — she recalled them now — there had been antennas rising from those roofs. The snow had been dirt-smeared; the smell of coal was in the air. On one of the houses the windows were boarded up. She remembered a pickup truck on oversize wheels parked next to one house whose clothesline had listed badly to one side. It seemed to her now that she had never been so attuned to the harsh side of things — not even in her short time with Martin. *Then* she had dreamed of getting out, getting away. *Then* she had planned her escape and daydreamed of being free.

"Honey?" Connally said.

She turned to look at him. They were sitting still, parked in the middle of the interstate, somewhere near Chicago. What was out the window looked like the end of civilization — the twisted mass of elements after the last explosion.

"I don't know what you want me to do," she said. And of course she did know. She hunched down in the seat, holding on to herself; it was almost a protective gesture. "Oh, God. Oh, Jesus Christ. Oh, Christ, Charles."

"What," he said. "What."

She couldn't look at him now.

"I didn't say anything," he said. "Did I?"

Outside, nothing was moving. Somewhere behind them horns sounded.

"I just wanted to talk everything over a little," Connally said.

She got out of the car and walked to the side of the road, into the gravel and down the steep little bank. The ground here dipped toward little crooked ridges of limestone and knife-grass, and was bordered by a short fence — wire cable strung between four concrete blocks.

"Carol," he called, standing out of the car. "Don't. Please come back."

She reached the fence and looked out at the rocky ground falling away, the wide concrete edge of what was built there, that stupendous collection of pipes and smokestacks and metal, the huge confusion of refuse and refinery and factory walls. She saw thousands of broken windows; she saw grime and paint-sided walls, signs faded under years of soot; she saw pockets of ice in the clefts of rutted ground. It was cold and bright here; the wind blew.

"Carol."

She heard car horns. When she turned, she saw that traffic was inching forward, and that Connally had pulled to the side of the road to let people go by him. He was walking down to her. "No," she said, turning from him. She thought of climbing over the fence and starting across the wasted landscape. Something scared and cowering in her soul urged her on. She put one foot on the rust-colored wire cable of the fence, and then he was holding her by the arms.

"For God's sake, will you get back in the car?"

"Leave me alone," she said. "Let go of me!"

He almost pushed her. She felt the shifting of his weight as he shoved and then held on, shaking her. "Goddammit," he said. "Will you listen? Can't you even listen?"

There were other sounds now. More car horns, and then two young men coming down the bank, sending little clods of snow and dirt before them as their shoes dug into the slope.

"Now hold on," Connally was saying.

The sun was blinding. Carol turned into it, then tried to face them all, crying, wanting them to move back and let her breathe. Connally had gripped her, held her tight to his side, and the two young men were standing before them.

"Nothing going on, nobody's business," Connally was saying. "Perfectly all right."

"I'm fine," Carol said into their noise. "Leave us alone."

". . . manhandling her, mister. It don't look good . . ."

"Leave us alone!" Carol shouted.

Then they were standing there staring at her. Connally had let go, and one of the men, a red-faced boy in a blue baseball cap, took hold of his arm above the elbow. Connally shook loose.

"Please," Carol said. "Don't touch him."

"Crazy," the one in the blue cap said, turning and starting up the bank.

The traffic was moving with some speed now. There was the sound of the truck doors opening and closing. Carol had moved to the wire fence and put her hands over her eyes, crying.

"Look, I didn't — please stop this," Connally was saying.

"Just go," she said.

He stood there. Up on the road the truck pulled away, and one of the men shouted something.

Carol let her husband lead her back up to the car. Her door was open. She got in and he closed it on her, walked around, and struggled in behind the wheel. For a moment the car wouldn't start. It groaned and he pumped the accelerator and cursed under his breath. Finally it caught. He raced the engine, looked into the side-view mirror. Cars were going by in a slow procession, and no one seemed willing to let them in. Carol looked out at the stacks, the rising smoke under broken white clouds with gray undersides. The sky beyond it all was bright blue.

Connally pulled out, racing the wheels a little. Almost immediately traffic stopped again. The car idled roughly, and once more he gunned the engine. They sat watching the back windows of the station wagon in front of them, where two children were wrestling with each other in the back seat. The children put their faces against the window, flattening their noses, contorting the flesh of their lips. It wasn't funny. It wasn't even amusing. Carol stared back at them, and her husband made a sound in the back of his throat. The snarl of cars began to unravel again, and soon they were moving with a little more speed. The station wagon changed lanes, went ahead. The children were making faces at someone else now.

"Look," Connally said, "I didn't mean what you think I meant, okay?"

"I'm not going to talk about it," she told him.

Perhaps a mile farther on, they passed a burned hulk and a badly twisted truck cab. There were several police cars and two fire engines. The whole scene was revealed to them as they came around a bend in the road, and so it was too late to look away. Carol's gaze was fixed on it all, and now the traffic stopped again. They were sitting in full view of everything while someone directed cars onto the shoulder of the road.

"Oh, God," she said, crying, "I can't stand it."

He put his hands over her eyes, and she covered them with her own. But then she couldn't breathe, and she pulled away. It was almost reflexive.

"Don't look," he said. "God."

The traffic was moving again. He changed lanes, went along the outside of the shoulder and on. The traffic thinned out, and everyone picked up speed. He had trouble shifting the gears, but soon they were near the speed limit. The road here looked dry, though a dust of snow blew across it in the wind.

"It wasn't anything," he said. "I mean — no one hurt, I guess. There wasn't an ambulance or anything."

She was silent.

"Did you hear me before?" he said finally. "I didn't mean what you thought. Really I was just talking. It was just anxiety talking, you know?"

She could not look at him or talk to him now, and why couldn't he see that she needed time to collect herself? She was sitting with her arms folded tight, as if trying to keep warm, staring out at the disastrous countryside, the sun pouring down out of the clouds.

"Okay," he said, and stepped on the gas.

"Will you please remember what we just saw," she said to him.

Gradually he slowed down. He lighted a cigarette, turned on the radio. When she asked him if he wanted her to look for a station they could listen to, he said, "It's all right." They traveled for miles in the chatter and cheer of the disc jockeys, and at last they had come across the wastes outside Gary, the tall columns of smoke and steam, the coal dust–stained brick façades, the miles of ashes. They were heading north along the curve of Lake Michigan. The snow had melted or been cleared away from the road surface, but there were piles of it along the streets, and it was all the color of smoke. Not many people were out. A wind came in off the water, which was almost black-looking in the sharpness of the late morning light.

Connally looked at it all and thought of saying something about it, some mild remark that might be neutral enough, friendly enough to bridge the distance between them now. She sat forward, seemed momentarily confused. They had entered Lake Shore Drive. She gazed out at the lake. He wanted to speak to her, wanted to tell her that it was all a mistake. He had not meant for her to think about an abortion; no, he didn't think he could have meant precisely that. The fact was he didn't really know what he had wanted her to come to, and then he began to admit to himself that if she had offered to get rid of the child he would've been relieved and happy. It would've been the thing he did want. It was something he had been afraid to think about in any specific way. And when she had got out of the car and walked away from him, crying like that, as if he'd struck her, he saw for the first time the reality of what he had been hoping for: until that moment, she had been a woman happy to be carrying her first child. And he had ruined that. He had ruined everything. And there didn't seem to be any way back from it.

He lighted another cigarette, and she rolled the window down partway.

That was a statement, too. The cold air came in, swirled around the inside of the car. He rolled his window all the way down and threw the cigarette out.

They pulled up in front of Leisure Village. It looked like any apartment complex or planned community. There were seven or eight buildings — high rises or towers, really — many windows, each sporting a balcony, and all the balconies decorated differently, with an impressive variety of furniture and patio paraphernalia. Winding among the buildings were streets with little cul-de-sacs and wide boulevards planted with willows and great oaks. It was a small city within a city. At the entrance gate was a very tall uniformed guard with small suspicious eyes, a bushy blond handlebar mustache, and middle-parted hair who looked like all the old images of nineteenth-century men — officers of Confederacy or Union, cowboys and desperados, and the proud, powerful barons of industry. He leaned down and peered into the back seat of the car, and then looked straight across Connally at Carol as if to be certain that she was a woman and that she was unarmed.

"Building number?"

"Tina Connally," Charles said.

The man stood back, produced a clipboard from somewhere, and began paging through it. "You don't have the building number?" He hadn't looked up from the clipboard.

Connally spoke to the side of his face. "No. Sorry."

"O'Connor."

"No," Charles said, "Connally."

"Oh, okay. Connally — oh, Miss Connie."

"Tina Connally," Connally said. "I'm her son. She's expecting us."

"Your name?" There was suspicion in the voice.

"Ernest Hemingway. She's expecting us."

The guard stared at the clipboard, seemed to be going down a list. "Oh, wait. Here. Yes, it says she's expecting a visit from her son and daughter-in-law. You must be the son."

"That's me," Connally said.

"All right. Go right on through, Mr. Hemingway. Building number six. All the way to the end of this road, past the hospital wing."

Connally drove slowly. The road surface had been plowed, but there were patches of ice.

"You could've got yourself arrested," Carol said in an even voice. It might've been a simple observation of fact, between strangers.

"Arrested? By a security guard?"

"They have all the powers of police inside the gates, don't they?"

"We weren't inside the gates. I thought you'd get a kick out of it. Didn't you get a kick out of it?"

"Cute," she said.

"Well, it got you talking to me. We've had a breakthrough. We can go ahead and get a divorce now."

She said nothing.

"What do you think?" He felt now as though he had begun to bully her. "Hey," he said. "Carol?"

"What?"

"I've just never done any of this before. Okay?"

"This isn't the time," she said. "Please."

Mrs. Connally's efficiency was in the last tower, the one whose entrance drive for perhaps a hundred yards ran parallel to a street of brick ramblers with identical-looking fenced yards and small concrete porches. That street emptied into a two-lane highway, and traffic was speeding by there. As Connally and his wife came along the walk, he saw that his mother was standing in the doorway of the building, wearing a nightgown and robe with frills around the neck.

"Charles," she said. "Hurry up here, I'm not dressed."

He quickened his step in spite of himself, and Carol hurried along, too.

His mother looked vaguely stupefied, coming out into the bright cold, breathing in little clouds of condensation, her eyes wide and moist and sad, hugging Carol. "At last, at last, at last," she was saying, patting Carol's back. Carol, who had always kept a certain restraint in moments like this — affection from friends, from her own mother and father — seemed to go limp, as if she had traveled here for this bumptious and bearish embrace.

"Oooo," his mother said, "it's cold. Let's get inside." She reached across and touched the side of his face. "You look tired." She'd put one arm over Carol's shoulder and turned with her, heading into the building.

"This is Carol," Connally said, meaning it as a joke.

"We've already met," said his mother. "Haven't we?"

"Yes," said Carol.

"What I want to know is, where's this Mr. Hemingway?"

"The guard called you."

"Yes, he said, 'Mr. Hemingway is on his way in.' And I said, 'Who?' And he said, 'Your son.' And I knew what you'd done to the poor man."

"He's happy," Connally said, stealing a glance at his wife, whose expression was hard to read. Carol seemed to be watching his mother, as if looking for some key as to how she should behave.

Inside, they went along the lobby to the elevators. The lobby was all shiny wood surfaces and cushioned furniture and statuary; there were paintings in ornate frames on the walls. Above the bank of elevators, a television screen showed them themselves, crossing the lobby; against one wall, two women sat side by side on a sofa, reading the same newspaper. Connally's mother had simply come out of her apartment in this state of undress, and made her way down to the entrance of the building. In the elevator, she examined herself in the mirror-like metal door.

"I look a mess, don't I?"

"You look fine," Carol said.

The older woman's robe had fallen open. Her hair, gray clumps showing scalp, was in curlers. Around her neck, the red scarf she had put on was loosely bunched, as if she'd been ruffled by winds. Connally looked at her and thought of inconsistencies, failures: his grandmother, in the last year altered by dementia, completely mad, and happy.

The elevator opened on the seventh floor, and Mrs. Connally led them out. They made almost no noise because the carpet here was so thick; there were dark wooden doors on either side of the hall, the fourth of which turned out to be the entrance to Mrs. Connally's apartment.

"Are all these one-bedroom?" Carol asked as they entered.

"The ones on this side. Over on the other side it's all penthouses."

The apartment was essentially three rooms: the living room/kitchen, the bedroom, and a small bathroom, like an afterthought, through a doorway to one side of the kitchen counter. Even with the closeness of the small rooms, the feel of the place was of a kind of luxury, a pinched opulence — the velvety plush furniture with its deep-pillowed look and its inviting contours, the royal red wallpaper, the wood-grain surfaces and counters. Deep shades of burgundy were everywhere — the crown molding, the small antique table, even the stereo. In one wall a large-screen television was embedded like a fake window, and in the other there was a grotto where a statuette of the Virgin stood, the globe and the snake under her little feet. Flowers were arranged behind her — a high crown of petals. Connally's mother walked into the center of the room and turned, assuming a pose of someone far younger, one hand outstretched, limp-wristed, as if awaiting a kiss on the back of her hand.

"Voilà!" she said.

"It's lovely," said Carol, walking into the room and letting her purse drop to her wrist.

"Make yourselves comfortable."

Connally sat down on the unreal softness of the couch. Carol was gazing at everything, still standing.

"I'll just change," said Connally's mother, opening a door near the television screen; it was a wet bar. "Make yourselves something to drink." Then she crossed the room and opened what turned out to be a closet, stuffed with clothes and boxes and smelling of naphtha. With the rustle of plastic cleaner-bags she took an outfit into the bedroom and closed the door.

"It's nice," Carol said.

"Do you want something to drink?" Connally asked.

"I can't have any caffeine."

"Right."

"Well, maybe there's orange juice."

"You want some orange juice?"

She made no answer. Over the kitchen sink there was a window, and she leaned up to look out. "You can see the Sears Tower from here."

"A selling point."

Either she didn't hear this or she chose to ignore it. She walked around the room, looking at the pictures. "Who's this?" she said, picking up a small framed photograph.

He took it from her, stared at it. Winnie Barthley, staring out of rainy light. "That's my grandmother."

"Nice face."

He said nothing.

"Did you know her?"

"She's the one I told you about," he said. "I lived with her for a time."

"Oh, it was *this* grandmother. She looks so clear-eyed." She put the picture back in its place, and Connally's mother came out of the bedroom wearing a black jumpsuit, the same red scarf. She'd brushed her hair, and now had it tied in back, an iron-colored ponytail.

"I thought we'd go somewhere and have lunch, and then if the weather's not too bad maybe go to the Sears Tower."

"It's Christmas week, Ma."

Mrs. Connally simply stared.

"They won't be open during Christmas week, will they?"

"I've got presents for you both."

"We have something for you, too," Carol said.

"Should we do that now?"

"Let's go get something to eat," Connally said.

Carol was reaching for her purse. The earrings she'd bought were in a little wrapped package there.

"I told you all that your coming was gift enough — you shouldn't have."

Connally watched his mother open the package and bring out the earrings; he sat through the thank-yous and the trying them on, the modeling of them. He was agitated and hungry, and wanted to get off by himself. He had the rest of the day to endure. "I don't feel very good," he said.

"What's the matter?" asked his mother.

"Maybe I'm pregnant."

Both women looked at him.

"Just a joke," he said. "I'm not always a dirty bastard. Sometimes I make jokes."

"What're you talking about?" his mother asked.

"Charles, please shut up," Carol said with what sounded like affectionate exasperation.

He smiled at her, and she gave him the trace of a smile in return.

"I have your present right here," said his mother, reaching under the couch where he was half reclining, one arm resting across the back. She brought out a package the size of a garment bag, and Carol knelt down to open it.

"Come on, Charles."

He got himself up, leaned down to help tear the paper, which was bright red with hundreds of small black shapes — marching English soldiers in tall caps. "Where'd you get the gift wrap?" he asked.

"I had it around."

Carol was tearing at it, pulling the ribbons off. It was a clothing box. He sat back and watched as she opened it, unfurling a heavy, dark tapestry that turned out to be a discouragingly overbright version of Da Vinci's *The Last Supper*.

"Like it?" his mother wanted to know.

"It's beautiful," Carol said. "Isn't it beautiful, Charles?"

Connally said, "Boy."

"It's beautiful, Mrs. Connally."

"Call me Tina."

"It's beautiful, Tina."

"I had a feeling you'd like it."

"Charles, won't this look good in the living room?"

"Much better than the old rug," he said.

"Rug?" said his mother. "It's a tapestry. You hang tapestry. Lord, I do wonder what he's learning in that college."

"Rug," Carol said. "Charles, I swear."

"I must have a headache," he said. "I can't think straight." He lay back and closed his eyes.

"Poor Charles," said his wife.

"You want an aspirin, Charles?"

"I'll let you know if it turns out to be a headache." He sat up. Everything felt false and somehow guilty, too, as if this teasing back and forth were a kind of cruelty, all at the expense of something or someone he couldn't name. Carol was admiring — or pretending to admire — the tapestry. "Let's just go," he said.

There followed a lot of confusion, packing the tapestry in its box and then deciding to leave it in the apartment for now, deciding where to go (a pancake house on Dearborn Street, and then to the Sears Tower, back home to watch a movie, perhaps; Tina would make dinner). They agreed to take Tina's Olds, since it was more roomy. But the Olds wouldn't start. Connally worked with it a while, pumping the accelerator pedal, thinking of it as somehow emblematic; nothing in his mother's house ever worked as it was supposed to, nothing in her life could ever be simple or easy. When the engine finally did turn over it sounded as though several pieces of metal were clanking around inside it.

"When was the last time you had this thing looked at?" he said.

"I only drive it once or twice a year," said his mother. "I can't imagine anything could be wrong with it."

"Listen to it."

"Well it's running, isn't it? Charles's always been so negative about everything. Always such a naysayer."

They rode on in silence for a time.

Carol gazed out at the establishments on either side of the street: boutiques, clothing stores, restaurants, banks. There was something vaguely gone-over about it all, as if this whole part of the city had been reclaimed from catastrophe or ruin: the walls were newly painted, and the façades and storefronts looked restored; new brick laid over old brick; new glass fitting old, rusty, iron-framed windows. The road wound north, through traffic circles and open areas of asphalt, and past a factory whose grimy bordering fence died out in a wall of weeds. Beyond this, the city stretched before them in its jagged enormity and sparkle: windows full of reflected sun, looking like plumes of flame in the sides of buildings; wedges of shade in the crevices and along the sheltered sides of the streets, a thrown pattern of triangular darknesses with all the logic of geometric design in them.

Everything was open; there were after-Christmas sales.

Connally parked the car on a quiet corner and the three of them walked for a few blocks along State Street. Instead of the pancake house, they stopped in a small delicatessen and had sandwiches, and Mrs. Connally asked to know what Charles was studying now, what his plans were.

"I'm thinking of teaching," he said.

"Not just thinking about it," said Carol. "That's what we've decided on, isn't it?"

"Well," he said, "if it works out."

"There *is* a baby coming, now," Mrs. Connally said.

No one said anything for a moment.

"You're going to have to get a job, son."

"We'll work things out," Carol hurried to say.

"Well, but you can't go back to work when the baby comes."

"For a while," Carol told her.

"Charles, you're not going to ask her to do that. Standing up all day like that."

"Really, Mrs. Connally. It's my idea."

"You can't live on Carol's salary, can you?"

"No," Charles said, "we can't."

"Charles can work part time or something," Carol said. When he looked at her, she thought she saw the phantom trace of a smile. But then he simply stared out the window at the sharp shadows of the street.

"Well, I wonder if you both know what you're in for."

"I think we have an idea," Carol said, managing an amused, rueful tone.

Mrs. Connally was already thinking of something else. "When we finish, let's do some window-shopping."

Outside, the air was stinging cold when the wind stirred, but neither Connally nor his mother seemed much bothered by it. In the partially enclosed entrances to the stores, protected from the wind, Carol paused and felt blessedly warm. The decorations in the shop windows were intricate and bright. In one store window a train set ran through fake mountain passes and little villages draped in cotton snow. She looked at her husband's face, ruddy and handsome, smiling automatically at something his mother said, and thought perhaps things would be all right now. After all, a man was entitled to some misgivings. She put her arm in his and then reached for her mother-in-law's too, and they made their way to the car.

On the way back to Leisure Village, Mrs. Connally, sitting in the back seat with her hands resting on her knees, looked to one side and then the other of the road, commenting on what she saw, and Charles began to make simple agreeing sounds, hums and mmms and yeses, glancing from time to time into the rearview mirror. Carol began to sense that something was being avoided. They reached the entrance to Leisure Village, and Mrs. Connally rolled down the back window. The guard had recognized the car, and he waved them through.

"I wanted to talk to him," Mrs. Connally said.

"He waved us through," said Charles.

"That was ridiculous. I had my mouth open to say something to him and you drove right by him."

"Next time, let's ask him if he wants my autograph. I am Ernest Hemingway, after all."

"I'm serious. You drove right by."

"He waved me through," Charles said. "I can't read your mind." He parked and they got out. Mrs. Connally walked on ahead. Carol put her hand on Charles's arm, and he seemed not to notice it. "We might just get our car and head back to the motel for the evening," he said to his mother.

Mrs. Connally stopped, turned. There was something between them now, and Carol wondered if she shouldn't remove herself a little, to let them talk.

"We're going to have dinner," her mother-in-law said.

"We don't want to be any trouble," said Charles.

"Trouble? What're you talking about? You live in Virginia. You drove nine hundred miles to see me."

And now Carol saw something sad and beset in the older woman's face, as if the prospect of spending the evening alone were frightening.

"I'll help with dinner, if you'll let me," she said.

"What is wrong with him?" said Mrs. Connally.

"Pay no attention to him," Carol told her. "Will you let me help with dinner?"

"I bought all this food. I don't normally keep much."

They walked on a few paces, then stopped. Charles was still standing where they had left him.

"What?" Carol said. She had tried to sound like teasing, but heard anger, and a demand. Straightening, she faced him.

He said, "Okay." Then: "Nothing, all right?"

She turned and took Tina's arm and headed up the walk. He followed them into the building.

•

For a substantial part of the first fifteen years of his life, Connally had lived in the houses of various relatives and family friends. Sometimes with his mother and sometimes not. Connally as a boy had seen the expressions in the adult faces whenever his mother's name came up, and had grown accustomed to the intuition that others looked upon him in the light of her troubles and worries: he was something else for her to think about, another complication in her very complicated existence. There was also the fact that for a long time the rooms of the various houses seemed sequestered somehow, as if in reaction to the sense that moving around out there on the dim outskirts of everything was Connally's father. The old man — he was almost twenty years older than Connally's mother — was inclined to fits of uncontrollable rage. The boy's own memory of him was confused and unhappy; there had been moments of the kind of excitement and pleasure he had seen other boys his age enjoying with their fathers, yet even the memory of happiness was freighted with the knowledge that at any turn he might start hitting. Even living in other houses, Connally feared what the old man might do, for the other adults were always talking about him, wondering themselves what was next. Storms and eruptions shook on the horizon, and now and again the boy's mother went off to contend with them.

There were times when she had stayed away longer than a few days, and when she came home it was always with a flurry of bustle and emotion, as if she had been hundreds of miles away. Yet one afternoon, walking to the corner drugstore with his grandmother, he had seen his mother framed in a window above the street, talking. She had been visible only for a moment, but it was enough for the boy to know she was near, and to understand, without words, that she was never very far away. It seemed to Connally in his young age that she moved at the very heart of mystery. And then he found out, sometime later, that she had been going back and forth from him to his father, that she had, off and on, planned not to return — had talked about staying with the old man.

This he had learned, not from his mother but from Winnie Barthley, when he was almost sixteen years old and living with her in an apartment in Point Royal.

Yet, when he was small, his perception was that his mother had stood between him and the dark, even when she was elsewhere, and perhaps this was in some way at least part of the reason he had felt so strongly the need to make this trip: the pregnancy had frayed some atavistic nerve in him, and it was true that he was shaky and uncertain inside — nervous, Carol had said to him — as a child.

Now, while Tina and his wife worked making dinner, he let himself out of the apartment and went for a walk, wending his way through the spruces and over a fallen barbed-wire fence to the street beyond, the neat row of houses there, with the dark awnings and the shifting motion of blue television light in the windows. It was almost full dark. He went down the street past parked cars, yards with bikes and toys in them, and real estate signs. Several of these houses were up for sale. Lights trailed along the wires bordering the road, and two trucks came rumbling past.

He had traversed the street of row houses before he realized how much he wanted to get himself out of reach of the voices of his wife and mother. Perhaps Carol would tell his mother what had transpired this morning. He couldn't bring himself to the point of curiosity about it. They would find whatever they would find to talk about, and he thought of the journey here as an aberration of perception, that he could've thought it would change anything, make him feel anything differently. He hadn't been with his mother five minutes before the old irritations began to work in him: the sensation that his life must be lived in secret, that he was a stranger, that something in him might perish for lack of air, for the suffocating necessity to behave as if nothing were ever wrong, as if there were no bad memories, no old complications and injured feelings between them, no sense of anger for the years living in other people's houses while his mother was working in another part of the county or trying to solve troubles with the strange, brutal man who was his father; there was always the sense that she was making a place for the boy, so he could have a real family. But something was always stopping her, and Connally got accustomed to living with other families.

In his teens, he had roomed with his grandmother in a small apartment on Mission Street in Point Royal, above the movie theater. She was seventy-nine and beginning to lose her memory. Afternoons of that second spring he was with her, he would come walking back from school — a boy not quite at home anywhere — and see her from the end of the block, sunning herself out on the theater marquee as though it were a porch. The windows of the apartment looked out on the roof of the marquee, and on soft, bright afternoons Winnie Barthley liked to sit out there in a wicker chair, with the telephone in the window sill and the cord stretched to the handset at her ear. She would drink iced tea and chat with a neighbor woman — someone with whom she had gone to boarding school — about the people his mother had grown up with: marriages, births, business failures, illnesses, divorces, failed reconciliations. It seemed that every one of that generation's children was in some trouble or other, she would say, and wasn't it a sign of something. She could remember so clearly the events of forty and fifty and sixty years ago; last night, this morning, the name of the boy she lived with, escaped her. Connally, walking back from school, could see her there in the distance, perfectly languid and peaceful under the sun, in plain sight of the whole street, like a preposterous advertisement for whatever movie was running below.

He stayed with her three years, through the slow loss of her own identity, and in the end he summoned his mother from the distance she had receded into, living with his father — the old man was dying in a home on the outskirts of Chicago, and some obscure need had demanded that she be with him in the last days.

"Ma," Charles had said. "Come home."

"I'm going to as soon as I can," she'd said.

"You don't understand. Your mother's calling me by other names." And it dawned on him that he had been put with Winnie Barthley not to *be* watched or tended, but to watch.

"Can't you humor her for a little while, son?"

"I'm moving out," he told her. "I'm joining the Air Force."

"You're not old enough."

"Oh yes I am," he said. "I have the recruiters calling me."

And then she was crying on the other end. "I can't do it all, son."

"You can do this," he said. He felt only anger.

"I'm sorry," she said. "I thought we were in this together.

I know you've suffered, too. I'm just trying to do what's best for everybody."

"Please," he said, "just get here."

Now, he crossed the highway and went along a path through the tangled growth on the other side.

He would see where it led.

The chill felt good on his cheeks, and he was curious now. He came to a hill, which rose to the level of a new development, brick houses on small plots of ground, many of them in some stage near completion. These were going to be big, roomy places, with bay windows and porches and sun rooms that opened out onto patios. They were all alike, with small separate features. In the dark they loomed on either side of him. He entered one, stood out of the wind, listening to it creak in the joists and boards, the unfinished rooms. The smell of plaster and paint was everywhere, and from below him came an odd, almost musical drip-drop of water. The baby would come, and he would have to quit school, find a job. Perhaps he would go to night classes for a while, but the pressures would build up, and he would have to settle for something. He saw it all — that old domestic drama played out so often in the generation of his mother and father, because there had been no choice then. It had been his own arrival, he knew, that had brought about the end of his parents' marriage, before houses gave way to apartment rooms and the low, garrulous murmur of his grandmother on the other side of a wall.

He went out through the open back door and across a little expanse of packed dirt and snow to the next house. This one was even bigger, its wide entrance opening into a high-ceilinged foyer, with a staircase winding up into the dark. As he stepped inside, he thought he heard voices. He paused, listened. The wind brushed his face and whistled in the eaves of the unfinished porch. He took another step, and two men walked out of the dimness of the next room.

"Hey," one said. "Hey, man."

Connally said, "Hey." He couldn't see them in the dark, and they stopped short of the line of light from the windows. One of them coughed and then hawked something out of the back of his throat. "You work here?" Connally said.

"Not exactly."

The taller one spit. "You?"

"No."

"We're basically just looking around, man," said the other one, the one who had spoken first.

"Me, too," Connally said. "Just looking around."

"We thought you might be the owner."

"No."

"Or, you know, a buyer."

"Nope," Connally said. "I'll never be able to afford anything like this. I'm broke."

"He's broke, Dwight. Just like us."

"You broke?" Connally said, trying for a joking tone.

"Broke as shit," the tall one, Dwight, said. He stepped into the light.

"Me, too," said Connally, returning his gaze. "Broke as shit."

"Well, let's go, Dwight."

They moved away, toward what must be the kitchen, and the back door. The one named Dwight looked around, seemed to want something else, but the other pulled his arm. "Come on, man. Let's not make a lot of confusion or anything."

"Hey," Dwight said, "you feel lucky?"

"Me?" Connally said.

"Come on, Dwight."

"A lucky son of a bitch," Dwight said, turning. They went out of sight. "Real lucky."

The other said something Connally couldn't hear, and then they stepped out into the snow between the houses, arguing back and forth about which direction to take.

Connally remained quite still until their voices died away. Then he went back along the road, hurrying through the shadows of broken streetlamps and the lights of passing cars. The moon was bright. Nothing stirred. In the apartment, he found Carol and his mother setting the table. Carol was wearing one of his mother's aprons, and she smiled at him. She'd put on more makeup. He wondered aloud what the two women had talked about.

"You, of course," said his mother.

"That's not true. You never even came up," Carol said.

"We were afraid you'd get mugged out there."

He decided not to tell what had happened. In fact, in the warmth and light of the room, he was ready to doubt that he had come to the point of any real danger: a couple of toughs with nowhere to go for warmth. They had probably decided about him when they understood he was not of those houses, but an outsider like them. "The whole area's deserted," he said.

"Tina says she'll come out and visit when the baby's born," Carol said. "And she'll come to Dr. Wilder and I'll clean her teeth for her."

"What a treat."

"Okay," Carol said.

Connally watched them work, watched the coordination of tasks, as if they'd been putting meals together for years. In the crimson-tinted light from the table lamp, Carol looked flushed and happy; her eyes shone. She had entered, with the older woman, into some province of simple comfort — the sense of warmth and ease and gaiety; the festive, bustling, benevolent racket and cacophony of holidays. On the table before her was a profusion of fruits and cheeses and breads, of luscious water-beaded vegetables, and she stood beaming, turning her bright smile in his direction, as if something in her feeling for him had brought forth this abundance.

He returned the smile. They sat down to eat, and then his mother remembered a movie she wanted to watch, so while they ate, the movie played. It was one of those perky supernatural comedies where death is borderless and people crossed back and forth from the darkness; ghosts, and living people falling in love with them, and moments of history replayed and neatly changed. There were outlandish special effects, and the soundtrack included a good deal of obnoxious noises and raucous music. Screams, breaking glass, the constant nattering of drums. It gave Connally a headache, and when he was through eating, he got up from the table and lay down on the sofa. For what seemed a long time there was just the commotion of the television. Now and again his mother laughed. The roar and chatter of the movie seemed to rifle something in his memory, and he thought of nights alone with her, in the silver-shifting glow of the television: the quiz shows and variety shows and sitcoms, the canned laughter, the police shows with their insistent and repetitive jazz and their gun battles. When he allowed himself to glance at her, his uneasiness increased: Carol was at the foot of the couch, crocheting something, looking like an incarnate version of the cliché about expecting a baby; his mother sat on the floor, one arm resting on the hassock there, her face frozen in the expression of a charmed child. The absurd business being transacted on the television screen ended, and now his mother yawned. The evening was over.

"Well," Carol said. "It was wonderful, Tina."

"Remember what we talked about for tomorrow," the older woman said, helping her into her coat.

Connally stood at the door.

"Look at him," said his mother.

"Good night," Carol told her, leaning over to kiss her on the cheek.

"You be careful with this young lady, Charles."

He kissed his mother's dry forehead.

"Tomorrow," she said.

"First thing," said Carol.

He followed her out into the cold parking lot, and he caught himself looking around for the two men. There was nothing. She walked quickly, with little mincing steps. He saw her small, bony ankles, the sweet curve of her calves. The wind moved, and lifted her hair. When she stopped at the car, waiting for him to open the door with his key, he thought of kissing her. Another time, he might have done so. But then she was gathering her coat about herself, shivering, and he had opened the door, was moving around the car.

"So cold," she said. "Hurry and get the heater on."

"I'm going as fast as I can," he said. "Merry Christmas."

"I'm just freezing. I'm sorry."

•

Driving through the dark, Charles complained to her about feeling restless whenever he was with his mother. "It's like somebody's lying," he said. "I can't explain it." Carol had discovered quickly enough that she liked Mrs. Connally, for all her batty notions and what turned out to be rather incessantly morbid talk. She told Charles that she supposed the older woman was simply preoccupied with something.

"Yes, that's right," Charles said. "Only I've never known which something it is. And every time I see her or talk to her some part of me expects to find it changed. Like maybe she'll open up. Or forget whatever the preoccupation is. I don't know. But I never end up feeling anything but this frustration with her. We went through some things together when I was a kid, and I still don't know the first thing about her."

"I liked her," Carol felt constrained to say. But it had thrilled her unreasonably to find that they were in agreement about something; she considered this fact and then she reached over and put her hand on his leg, just above the knee.

"Did you tell her anything?" he said.

"Tell her?"

They rode on in silence.

"Did you say anything about me?"

"She talked about you," Carol said. "When you were a little boy. Some of the trouble she had trying to raise you alone."

"She didn't raise me alone."

"She meant without your father."

"Yes, but *she* wasn't alone a lot of the time. That's my point."

Carol left a pause. "Well. She also talked about your grandmother some, and about the work she's been doing with the hospital wing of that place. Some volunteer work. She talked about all the diseases and the ways people were dying."

"Okay," he said. "Okay."

"What did you think I'd say to her, Charles?"

"Nothing," he said. "I feel so bad about — earlier. You know."

She kept her hand on his leg; she would make him see that she loved him, that no change would make loving him cease to be so.

"What did she tell you about my grandmother?"

"Oh, just that she was lonely and afraid in the last years. Nothing specific." Carol might've gone on to say that she wished his mother would've wanted to say more. Upon seeing the old photograph of Winnie Barthley, she had felt an immediate sense of curiosity and recognition, too, thinking of her father's chronic troubles.

"Lonely and afraid and completely crazy," he said. "And I lived with her through most of the end of it."

"Well."

"She didn't tell you about that?"

"I'm sure she's aware that I know."

"I don't know what I thought I'd find here," he said.

"Don't be so negative," she told him.

He put both hands on the wheel and sat forward slightly, speeding up. "You sound like her, for Christ's sake."

"Slow down," Carol said.

They had entered the highway east. There were trucks in a line, all traveling too fast, all in the left lane. He pulled behind one of them, too close, the big iron-looking trailer door looming. Carol covered her eyes. Everything was a blaze of light, and she drew in a breath, feeling the huge sound of horns thrumming against her face and neck. Finally they had come out and were in their own empty lane, the big trucks rumbling past on the left.

"Sorry," he said.

She was sitting straight up with her hands on the dashboard. "It's just — we have to think about the baby," she said.

This irritated him unreasonably. "Oh, come on. The baby's no bigger than a tadpole. You're worried about upsetting the fucking baby?"

A little later, he said, "I'm sorry for that, too. That was just being grouchy."

"It's all right," she told him.

"Look," he said, "from the time I was two and a half to the time I was fifteen I lived in different houses with relatives — a lot of the time with my mother living elsewhere —

and then I lived exclusively with my grandmother. You know why?"

"I didn't do that to you, Charles."

"Do you think you could leave yourself out of this for a minute?"

She was silent. The windows of buildings looked like glimmering aspects of a single massive shape outside her window.

"My father didn't like having me around," he said. "I made him nervous. *I* drove him to the various beatings he administered. And she put up with it."

"All right," Carol said, touching his arm. "We'll make up for it. We'll know enough to do differently."

"Look, the baby's a fact. Okay? But that isn't what I was talking about."

She moved over in the seat and put her hand on his shoulder, but she didn't feel any welcome there; his arms were stiff, the muscles hardened, tense. He was gripping the wheel.

"I didn't mean anything," she said. "I can't help thinking about it. I mean, that's sort of understandable, isn't it?"

He made no answer.

"Isn't it?" she said.

Outside, the muddle and radiance of the city shone like a kind of peril. She wanted so badly to have this baby. She couldn't think otherwise; the child was real to her, inside. It was impossible to think of stopping it. But she had wanted it all to be so different, wanted the suffused warm glow and the sense of anticipation and joy. Slowly she moved back to her side of the car, gazing out at the wintry night, the luster and brightness of Christmas showing in windows and along the eaves of houses.

When they arrived at the motel, she opened the door to the room and hurried inside, breathing the odor of gas again.

She said nothing. But her husband noticed it, and opened the door, stood fanning the air. "I'm going to complain," he said.

"Maybe we can get another room."

"They probably all smell like this."

Someone had made the beds and put fresh coffee packets on the bureau. She sat on the bed and reached over to try the television. "Still no television."

"I'll be back," he said.

And before she could say anything he was off, going across the dimly lighted lot to the motel office. She watched him go in — he hesitated in the open door — and then she turned and, on the chance that he would come back with the key to another room, began to pack their things. But he didn't come back for a long time. Twice she went to the door and looked out, and she could see him in the window, talking. She saw him smile. All right. She got out of her clothes and crawled into the bed, and she was half asleep when he came in.

"Awake?" he said.

"Little," she told him, only half awake. Yet some part of her was attending to everything.

He began to undress.

"What did they say?" she asked.

"It's nothing," he said. "Nothing to worry about. It doesn't smell now, anyway."

He moved out of her line of vision, and she felt his weight on the other side of the bed.

"I got sleepy," she said.

"Sorry I took so long."

"Want to make love?" she asked.

He said, "That would be nice."

She turned. He had lain down, was on his back, staring at the ceiling. "You didn't get the light."

He got up, turned it off. When he came back, she reached for him. His hands were cold; he was shivering.

"Here," she said, snuggling.

"Carol," he murmured, "I'm so sorry. I don't know anything."

"Be quiet," she said.

He lay very still, and the shivering gradually ceased.

"Warm?" she said.

He had gone to sleep. She lay there holding him, knowing that he had fallen off, glad of it, feeling oddly that sex between them now would have been too weighted down with worry, would have somehow made them both unhappy. When he moved out of her embrace, she pulled the blanket over their shoulders and hid her face in the middle of his back.

Once, she woke to the feeling that he was also awake; she thought she could feel his body tensed and breathing at her side. "Charles?" she whispered.

"What?"

"Can't you sleep?"

"I had a nightmare."

She waited.

"Want to talk about it?"

"It's silly. I saw some men tonight when I went for a walk. I dreamed about them."

"What about them?"

"It's just silly. They were — it was a choir and they were singing."

"That doesn't sound like a nightmare."

"They were covered with blood."

"Oh, God."

"But I couldn't see it. It was supposed to be perfectly visible, you know. And yet they were wearing white. It was all white."

"I have such nightmares," she whispered.

He sighed. And in the dark his hand groped, patted her wrist.

She moved closer, kissed the side of his face, then licked the lobe of his ear. "Darling?"

He said nothing.

"Baby?"

"Oh," he murmured. "I'm sorry. I guess I went under a little."

She kissed him again, lightly, meaning it to seem casual, perfectly all right. Then she turned her back and, pulling the blankets high over her shoulder, tried to fall asleep.

•

Perhaps once or twice he might've drifted, but then he was wakeful, lying on his back listening to the whir of the heater fan, in which he thought he could hear the traces of music, sirens, even voices. It was his imagination, he knew. He couldn't sleep. Finally he put the light on and propped himself on the pillow to read. For a while he gazed distractedly at impossibly vivid photographs of natural phenomena in a travel magazine; then he was reading the Bible, or trying to, his mind wandering, going over everything; he was thinking about his failure to keep from being peevish with her.

"I can't sleep with the light on," she said suddenly.

It startled him. "You *were* asleep."

"How can I sleep?"

"I thought you were asleep."

"I can't sleep with the light on," she said. "Turn it off. Think of somebody besides yourself for a change."

He reached over and flicked the light off.

"Thank you."

"You're welcome," he said, and threw his part of the blanket off, getting out of the bed.

"Where're you going?"

"Out," he said, pulling on his pants.

"It's past two o'clock in the morning."

"Yeah, thank you. But I don't have as much trouble with these digital clocks. I just read the fucking numbers."

"Are you going to get drunk again?"

He didn't answer. He'd got into his clothes. He would spend a long time out in the night; he would give her something to worry about.

"This is a tantrum," she said. "Right?"

"I don't know," he said. "I think I'd recognize the signs."

"Charles."

"I'm going out for some air," he told her.

"Charles, stop this."

He got his leather coat on and opened the room door. The cold blew at him.

"Charles."

He slammed the door behind him, and the sound of it went echoing out into the parking lot. Across the way, the candle glowed in the office window, and there was a shadow of blurred moisture on the glass. He turned from this and made his way along the row of doorways, to the hedge and through it, down the long hill in the direction of the convenience store. He felt wrong, felt his own childishness like a fever, and this made him all the more angry, all the more intent on carrying his fit out to its end.

The cold air stung his breathing passages. He pulled his coat collar up, gripping it at his throat with one gloveless hand. Almost all of the apartment house beyond the mall was dark at this hour, and it gave the whole scene a denuded look; it had all shone so colorfully with decorations earlier. The few lighted windows were so widely separated as to suggest something meager and sad. Even the interstate was quiet — one truck rattled past, speeding. He paused in the chilly stillness, feeling his mood change, so far from home, adrift and tired and sick with the sensation of futility. He almost went back to the room.

In the convenience store, the small oriental woman behind the counter looked at him with something like wariness, but then she smiled. Her teeth were an amazing shade of yellow. He nodded, walking past her. He had come in simply for the light and the heat; there was nothing he wanted. Standing between two rows of merchandise, he looked at the bottles of antacid, containers of aspirin.

At the end of the aisle someone moved, and he turned to see the motel proprietor, old Uncle Arlen, standing with a lighted cigarette in his mouth, reading the label on a big can of coffee. Connally had sat listening to him talk earlier, waiting for him to offer a beer, which he never offered. He didn't feel friendly toward Arlen now, and he was pretty sure the feeling was mutual. Now he made an involuntary sound, and the old man looked at him through the smoke of the cigarette.

"Hey."

"Hey," Connally said.

A perfectly indifferent exchange.

The old man returned to reading his label, and Connally remained where he was, not wanting to seem to avoid him by moving away too quickly, yet wanting very much to keep from having to say anything else to him. It was absurd — this abrupt anxiousness to get back to the confines of the motel room. But it crossed his mind that the old man would know he was in an argument with his wife, and would want to give advice about it. He glanced at Arlen again, and saw that Arlen was looking beyond him, something changing in his leathery face. Connally saw surprise, then understood it as alarm. He turned and was confronted with a man wearing a nylon stocking pulled down over his head, the foot part of it dangling like a clownish appendage to one side. The man held what Connally realized with a spasm of the muscles around his heart was a shotgun.

"Jesus Christ," he said. "Don't shoot."

"Good evening," said the gunman. "Welcome to the end of the fucking world."

The face was twisted and flattened, the eyelids pulled into a droopy swollen frown, the nose looking mashed, like a child's pressed against glass; yet Connally knew him. He held his hands up and tried to breathe, and somehow he kept from saying the name. The one named Dwight raised the shotgun slightly and made a prodding motion, as though it were a stick. "Over here," he said through the nylon. "You and the old guy. Quick."

"I didn't come in here for anything," Connally heard himself say. "I don't have any money."

The other stared at him, then seemed to shrug something off. "It's gonna be a terrible night."

There were others in the store: a black man in a parka and sweatpants, a black woman in what looked like a nurse's uniform; and now Connally saw Dwight's companion — the smaller, thinner man, very agitated and shaken-seeming — holding a pistol with both hands and aiming it first at one person and then at another, as though he expected to be ambushed at any moment. His twisted features under the mask were somehow more pronounced, as if the stocking had been pulled over a permanent scream of pain. Moving to the counter, he grabbed the wrist of the oriental woman, who was no more than four and a half feet tall. She began to cry and moan, like someone about to be punished. She sounded exactly like a guilty child.

"All of you," the man with the shotgun said, "move."

They were all standing in a little knot by the cash register, and the one with the shotgun kept gesturing for them to back toward the doorway along the rear wall. Everything was blurred and confused, but they were all moving toward the door, which led into a foyer-like space, the entryway to the store's room-size refrigerator, with its thick walls, its feeling of moisture in the air, and its generator fan running. There were crates of merchandise stacked along the left wall — kegs of beer, cases of soft drinks and bottled soda, piled wood and boxes, and big cans of refuse. The right wall was a series of shelves with refrigerated products on them, on the other side of which were glass doors the customers could open. Connally was the first inside, and immediately he thought of the doors, looked through the carefully arranged packages of cheese and dip and milk, the cartons of eggs, and the bottles of beer and wine. The shelves did not look removable; there was no way to crawl through, and yet the open space beyond seemed tantalizingly possible.

Dwight stood in the entrance of the room and regarded them — Connally, who kept rubbing his mouth, trying to keep from showing his face to him too fully, the black man, the nurse, Arlen, and the oriental woman. When Dwight spoke, the nylon showed a tiny bead of spittle. "Here it is, I'm afraid. The absolute worst night of your lives."

Everyone remained quite still, and there was a quality to the silence — a pathological, barely breathing hesitation. Behind Dwight, the other, smaller man seemed to be rushing from place to place, opening boxes and throwing things. Then he opened one of the cooler doors, and Connally saw him take a carton of milk out, open it, pull the stocking from his lips, and drink.

"Well?" Dwight said.

"Eighty-two dollars in the register, man."

"You — looking out the glass. Get away from there."

Connally did so.

"You know what a nightmare you're in?" The voice was soft, almost caressive. "I'm talking to you."

"Let's just cool it," said the black man. "Everybody's doing what you want."

"What if nobody's around to tell how brave you were, nigger?" That soft, confident voice.

"Oh, please," the motel proprietor said. "Let's not get out of hand here."

"Everybody just be still," the black man said.

"Are you giving orders now?" Dwight said.

The other man called to him from the counter. "It won't open. It must be different at each store. I've tried all the numbers and it won't budge." There was something frantic in his voice.

"We've got a nigger giving orders," said Dwight, aiming the shotgun.

"He's not ordering any of us around," the motel proprietor said. "We won't listen. We're listening to you, sir."

"I have your full attention."

"Yes, sir."

"You think I ought to shoot this nigger?"

The motel proprietor's face seemed to twist then, as if he were in some pain.

"Let's shoot him, what do you say?"

"Oh, please," said Arlen.

"You want me to shoot him." Dwight put the twin barrels of the shotgun against the side of the black man's head. The black man had straightened slightly; beads of sweat stood out above his lips. The small muscles of his cheeks were jumping, but there was no other sign that he would give way. He did not. He stood there, and gradually the jumping in his cheeks stopped.

"Jesus," said the motel proprietor, covering his ears.

The gunman actually laughed. For an absurd moment it

all looked like a joke, the way he punched the black man's shoulder and stepped back, laughing, holding the weapon as if in mock aim, like a boy playing at guns. He seemed almost innocent.

"Hey, admit it — you're about to shit in your drawers."

"Our Father, who art in heaven," the motel proprietor said.

"Shut up about that Our Father stuff. It's time to be serious and real practical." Now Dwight turned to the oriental woman. "You speakee English? Out here." She had been whimpering the whole time, and at his gesture that she follow him, she fell to her knees. "You'll get your knees dirty," he said, pointing the shotgun at her.

She made a sound, "Ahhhh," not looking at him, her small hands outstretched. Connally thought absurdly of Buddhists praying in the temple; the almost concave flatness of her face was shining with tears, and she brought her hands together over her head.

"Hey, Darvon," Dwight said. Then he seemed to smile — showing, through the moist nylon, a gap in his teeth. "Hey, Hughes."

Connally saw himself describing this to the authorities, or to a sketch artist. He thought of television newscasts.

The other gunman came to the doorway. "It won't open, man. It's fucked up."

Dwight put the shotgun under one arm and began wrestling with the oriental woman — hauling her, kicking and begging and fighting, out of the room. She sent up a terrible racket, an ear-piercing scream. Her flesh shook through the black silk cloth of her slacks. The other gunman, Darvon or Hughes, kept looking over his shoulder as if to check her progress across to the counter.

"Nervous?" the nurse said to him.

Wielding the pistol as if to fend something off, he started, then crouched slightly, pointing the pistol at her and at the black man in turn. "I'll use this. I mean it."

"Calm down, son," the black man said.

"I'll calm *you* down, man. I'll calm you right down."

The black man moved his head slightly aside from the barrel of the pistol as the gunman thrust it at him.

"I'll calm you down for-fucking-ever."

"Okay. We're cool."

"Man, you got a lot of nerve fucking with me at a time like this."

"Nobody's fucking with you," said the black man.

"Just don't say anything," the old man said.

Out front, the oriental woman had stopped yelling. It had grown quiet.

"What're you doing, Dwight?"

No answer came.

"Man, Dwight — what's the deal?" The one with the pistol shook, seemed to quaver. Something like a whimper came from him.

"Can I tell you something, son? Is it Hughes?" the black man said.

The gunman stiffened, grew visibly more shaky.

"Hughes, right?"

"Man, why do you think you know anything?"

"If you hold the gun too tight, it might go off before you want it to."

"It's going to go off in your *face*, man, if you don't stop fucking around."

From outside came the shriek of the oriental woman again.

"Jesus — come on, Dwight." The nervous one was now holding the pistol with both hands, pointing it at the black man's face.

Dwight came back into the room, dragging the oriental

woman. Her pant legs had been pulled up, and her stockings were torn and besmirched. A gum wrapper adhered to her thigh, like a horrible sign of indignity itself. She lay there crying while the one named Dwight stood over her. "Fucking hopeless," he said.

"Did you get it open?" the smaller gunman, Hughes, asked.

"She can't open it."

"I could've told you that, man. Jesus, everybody knows that."

"That's what they want you to think."

"Aw, Christ. Let's go. Let's get out of here."

"Let's do some shooting first."

"Shit, man. Somebody's going to pull up or something."

Connally heard all this as if from a great distance. He looked at the unreadable yet greatly interested face of the black man, and at the bald panic in the face of the motel proprietor. And now, as if he had been blank for a moment, he saw the gunmen backing out of the room, pulling the other woman, the nurse, with them. She was protesting. "Get your hands off me, turkey. I can walk on my own."

The one with the shotgun, the one called Dwight, twisted her arm and held the twin barrels of the gun to the side of her head. "Be quiet," he said in that voice. "Be very quiet, now."

"Fool. I'm not afraid of you."

"In a little while that won't make any difference at all." He backed out, still holding her arm behind her, and the other gunman followed, closing the door. In the quiet that ensued, Connally breathed, and realized that he might live.

The motel proprietor said, "We'll freeze to death, won't we?"

"They won't leave us here," said the black man. "They're not through."

"What do you mean?"

"I mean one of them isn't interested in just the money."

"How do you know that?" the motel proprietor said.

The black man shrugged. There was something almost forlorn about it. "Just do."

"They're going to kill us, right?"

He held one hand up, as if demanding quiet.

"That's it, isn't it? This is the goddam eleven o'clock news happening to us here, isn't it?"

"Please," Connally said to him.

"You don't think so? This is America, boy. This is what we got ourselves into now. At this time of the morning."

"Oh, no," the oriental woman moaned. "No, no, no, no."

Connally said, "We wouldn't freeze to death anyway, right? If they left us."

The black man apparently considered this a moment, then seemed to dismiss it. Clearly, he was holding something back. Connally studied his face — large-featured, inky black, with wide, flaring nostrils and downturned mouth; a set look to the jaw, as if he had stood stubbornly in great storms of protest. The hair above his ears was lightly brushed with gray, and along one dark cheek was a beaded scar that looked ill-healed, as though it might start bleeding again if it was touched.

"It's not freezing temperature in here," Connally told him.

"They'll just go, won't they?" the old man said. "Maybe they'll just go."

The black man moved to the shelves and peered out. "Can't really see anything."

"You think they left?"

He waited a moment. "No."

"Why don't they leave," Arlen said, sounding as if he

might start to cry. "There's nothing to stop them from leaving."

"Maybe they'll leave," said Connally.

"The thing is to keep cool. Not get panicky, right?"

Connally looked inside himself for panic. He felt nothing. There was a deep numbness in him now. "No panic," he said, not really hearing himself.

An instant later, they heard a shot. It sent the oriental woman into a fit of screaming, and the old man fell to his knees, his hands folded tight under his chin. "My God. Oh, my dear God," he kept saying. "Oh God, oh God."

The black man was peering out through the openings in the shelves. "Everybody be quiet," he said. The steadiness in his voice made Connally feel almost light-headed with hope. But he was talking at the black man, and it was all coming out of him like something in a dream. "I had an argument with my wife. I shouldn't even have come down here. I don't even live here." The black man pulled a revolver out of the parka, and Connally took a step back from him.

"Take it easy, sir. I'm a police officer."

"Oh, Jesus Christ," the motel proprietor said. "Save us." He and the oriental woman were cowering against an aluminum rack of packaged meat; she had grasped him about the waist, and the two of them looked like one of those old silent-movie tableaux — the poor wife begging the determined husband not to leave her. The latch on the door made its metallic little sound, almost bell-like, and the black man moved to shield himself behind a stack of beer cases.

"Get back," he said. "Get down."

The two gunmen were framed in the doorway an instant, and then everything went white, the one with the pistol firing — or his gun going off — the black man kneeling and falling forward and firing, and simultaneously the shotgun exploding, the huge sound of it, and the gunman named

Dwight being blown out of the doorway as if he had dropped through the floor backwards, falling out of the screaming, out of the flashes of fire, everything piercing, the room quaking as if the walls might give way, then the sound dying into the long, tearing shriek of the woman, the concussive feel of the explosions still prickling on the skin, and Connally realized that the black man was lying face down on the floor, that his own hands were down on the black man's massive, muscular back, something fluttering there under the shirt — a spasm or paroxysm, then a stillness.

The smaller gunman, Hughes, was kneeling in the doorway, pointing the pistol with both hands. He stood, he was gasping or sobbing. "Okay, everybody down. Everybody get the fuck down!" He moved toward them, toward Connally. "Down. EVERYBODY DOWN!"

They did so, waiting for him to tell them what to do. They were all on the floor, in the wailing and crying of the oriental woman, and for a moment it was as if they had all joined in the same immense grief. "Okay," Hughes said. He was shaking; Connally heard fright in his voice.

"Okay. Okay. Okay, okay, okay."

"Please," said the motel proprietor. "There's been enough. We won't tell."

"You better shut up, man." The voice was pinched with something frantic. "Oh, Jesus. Jesus. Don't anybody — you better stay still, goddammit."

The first thing Connally thought about when he got to the floor was that it smelled strongly of ammonia. He saw a stain coming from the base of the wall; he looked at it, marked it, hearing Hughes moving in the room. Something metal clicked against metal.

"Don't look at me, you — goddam you."

"No one's looking," Arlen said.

"Just everybody stay still and let me think."

"Please," Arlen said. "It might be best if you —"

"Shut up. Man, will you shut up?"

"I'll shut up."

Connally's face was turned away; he was watching the wide, crying face of the oriental woman.

And now it seemed to him that Hughes was crying.

"Son, there's a way out of this," Arlen said.

"I said goddammit shut up!"

There was a pause. The only sound was breathing now. The gunman took a step. "Lay still, man."

"Oh, God," Arlen said. "Please don't."

There followed a moment's quiet, and then the tremendous shock of the gun going off. It caused the oriental woman to begin screaming, though Connally could see that she wasn't trying to get up. She was all right; she was a person yelling. "All right," he heard himself say. "All right, all right." He saw the gunman take a step toward her, and cried out once, or tried to — a tearing something, escaping him without sound. Then he was hearing himself breathe, was intensely, almost exquisitely aware of his own lungs filling with air, beginning to feel a prodigious horrible peace settling over him. And feeling something else, too — a thing like being the smallest child. He looked at Hughes and experienced a strange infantile devotion, like a kind of yearning. The gunman's features, the skin of his wrists and the muscles in his neck, took on an aspect of great sensual beauty.

"Lay still," the gunman said to the oriental woman, ranging himself above her.

Suddenly she began scrabbling toward the door, and Connally simply stood up. He couldn't believe himself. The poor motel proprietor lay on the floor, face down in blood, an impossible amount of blood. Connally had stood, and was watching Hughes push the woman to the floor. Now Hughes aimed the pistol at him. "Godammit, man. Get back down where you were."

The woman was still struggling to get away, her wide flesh working. Hughes struck her on the back of the head with the barrel of the pistol. "Lay down."

She only cried louder, and Connally heard himself say, "Let her alone — Jesus Christ, that's enough. That's enough!"

Hughes looked at him. "Yeah," he said. "Yeah, I know who you are. We saw you at that construction site. Dwight wanted to do you then, man. Dwight was a fucking killer. We're fucking killers, man."

"Just let us go," said Connally. "We won't tell anyone."

"*Fuck* it," said the other, brandishing the pistol at him again. "You're not in control here. Come here."

Connally found that he couldn't move.

"Now, man! I'm gonna shoot you."

He took a step. The other man backed up a little, then was looking toward the front of the store. It came to Connally with a species of bewilderment that sirens were sounding, that there was a commotion somewhere outside this small space. "Stay away," the little gunman said to someone. "Stay away, man. I've got hostages here. I'VE GOT HOSTAGES HERE!"

The moment's hesitation allowed the oriental woman to crawl toward Connally, and on impulse he tried to block her, thought of trying to shield himself with her. He had his hands on her arms, and then he was holding her wrists, holding her up. He could've struck her full in the face without the slightest compunction. "Stand up," he said to her. "Christ." When she looked at him, the expression on her face, of a kind of frantic gratefulness, made him turn slightly, allowing her to move by him. She got to the farthest corner of the room and lay there on her side, her legs drawn up, her dimpled hands over her face.

Now the gunman seemed to have forgotten her. He pointed the pistol at Connally. "Okay, move it. Get over here."

"Don't shoot," Connally said, advancing, feeling again that sense of abject child-love toward him. "Please."

The other man put his free hand on Connally's shoulder and stepped behind him. "Okay. Walk."

He did so. In the storefront window now there was a blaze of lights. They made slow progress across the floor. He held one hand up to shield his eyes, couldn't see to take a step.

"I'll blow his brains out if you don't turn the lights off!"

Some of the lights went down. They were standing a few feet from the bank of coffee machines and condiments. They waited, and then Connally felt the barrel of the gun at the base of his skull; he was being pushed toward the entrance to the store, past aisles of scattered merchandise and a trailing pool of blood. He thought of the nurse, then saw her sitting against the inside of the counter, her hands open on her lap, her dark eyes staring. Out in the cold, he came to know he had made his way here, and didn't remember having done so. The gun barrel hurt. He was jostled toward the edge of the sidewalk. "Where?" he said, feeling the other man's grip tighten on his shoulder. "This way?" Some part of him marked the absurd consideration in his own voice. Everything was out of focus now, pulsing with light, distant sirens coming closer; there was a bluish cast to the air, and he heard a sputtering of voices in static.

"I'll blow him apart."

Police officers were crouched behind several cars in the lot. Somehow all these people had become involved.

"Everybody back."

For a long time they stood there shivering while other cars pulled in, other lights flashed and stopped.

"Stand still," the gunman said.

And then a voice spoke out of the confusion of open car doors and lights. "What's your name, son?"

"Everybody back off, I mean it."

"Talk to us."

"I'll blow his head off."

"Tell us what you want."

Hughes's voice was almost tearful. "I want everybody to get out of here."

"We can't do that, son. Why don't you just put the gun down."

"It's not my fault."

"We'll get to the bottom of it."

The gun was now pushing Connally's head forward slightly. "Could you please —" Connally began.

"Everybody be quiet," said the gunman.

"Just put the gun down and nobody'll hurt you. It's easy. It's the easiest thing in the world. Come on. Nobody here wants to hurt anybody. We're all just folks, you know — at work, sort of. We'd like to see you get out of this in one piece."

"You better think about *him*," Hughes said, and Connally felt another increment of pressure from the gun barrel.

"We're thinking about both of you. We don't want anyone else to be hurt."

Other vehicles were pulling in. And after what seemed an endless wait the gunman began pushing Connally toward the edge of the sidewalk. They had got to the single step down in the parking lot, but then Hughes was pulling him back toward the wall of the store. It was amazing that they could have come so short a distance in the great length of time since they had left the refrigerator.

Looking into the profusion of vehicles and lights, Connally felt something change in him. His memory went away and he was a blank, he was empty, feeling nothing, believing

nothing, only a pair of eyes, an aggregate of senses, connected to no history or past. It was a moment of such
vividness — the colors, the little clouds of breathing on the
air, the smell of gasoline and gunpowder, and the squawk
and static of the sirens and radios — that he almost cried
out. But then in the next moment, he began to experience
something else, a stirring, a shifting of blood, an impulse no
more substantial than the merest urge to whistle, except that
now, from the new hollowness inside him, it seemed to flare
up like a pulse, something utterly new, rushing in to fill a
vacuum. With the sensation of having given way to some
other self inside, he wrenched himself from the other man's
grasp and dove toward the confusion of lights in the parking
lot, feeling nerves and synapses arcing in the moment of
falling. He was free. He had done it. He had taken a running
step, and then another. He was on the ground now, moving
through slow time, separated, pulling himself forward, hearing, from too near, the concussion of the pistol and the
exploding guns, rolling hard on the cold asphalt, scrambling
across a patch of jagged ice, his face in the oil-smelling grit,
hearing more shots, hearing screams, coming to understand
that one scream had issued forth from his own mouth. He
lay on his hurting stomach, peering at everything through a
small foot-high space, and realized that he was under an
automobile. He had pulled himself under a car. Somewhere
a tire whistled piercingly, and there had also been the sound
of shattering glass.

He was alive. He had lived through this, had made it.

The only pain was in his stomach and knees where he had
scurried across the surface of ice and asphalt. He heard
more sirens. Shouts, shrieks of brakes, and the absurd dying
squeal of the leaking tire. He looked across the ice-veined
surface of asphalt and saw the gunman, who was lying on
his back with his hands thrown out from his body, broken

glass all over his chest. Hughes looked at him and said something, and then he was talking to a police officer who put a hand along his neck.

"Need medical help here," the policeman said.

Now someone was speaking to Connally from the other side of the car. "Sir? You all right?"

Connally nodded at him, then looked back at Hughes, who was being tended to.

"You can come on out of there. You need help getting out of there?"

They were all around him as he worked his way from under the car. They moved with him to the back end of an ambulance, where he sat down and others began looking him over and talking to him. He couldn't make much of any of it out. There were people with cameras now, and a big van from a television station, and he saw more vehicles and emergency lights and camera crews. Cables and wires were being laid down everywhere. A crowd of onlookers had gathered from the apartment house across the way — people in robes and with parkas on over pajamas, some of them holding children in their arms, standing behind an orange ribbon someone had put up, moving to keep themselves warm, yet still watching, staring at everyone in the lights. The lights were blinding.

"We're going to give you a mild sedative," a voice said.

"Sir, could you tell us what happened?" Someone thrust a microphone at him.

He turned away from it.

"Hold still," someone said.

He looked at the faces. Medics, or doctors. Police. News people, cameramen. Some people in uniforms. Beyond them, another ambulance had pulled up, and others were putting a gurney into it. A man with a parka hood on, so that his face was in shadow, thrust himself at him from the cordoning arms of police.

"We need a statement. Would you make a statement, sir?"

"Let us just do this, will you?" one of the medics said.

They took Connally's blood pressure, and someone draped a blanket over his shoulders.

"We need your name and address," a woman said, holding a pad and not quite looking at him.

"We're going to take him in for observation," said one of the people in uniform. It was a white uniform. "You can talk to him after we make sure he's all right."

"The Chinese lady says he's a hero," said the woman with the pad. Then she leaned toward him, as if to get a closer look at his face. "Do you know you're a hero, sir?"

"Okay." A man's voice came from the other side of the open ambulance doors. "We've got two dead in the refrigerator room, and two dead in the store, and one with gunshot wounds in the hip, thigh, and neck. Medic says he thinks it's not fatal. He'll make it, believe it or not."

"Sir?" the woman said.

"Who are you?" Connally said.

"I'm with the *Chicago Daily News*."

"Leave me alone. Get out of here."

"People want to know what happened to you. It's natural for them to want to know."

"Okay," someone said. "Back off a minute."

The woman turned, moved away a step, and a man with thick, trunk-like legs and a wide, jowly face stepped through the bedlam of lights and shadows and moving bodies. He was wearing a tie, and it seemed to lie out flat against his heavy chest. "You all right?"

Connally nodded at him. He recognized the voice. This was the man who had tried to negotiate with Hughes.

"Rough time."

"Yes, sir."

"It's gonna be rough a while."

"Yes."

"I'm Sergeant Donovan."

"Yes, sir."

"I'm sort of in charge of all this confusion here. You feel like talking a little?"

"Oh, Jesus Christ," Connally said.

"I don't blame you."

"I don't even know."

Sergeant Donovan reached over and patted his shoulder. "Oriental lady says you saved her life."

"I don't think so."

"That's what she said. We can't get much else out of her."

"I don't know," Connally told him.

"Look. I think I can figure some out for myself, but — we need to talk about it."

Connally stirred. "I want to tell you about it —"

The man spoke gently. "There's a few things we have to ask, and it'll take a little while. You up to it?"

"Let's get it over with now," Connally said. "I want to get it over with now."

"I'm sorry for it."

Connally put his hands to his face.

"Get back," someone said. "Hold it. Give me the light."

The big man's questions at first were ordinary—name, age, address, marital status—but gradually they became searching, and forced him to look at everything again: the detective wanted to know what was said and done, how the murders began, the order of things. He wrote in a pad some of what Connally told him, though another man stood by with a tape recorder. The words describing the shootings began to sound almost reasonable. It was safe and warm here in the lights, in the idling ambulance. A doctor put something in a syringe and gave him a shot. Nearby, sirens went up again, and he had to speak louder. He saw that out in the night it had begun to rain. He thought of his wife, and looked at all the faces.

"I think Hughes's pistol killed the policeman," he said.
"Well, we'll know when forensics gets through."
"It looked accidental. But Arlen and the nurse — that was cold-blooded murder."

The questions were done with. "We'll talk more," the big man said, "after you've had some time."

"Yes, sir."

A doctor stood by with his hand on Connally's wrist, looking at a watch on his own wrist. And now a stooped, willowy man pushed through the crowd of others and put one hand on his shoulder. He had bushy eyebrows and a long, splayed nose, and he looked vaguely familiar: Connally thought he'd seen him on television, though that couldn't be, since this was Chicago. But then he recognized him; he was someone who had left a Virginia television station for opportunities elsewhere.

"Excuse me," the man said. "I'm Mike Sawyer."

Somewhere, another voice was going on about murder.

"I'm with the news channel, and I'd like to do an interview at the scene with you, if you don't mind. I told these people you ought to at least get to decide for yourself whether or not you want that now."

"Not now," Connally said.

"Don't you want to be on the news?" the man said. "You did something brave. It'll be a minute or two before they can take you anywhere."

"I don't want to go anywhere." The sedative — whatever they had given him — was working. He could feel the tightness in the sinews of his back begin to loosen slightly.

"It'll just take a minute," the bushy-browed man said.

Connally allowed himself to be led through the rain to the television van, where other people were standing with hand mikes and mini-cams and wires. Mike Sawyer took a hand mike from someone, and pulled the wires around behind him. He took Connally by the elbow and turned him slightly. "What's your name?"

Connally told him.

"Okay."

He looked through the rain at the dark shape of the motel on its hill above the highway.

". . . one of the two survivors of the tragedy here." The man was holding the microphone toward him.

"I didn't hear the question," Connally said.

"Start over," said the television man.

"I didn't hear the question."

"I was talking to the camera."

And Connally began to laugh. It was like someone else; it was a sound coming from somewhere.

"Are you all right? Can you do this?"

"I don't really want to do it."

"He doesn't want to do it."

"Will you just answer a couple of questions?" someone asked out of the dark on the other side of the lights. The rain was coming harder now.

"Shit, let's hurry if we're going to do it."

Connally couldn't stop laughing.

"Okay. Just hold it. Christ."

"I'm sorry."

"Just one twenty-second thing, all right?"

"Mr. Connor, could you describe what happened here tonight?"

"Conn*ally,*" he said.

"Ah. Christ. I'm sorry. Okay, from the edge."

They waited.

"Mr. Con-*nally* —"

"It's just Connally."

The man sighed. "I'm a complete idiot tonight, folks. Jesus pleasus. Listen, will you just let it roll, Harv, and we'll take care of it in the truck. Mr. Connally, could you describe for us what happened here tonight?"

"Murder," Connally said, and something moved under his heart. "Killings. Goddam. *Killings.*"

"Shit. Back up."

"One of us was a policeman."

"Back it up."

Connally waited.

"I know you're upset, son. You have a right to be. But try to concentrate here, a little, okay? You're a hero, for Christ's sake. You tried to shield that lady and you saved her life at the risk of your own. Don't you want to say anything about it?"

"I don't think I saved anybody's life."

"She says you saved her."

"I don't know how that could be true."

"She believes it to be true. How do you know it's not true?"

"I don't know. I don't think so."

"The version we have says you acted to save her life. That's what she told us and we have no reason to doubt her."

"I didn't save her life," Connally said. He might have gone on speaking; he wasn't sure if he'd spoken aloud: "I wanted her to stop — if she kept up — he — he shot the old man for *talking.* I didn't even see her after he aimed the pistol at me."

"What?" the television man said. "Speak into the microphone. This is no good. This is no help. Let's go with Mrs. Wu."

"That's her name?" Connally said.

"All right. Let's just try it one more time. Mr. Connally, Mrs. Wu is the woman you acted to save tonight. Could you tell us what you were thinking when it happened?"

"I just wanted the shooting to stop."

"Did you say anything to the gunmen, sir?"

"I don't remember anything."

"Can we use any of this?" The television man was talking to others now. "It's pretty scant, isn't it?"

"Get him to say what he did."

"I didn't do anything unusual," Connally said.

"Did you get that?"

"Check," came the voice from behind the lights.

"I'm sorry we bothered you," said the television man.

"I didn't think I saved anyone's life," Connally said. Now someone had taken his arm and was guiding him back toward the ambulance. The sedative had made him woozy. When he reached the ambulance, he recognized the face of Sergeant Donovan.

"Some scene," Sergeant Donovan said. He sounded out of breath. Between the heavy fingers of one puffy hand, he held a cigarette. There was something almost dainty about the way he brought it to his mouth and took a draw on it. "The cop they killed was a fella by the name of Jack Shelby."

"He tried to help us," said Connally, feeling as though he might start crying. It seemed tremendously important not to let down in front of the other man. Somehow, he held it all back, turning from Donovan, feeling himself begin to quaver inside, deep. Another voice said his name from nearby, and he heard something almost pleading in the tone. He remembered, with a strange little leap of his blood, that he didn't live anywhere near here.

"You want to go with these people?" a woman asked.

He looked into the face, violet with cold and livid around the eyes. "No," he said. "I'm all right. I just want to go."

The rain swept down out of the eerie pulsing of the emergency lights, and now another siren began to sound.

"You're all right?" Donovan asked him.

He nodded.

"Sure?"

"Yes."

"You need anything?"

"We're staying up the hill there."

"Right."

"I just want to go to sleep now."

"Hell of a thing, id'n it?" the big man said.

Connally thought he said it was.

"You take her easy now."

Cars were moving out of the lot. The crowd was beginning to disperse. All these people had come from the apartment building behind the store, having awakened to the sound of sirens and to the ghostly shiftings of light through their closed curtains. They were all subdued, walking quietly back to their rooms and their beds, and as Connally moved past them they stared with the simple frankness of expectation. He had come from the encircled area, from the television van, but they would hear nothing from him, and they seemed to sense it; perhaps it was the way he walked through, looking straight ahead. "I was sound asleep," a woman was saying to others. "I thought it was a fire."

Connally climbed the hill, parted the hedge, and stepped through. He saw two policemen enter the office: they would inform the nephew of poor Arlen's death. Arlen, who only minutes ago had stood in that absurd silent-movie stance, the oriental woman clinging to his waist. Back down the long hill, the convenience store shone in that ominous blue pulsing. Connally turned the key in the motel room door and stepped inside, closing it, feeling the quiet and the warmth like something coursing through his veins.

Carol apparently had not awakened.

He stood absolutely still in the dark, and it seemed that the whole of life was freighted with pathological possibility:

murder, catastrophe — the blackness outside, the vast piti-
less natural world — it all seemed terribly near and threatening. From his soiled coat, the odor of blood rose. He
stirred, went into the bathroom, closed the door, and turned
the light on. In the mirror over the sink he looked at himself.
Perhaps if he had waited with the doctors and taken some
more of the sedative. His leather coat was spattered with
blood. At some point he had bruised his forehead, and a
small red welt stood out on his chin. One elbow of the coat
was barked and torn. Even when he thought about it, he
couldn't remember getting under the car. In fact, the whole
event seemed to be fading quickly around the edges of one
image — that of the nurse sitting in the pool of her own
blood. It seemed now that the belief in the brutal reality of
the thing had come to him, not with the deaths of the others,
but in the moment of seeing her sitting there so matter-of-
factly with her hands in her lap, dead.

Remembering this, he began to cry. He sat on the edge of
the bathtub and, putting his hands to his face, cried silently,
with profound exhaustion, like a spell of madness. At the pit
of his stomach, but in a way which was more than that — as
though it moved on the surface of the little trembling core of
his deepest being — he was mortally, wholly afraid.

He cried for a long time, then stood and took the coat off,
washed his face and hands. The water was rusty, and he
turned it off. With his face in the fresh-smelling towel, he
felt hidden briefly. The bathroom was a plain, recognizable
room. Here were his wife's hairbrush and hand mirror; here
were her curlers, her bottles of toilet water and perfume.

He was crying again.

Finally he got out of his clothes and went back into the
room, in the dark, feeling for the edge of the bed. She muttered something sleepy, stirring — and then she reached for
him.

"I'm sorry," she said. "Forgive me?"

He had got to the bed, was holding her, looking at the fabric of the dark, the texture of it, which was somehow the texture of his sight. He didn't know where to begin.

"I don't know what gets into us," she said, snuggling. "But it's over now. It's okay now."

He waited a moment, then took a breath to speak, and couldn't. She was resting so peacefully, with such relief, in his arms: she was so sure everything was all right. And, he told himself, everything *was* all right. He lay quiet, trying to believe it, trying to draw the assurance out of himself.

"I thought I heard sirens and got scared," she said. "There must've been an accident out on the interstate. I didn't want to see, and then I just went out."

He patted her shoulder, hoping this was answer enough.

"Where did you go? Did you see anything?"

"A walk," he told her. "No."

Sometime after she'd drifted back to sleep, he removed himself from the bed and crept to the chair by the window. He looked out at the lot, the plane of the highway going off to the west. From this angle, it was impossible to see the convenience store, and even so he put the side of his face against the cold glass and tried to look down that way. The lights seemed to have diminished, but something still flashed, some arterial pulse of illumination. Up the other way, the police car was still parked in front of the motel office. He had made it here, was not so frightened now, though he was obscurely aware of a pressure building up inside, and this had begun not while the shootings were taking place and not while he was being held at gunpoint, but later, here, in the motel room bath. It was as if he had been shown something about himself that he hadn't known before, something unpleasant and shameful. Yet no matter how hard he tried to look at it, set it out in some sort of reasonable shape in his mind, he could come up with nothing concrete enough to explain; he felt only the bottomless sense of what the fear had been.

•

In first light she came up out of a dream that she was running in bright sun — winded, her arms futilely outstretched — pursuing a little blond girl who happened also to be herself. Connally lay with his back to her, inanimate as wood. She sat up, looked at the room, her own amber reflection in the blank television screen. When she stood, she paused a moment, expecting to feel woozy. But nothing happened. Quietly, she got into a pair of jeans and a blouse, retrieved her brush and comb from the bathroom, and sat at the small bureau, trying to get the knots out of her hair. Connally moved in little jerking motions, dreaming. The blankets were twisted around his waist. She put the hairbrush down, stepped to the window, and looked out. The sky was cloudless and bright blue now, and most of the snow had melted. Everything seemed quite reasonable and clear, and she felt happy. She fixed some of the instant coffee from the packets on the bureau, and sat in the chair in the sunlight, watching the traffic speed by on the interstate. In a little while, she heard him stir in the bed. He turned slowly and gave forth a little groan, then sat straight up. He blinked.

"Morning," she said.

His hands went up to his face, and when he brought them down she saw the welt on his chin, the small violet place on his forehead.

"Honey?" she said, sitting forward.

•

Somehow, he managed to tell her everything. At least he told her what he could clearly remember: the stocking masks

like so many they had seen on television, the off-duty policeman, the shots. The end of it. All of it. She sat very still,
not quite looking at him, and he remembered that as he had
walked through the store with the pistol at the back of his
head, he had seen the nurse sitting like a big doll thrown
against the inside of the counter, and believed fully — for
perhaps the first time in his life — in his own death. He
halted, unable to speak for a moment, unable to keep from
seeing the image in his mind.

"Don't," his wife said. "Don't say anymore."

For all the fading imagery of the thing, he began to have
an ever clearer sense that he had seen part of Dwight's head
disarrange itself on one side at exactly the same second the
off-duty policeman fired his weapon and went down.

He shook, thinking of it. "I think the little guy's pistol just
went off because he was holding it so tight. And the shot
killed the policeman just as he — shot Dwight."

"Don't," Carol said. "God, stop. It sounds like you knew
them."

"They had television cameras —" he began.

"Charles."

"I'm all right," he said, trying to get his breath. "I can't
stop seeing it, though. I looked right at her face."

"I wonder if it's on the news."

He was rubbing his thighs with the palms of his hands,
and when he realized this he stood, began to get into his
clothes.

"Honey?"

And it came to him with a kind of sick recognition that he
wanted to get off by himself; it was actually as if he needed
a few moments' respite from her.

"Do we have to stay here, now?" she asked.

"I'll have to come back for the trial, I guess. I don't
know."

"I want to go home," she said.

He had pulled on his shirt, and was trying to button it with trembling fingers.

"God," she said. "Christmas." In the brightness of the window she looked bowed, staring out, her hands working in front of her, the fingers knotted, moving in and out of each other, her every motion expressing fretfulness and the sense of things getting out of control. "What about your mother?"

"Jesus." The word had escaped from him like an involuntary tic at the thought of his mother — the sudden recollection of everything for which he had begun this journey westward: the fact of Carol's pregnancy blew through him.

"Well?" she said.

"I'm sorry — Jesus — I can't think right now."

"Do you want me to call her?"

"No," he said. "We'll go into town. I'll get the car warmed up. I want to go into town." He got into his coat and she gave forth a little gasp. "I'll wash it," he said. He was all action now, crossing to the door and pulling it open on the wind and chilly sun. "When we get there."

"She's not expecting us for an hour, Charles."

His wife stood in the cold blast from the door, her thin arms wrapped tight around herself.

"Shouldn't we call her?"

"I'll warm the car up," he said. "There's no need to call her. I don't want to tell her something like this on the phone." He stepped away from the door, looked at the cordoned building at the bottom of the long hill, its cars and its city vehicles and police wagons parked in front of it. Nothing moved. The motel office was closed, and there was no sign of Arlen's nephew. All the other rooms were closed and locked, the curtains drawn. Carol came out in her coat, looking frightened.

He got into the car and started it, experiencing an odd, transient sense of well-being at the simple fact of his control of an engine. He gunned it, waiting for Carol. When she got in, he saw that she was fighting back tears.

"I don't understand what we're supposed to do, now," she said.

"It's over," he told her. "We don't have to do anything."

"I don't want to go into the city, Charles."

He backed the car out and drove to the entrance of the interstate. The surge of power when he pulled into the flow of traffic made him feel as though he were rising out of deep water, toward air.

"Slow down," she said in a small voice. "Please."

He eased up slightly.

"Charles," she said.

"It's going to be fine," he said. "We don't even live here."

"I wish we'd never come."

"Don't cry," he said. "Don't worry."

"You're going too fast."

Her face was heart-shaped. He felt as though he had never noticed this before; it was quite like a heart, with its soft convergence of angles at the chin and its dark hairline, the suggestion of a widow's peak. For some reason, thinking of this made him feel that he might begin to slip toward panic, and he tried to concentrate on the road ahead. When she fumbled with the radio, he asked her to leave it alone.

"I want to see if it's on the news yet."

"It's over. All right? It's done with and we're going to forget about it."

They were quiet. She huddled on the seat and stared out the passenger window. It was exactly as if they were irritated with each other. Before them, the city shone in a spectacular shower of sun pouring through a vast, smudged escarpment of storm clouds. It looked extraordinarily peace-

ful, gloriously immutable and solid — the world's one answer to every consternation. Connally found it difficult to
imagine that people killed there, or that its shining towers
held anything less than sanctuary. He was afraid of the flat
expanses of open plain, the brown spaces and distances and
faceless suburban streets.

He was speeding.

"Charles, please," she said in a small, hurt voice at his
side.

He apologized, feeling the urgency of putting miles between himself and the motel, that complex of stores and
establishments, the black flatness of the surrounding fields,
the grit and refuse of the broken, grass-sprung asphalt —
the desolate, pathological feeling of the place, with its winter sky and its distant hulks and silos, its smell of gasoline
and blood.

•

His mother had seen it on the morning news. She was awake
and dressed when they arrived, and she wanted to hear
everything. "You're a hero," she told him. "They're touting
you. Really."

"Touting me," he said.

"No kidding. The reluctant hero. That was the phrase he
used. I saw you on television not five minutes ago. It's the
top story. That Chinese lady crying and saying you saved
her life. On the scene. They took it on the scene, right?
Minutes after it happened, they said."

"Jesus," said Connally, "I don't believe this."

"The one killer got a bullet in his neck but they think he'll
make it. And that poor police officer. You know he was off
duty?"

"I was there," Connally said. "Christ."

"I'm sorry."

A moment later, she said, "I thought we might go to the aquarium today. But I guess you won't want to do much of anything now."

The thought of a public building where people gathered and were safe seemed remote, nearly unimaginable.

"I don't think we should sit around and think about it all day," Carol said.

They were both looking at Connally now. Something had passed between them — a look, some muted gesture of Carol's. And now his mother was urging him to her side, guiding him toward the open door.

"We'll go right on with our visit, won't we," she was saying. "We won't let it get the best of us."

"This isn't bad weather or money trouble," Connally said.

They drove to the aquarium in a quiet that seemed to feed on itself; it would be harder and harder to break. On the street outside the building was a small newspaper stand; the headlines were about an economic conference in Europe. Connally's mother hesitated, then seemed to remind herself. "The news is always two days old."

In the aquarium they strolled through wavering emerald lights, among the floating shapes of sea vegetables, the darting smaller shadows of fishes: starfish, sponges, the columnar, tentacle-crowned, current-dancing sea anemones. It seemed to Connally that the fish all had the same staring eye. In one large chilly room they watched sharks glide and shift, opening their mouths with the unreal, saw-toothed curving. In another tank a killer whale dove and played, and they could see the window of the other side of the building, the people standing there. It was not very crowded. They went from room to room and along the corridors, and occasionally Carol called their attention to what she saw — the electric eel interested her, as did the strange ghost-cape of a manta ray. Connally felt weirdly empty. When he looked at his wife, the features of her face seemed to change, momentarily to separate; it was the countenance of a stranger, the bones showing through. Under the watery green light he thought he could see the curve of her scalp, and he looked away.

They went to the sandwich shop on the top floor and sat in a booth by one of the aquarium tanks, a window looking into another green world — enormous, waxy-looking leaves, dark grasses, algae and floating weeds. Carol marveled at the shades of the one color, and Connally's mother asked for menus. They ordered sandwiches from a slight, handsome black waiter whose smile was perfectly straight and white.

"Beautiful young man," Connally's mother said. It was not the sort of observation she had ever been prone to make.

"I didn't really see him," Carol said.

"I sometimes come in here and have something even when I'm doing other things in town. They're very nice here."

"It's a little early for the lunch menu, isn't it?" Connally said.

"Well, I didn't have breakfast and I'm starved."

The room was decked in pine boughs and holly. In one corner, a false hearth was festooned with poinsettia, bright red ribbons, more pine boughs, and green candles. From a speaker in the wall, a Christmas song came: a familiar male voice and a chorus of female voices.

"Is that Perry Como?" Carol asked.

"I'd recognize Perry Como," Connally's mother said.

The song ended, and something else began, an instrumental version of "The Little Drummer Boy." They all listened and waited.

Finally Connally's mother said, "I wish there was something I could say."

"There's nothing to say," Connally told her. "I want to forget about it. I don't want to talk about it."

"It might help to talk about it," Carol said.

"There's no sense keeping it all inside, Charles. That can't do you any good."

"What do you want?" Connally demanded. "You want an inside interview? You want to know what it was like when the shooting started and people started dying in front of me? Is that it?"

His mother looked down at her hands, and now Carol had taken hold of his arm at the elbow.

"Stop this. You're shouting — you don't have to shout."

"I can't believe this," Connally said. "I'm sorry. I don't know what I'm saying."

"We should've stayed home," Carol said.

"I don't want anything anymore," Connally told them. It had just come into his mind to say it. He could not quite understand it himself. They looked at him, and then the waiter was setting their sandwiches down. He carefully avoided any eye contact now.

"I can't eat," Connally's mother said.

They sat there with the food before them, while others walked in and took the surrounding tables and ordered from the same waiter.

"Is everything all right here?" he said, passing them with a tray of emptied drink glasses.

"Fine," Connally's mother said.

She paid the bill and asked to have the sandwiches wrapped. It took a while for the kitchen staff to accomplish this, and there was a space of pained silence in which the three people waited to be able to leave. Outside, it was bitter cold. Clouds were rolling in off Lake Michigan. Carol remarked hopelessly that the wind smelled of snow. No one responded. They made their way to the car, and then the car took some time starting again; it almost quit as they entered the highway. The traffic was heavy, and by the time they reached Leisure Village, a windy powder of snow was blowing down from an ashen, ragged sky. They went past the archaic-looking guard and walked quietly into the building. On the elevator, Carol sneezed suddenly, and Mrs. Connally said, "Oh, bless you."

"Allergies," Carol said.

They filed into the apartment and got out of their coats, and then Connally's mother sat at her small table and ate one of the sandwiches, staring distractedly at her own dim reflection in the dark television screen. Carol had gone into the bathroom.

"Why don't you turn it on," Connally said from the sofa.

"Do you want it on?"

"Don't you?"

His mother went on eating the sandwich. "I think curiosity is natural, son. You went through something extraordinary."

"It's not so extraordinary these days," Connally said.

"Just because it's on television?"

He got up and turned the set on, flipped through the channels: cartoons, game shows, soap operas. Old movies. A man held a pistol to another man's head. A western: the tramp of horses sounded in the background.

"It's Randolph Scott week," his mother said.

The absurdity of this remark brought a small sound up out of his throat.

"What?" his mother said.

"This country," he muttered.

"What's wrong with Randolph Scott?"

There was shooting on the screen now, men falling in dust, pitching forward off the seat of a stagecoach. Music, excited and percussive, like a sort of aural thrill, rose through the firing, the shouts. Connally watched with unhappy fascination.

Carol came into the room, smelling of lotion. She had washed her face and treated her dry hands. The pregnancy was having all kinds of effects on her metabolism and she had been given a minor regimen to follow. She had not done very well keeping to it on the trip, she told her mother-in-law. The two women sat at the table and talked quietly about the changes of age and pregnancy; it was clear that they were not quite hearing each other, that they were keeping an attending ear on Connally, who went back to the sofa and lay down, wanting sleep, wanting the release of unconsciousness. But now the afternoon news was starting, and his mother turned to the channel she had seen earlier. The top story was the murders in the convenience store. They all watched it without speaking. The bushy-browed Mike Sawyer stood in front of the store — live, in the gray light of day, the blowing, dusty drift of snow — talking with all the frowning concern and barely suppressed gusto of television news, about the drama that had unfolded during the night in the little store at his back. What was left of the big front window had been marked with some chalky substance, but everything else looked normal enough; people moved in and out of the picture, sweeping, carrying boxes. The parking lot was still cordoned off. And now a woman was talking with Mrs. Wu. The two women were seated in what looked like a small library; books lined the wall behind them, and someone moved across from the left and sat at a long table.

"Mrs. Lucille Wu was working her shift as night clerk in the store. Mrs. Wu, could you tell us what happened?"

Mrs. Wu began to talk, in her broken English, about the men walking into her store with guns and masks. She began to cry; it was all very dramatic. The camera switched twice to the face of the newswoman, which was sober and imbued with compassion. Mrs. Wu couldn't continue. She mentioned the young man who saved her life.

"That young man, apparently only visiting Chicago over the holidays, did not want to be interviewed. Mike Sawyer did talk to him at the scene. Mike?"

"Christ," Connally said. "It's a mistake."

"You're a hero, son."

On the screen, Mike Sawyer was standing in the dark and the misting rain, the pulsating light, talking about the tragedy. Then he turned and held the microphone toward Connally, shaken and pale, disheveled, bleeding from the chin. There was a voice-over. Connally saw himself talking, saying something, but the voice-over was what you heard. Then Mike Sawyer spoke: "Mr. Connally, what happened here tonight?"

And Connally heard his own voice: "I didn't do anything unusual."

"Apparently, Jane, for some people, heroic action is second nature," Mike Sawyer said from the same dark and rain, though the scene behind him was changed, the open doors of a television van with all its equipment glaring in the light. Then he was sitting in the studio, next to the woman named Jane, who waited, all interest, for him to continue.

"One of the gunmen, Mark Hughes, is in serious condition at Mount Sinai Hospital in Oak Ridge. Doctors say he is stable, and indications are he will survive to stand trial."

"When we come back," the person named Jane said, after a brief pause, "we'll have more on the story, including a report from Diana Moore with the family of the young off-duty police officer who gave his life in an effort to stop the gunmen."

Now the screen was glowing with light, and someone was pouring syrup into a bathtub. Then an astoundingly beautiful dark woman wrapped in a towel looked at the camera and seemed surprised. "Now why would a woman like me want to take a bath in maple syrup?" she asked.

Connally's mother had got up, and now she turned the sound down.

"Let it play," he said. "It's perfect."

"I want to talk to you," she said. "You could be on *The Tonight Show* or *Nightline*. You know it? This could be big. I mean, you could get into the magazines and everything. Couldn't he, Carol?"

"I don't think that's the point," Carol said.

"Charles, you're alive. You made it. You did something good and people want to thank you for it."

He stood. "It's back on."

In a modest room, under a lighted painting of Christ with children, a very dark woman sat holding a baby, who tried to climb her slender body, pulling at her blouse. Beside her, another baby sucked passively on a bottle. The woman was trying to hold back tears, and when Connally's mother turned up the sound her voice came through, a rich contralto, breaking with grief, with the strain of trying to speak. Her husband had stopped to buy milk, coming home from an uneventful shift at work. The convenience store was only minutes away. The baby on her lap began to protest, reaching for her face, and then the picture was of the street outside, a row of fenced lawns and concrete steps leading up to porches. The newswoman stood on the grass talking about one family's tragic Christmas season.

"Turn it off," Connally said. "Jesus God."

"Maybe they'll mention you again."

But when the picture changed, someone was putting batteries into a flashlight. "You spend your hard-earned dollars on what you hope is dependability," a gruff male voice said. His mother turned the sound down again.

"You're worried about money," she said, turning to

Carol. "Both of you. Right? I know this sounds awful, but you really can't help the way the world is, can you?"

"I know what we can do," Connally told her. "We can call a news conference. I'll put a cape on and paint something on my chest."

"I'm just thinking of you."

"Well, don't."

"You've got a wife and child to think about."

"Please," Carol said, "I'm not part of this."

"You act like it would be a fraud or something."

"What?" Connally wanted to know. "What would be a fraud?"

"Just — letting them talk to you a little. Telling them what happened."

"Then it's a lucky thing, right? A lucky stroke I saw four people killed. It means I can pay for this baby I'm already terrified about."

Carol gave forth a little shuddering sound.

"I'm sorry," he told her. "I didn't mean it like that."

"The thing happened," his mother said. "You can't change that. People want to know about it. I don't see what you'd be harming by talking about it. You could be an inspiration or something."

Connally stood. "I'm going outside. I'm going home, in fact. I'm getting the fuck out of Chicago."

"Don't be ridiculous," said his mother. "And watch your mouth in my house. And in front of your wife."

"You think Carol cares how I talk?"

"I'm not saying he has to do anything," Mrs. Connally said to the younger woman. "But I won't have him act like I'm horrible for even thinking of it. The world happens to think a certain way, and if a person does something brave, people want to tell about it and broadcast it. I personally don't see what's wrong with that. He doesn't have to do anything or change anything, just because he's upset. But to turn it on me, as if I made it all up or something . . . well, that's just the kind of judgmental behavior his father — that's just like his father."

Connally had got into his coat. "Let's go, Carol."

"You go right ahead," his mother told him.

"Carol?"

She was aware of something gathering inside her, like a scream — that they could so matter-of-factly use her for leverage against each other, that he could speak so coldly about the child she was carrying.

"Are we going back to the motel?" she managed.

He said nothing for a moment. "Just to get our things."

"Where then?"

"Home."

"Home," said his mother. "Look, I'm sorry."

"It's not that," he said. "I can't — we can't stay. I have to get back."

"You can stay here, honey. Of course you don't want to go back and stay in that motel. We can put the sofa cushions on the floor and make a bed."

Connally and his mother were standing near the door, Charles with his spattered coat on, unzipped, his hands in the deep pockets. He was searching for his car keys, not looking at his mother, who stared at him in an attitude of helpless consternation. Carol felt sorry for her, gazing at the veins in the side of her head. She looked old and worried and frightened.

"It's not even New Year's yet," Mrs. Connally said, and seemed on the verge of tears.

"I hate it here," Charles said.

"No, you're just angry with me. Son, I'm sorry. I won't talk about it anymore."

"It's not that," he said.

"But you can't go now."

Carol stood. "Take your coat off, Charles."

He looked at her. There was nothing in his eyes. She met his gaze as coldly as she could.

"Do you understand?" he said. "I *need* to get away from it."

"Absolutely," said his mother. "And we'll stay here where it's warm and safe. We'll have a quiet, cozy celebration of the new year, like we planned. We won't let them take it away from us. Please, son."

Carol touched the older woman's arm. "We'll stay."

Mrs. Connally looked back and forth, from Carol to Charles, who now began to slide his coat off.

"And we won't say anything more about badness," she said, turning to embrace Carol. She smelled of the sandwich she'd eaten, and of something else, too, some alchemy her anxiety had worked with the pores of her skin. Her hands were moist; there was a faint lividity around her eyes. "Well, let me sit down a minute."

Carol took her arm. Charles went into the bathroom and closed the door. It was quiet. On the television screen people moved in a line past a marble shrine. Blue sky was in the background. Mrs. Connally breathed, held her veined hands fisted into her lap, and rocked slightly back and forth as if listening to some inner melody of anxiety and alarm. Her eyes were wide. "You know," she said quietly, "you have them, and you try to love them, and you do. You think you do, anyway. But you're human, you make your mistakes, too — and then when they grow up there's nothing you can do to make up for it. The only way to make up for it is to be somehow different than you ever were, and you can't find the way to change."

Carol touched her shoulder, then drew her hand away.

"Life's so . . . unforgiving, Carol."

"We're here now. We'll have a quiet celebration, like you said."

The older woman looked at her, the clear eyes swimming. "You're not angry with me, too?"

"No."

"There are things I should've done, you know. Long ago, of course. Before I knew how to do them. That's what he can't forgive me for."

"Let's not talk about that now," Carol told her.

"I suppose you think I'm justifying myself."

"No." Again, Carol patted her shoulder.

"Well, maybe I am."

Charles came back into the room and seemed to have to remember what had been decided. He picked up his coat, opened it, then put it across the top of the sofa. He was standing very close now. "I'm sorry," he said to the room.

"What you've been through," said his mother, rising.

He moved away, as if to avoid contact with her. "I can't stand anything right now. I don't know what it is."

"It's a shock."

"I can't stand the sound of anybody's voice right now."

For a moment, the two women simply gazed at him.

"Why don't you go in and lay down on my bed," said his mother. "Take a nap."

"I just need to be by myself a little." Again he picked up the coat.

"Oh, don't go out, son."

"Charles," Carol said, "it's over with now. Go lay down if you need to."

"I don't need anybody telling me what to do," he said. Then he added, "Please."

Carol stepped away from him.

"I feel like I should curl up in a hole. I don't want to give in to it. I'm going outside — just out to the front of the building — and breathe a little."

"Do you want me to come with you?"

"I'm fine," he said. "I'll be fine."

"We'll get something ready for dinner," said Mrs. Connally, all false cheer. "It'll be fine. You go get some air, and when you come back we'll have a nice quiet dinner."

Carol accompanied him out and along the polished corridor to the elevators. They waited quietly for a moment, staring at the little lighted number changing above the doors.

"I don't think I can do it," he said.

She waited.

"I have this feeling — I've got to get home."

"That's what you said about coming out here, Charles."

He gave her an aggrieved look. "You're not going to understand, are you? Carol, everything's changed. It's all different. I can't explain it."

"What do you want me to do?" she demanded.

"I'm scared," he said. "Do you understand? I'm terrified."

She was, too, now. The elevator doors opened and he got in, turned to look at her. "We're all right," she told him. "We'll be all right."

The doors closed. The bright numbers counted down. She went back along the corridor, feeling light-headed and weak. In the apartment, Tina Connally sat holding a handkerchief to her mouth. She seemed almost startled when Carol entered.

"I thought you might go with him."

Carol wanted to walk over and put her arms around her. But then the older woman was up and moving about, putting the bag with the sandwiches in it away, wiping the tabletop, and there was something nervous and awkward about her movements, as if she had sensed that Carol might

reach for her. What was it about these people that caused
them to be afraid of solace? It seemed to her that whenever
Charles had been most in need of her affection and her care
he had shied away from it in just this embarrassed hurry,
this meaningless bustle. "We'll just — get started with something, here," Mrs. Connally said, bringing a huge, lavender-
colored book out of the bureau and carrying it as if it were
a holy text over to the sofa, where she settled with it on her
lap. It was a cookbook. "Maybe I'll try to bake something.
You know I'm a terrible cook. I always was. Can't tell you
how many meals I've ruined. I don't bake things, I just
reduce them to coal."

Carol sat down across from her.

"Do you like to cook, dear?"

"I'll make something if you like."

"Do you like it?"

"Sometimes."

Mrs. Connally stared off. "Charles's father was a violent
sort of person, you see."

Carol waited.

The other woman shrugged. "Maybe they all are."

A moment later, she said, "I was young. I didn't know
any better. I put up with it longer than I guess I had to.
There were times, when Charles was a baby — I mean it
was hard to feel very good about life."

"Charles doesn't talk about his father much," Carol said.

The older woman was distractedly turning the pages of
the book. "Well, he couldn't remember a lot of it very
clearly. Charles and I got out of the house when he was still
pretty small, and he didn't see much of his father after that.
An occasional weekend, and sometimes in the evenings, with
people around." She shook her head, staring now at the
other side of the room, the statuette of the Virgin in its
lighted shrine. "That man just wasn't cut out to have chil-

dren. He was older, you know. Set in his ways. I did everything for him, and he just didn't know how to be loving. He
meant to, and he tried so hard." She sighed. "Anyway, you
know — when he got after Charles it was almost always to
teach him. It was only with me that he got really bad. I
mean, I think he thought he was doing what he was supposed to do with Charles. That was how *he'd* been raised,
see — and you have to understand, I'd been so lonely as a
girl. I was so very — frightened of being alone." Now she
seemed to throw something off. "Well, we couldn't make it
work anyway. Not even after I tried to solve his trouble with
having — with having a baby around."

Carol was momentarily at a loss for something to say.
She'd had a feeling in the first minutes she'd spent with this
woman — though it hadn't quite made itself clear to her
until now — that Mrs. Connally was the sort who yielded
up personal revelations with a kind of haphazardness that
left no room for comment. Somehow, the only way to respond was to provide a revelation of one's own, and Carol
had found herself barely skirting the subject of her trouble
with Charles concerning the pregnancy, tempted to tell
everything — what she now understood to be the real reason for this disastrous westward journey: her husband's
anxiety about having to take on life and be a grown man,
a father. The thought went through her like a memory.
She almost spoke it aloud. And she thought of her own
father: how many times over the years she had wondered
what her presence in his house meant in terms of his recurring troubles, his darknesses. She knew, for instance, without words, without any expression or hint from either of her
parents, that before her birth he had shown no signs of
illness.

"Is there something wrong with that?" Mrs. Connally
was saying. "I keep thinking now that there was something

wrong with wanting so badly not to be alone — well, not to be without someone. I loved him, you see. So much. And — I don't know — maybe that means there's something missing in me."

"You're fine," Carol said, and felt the absurd inadequacy of it. There was nothing unfamiliar about the feeling. "I'm sorry," she went on. "I know that's not much for someone to say. I mean, I don't know what to say. It seems I never know what to say when something needs to be said. My father would start to go off on one of his — flights, and when he'd come to me, I — well."

"I don't require anything," Mrs. Connally said.

Carol remembered the murders. "God," she said. "I wish we'd stayed home."

Her mother-in-law was staring at the book, following the nervous tracing of one bony finger. "Something we can make," she murmured, as if to herself.

Carol said nothing.

Finally the other woman looked at her. "It's going to be all right, isn't it?"

"We just have to get past it," Carol said.

"I'm proud," said Mrs. Connally. But she looked as though she might begin crying. "That's all. You know."

"I'm sure Charles knows that, Mrs. Connally."

"No, you see — that may be the thing he doesn't believe."

"Of course he does."

The other woman smiled weakly. "You're sweet."

"Now let's see," Carol said, moving to her side. For a few moments they stared at the cookbook as the older woman turned the pages. The book was illustrated with glossy, colorful photographs of various fancy dishes, some of which looked more like decorations or sculptures than food. Mrs. Connally's crooked finger trembled over the lists of ingredients and the names of various dishes, and finally Carol took the book from her and closed it. "Let's just see what you've got in the refrigerator."

"I'm so bad at making do," Mrs. Connally told her. "I eat out so much."

The refrigerator turned out to be almost empty, except for what was left over from the day before — the salad, a few cold cuts, bread and crackers, part of a bottle of white wine.

"I guess we can make something from this."

"I don't cook much."

Carol said nothing.

"It's just easier to eat out."

A moment later, Mrs. Connally said, "Would you care to pray with me, dear?" She was standing by the little shrine in its soft illumination. The look in her eyes was almost pathetic. Carol knelt with her and was surprised that she simply closed her eyes and was silent. Apparently, each of them was to say her own prayer. Carol prayed for safety, then for her husband and her unborn child. Beside her, Mrs. Connally gave forth a soft murmur of supplication.

The phone startled them both.

Mrs. Connally got up and answered it. "Who?" she said. Then she sighed. "Connally. Yes."

Carol stood, and the other woman indicated that the call was something unwanted, rolling her eyes to the ceiling.

"Look here, young man. How did you get this number?"

"Who is it?" Carol said.

"My son just wants to forget the whole thing. He wants to be left alone."

"Let me talk to him," Carol said.

"Well, you're very kind," said Mrs. Connally, "but I really feel I must respect my son's wishes. I'm very proud of him, yes. Very proud."

"Tell him not to call again, Mrs. Connally."

"Well, thank you," the older woman said. "Thank you and good day." She hung the phone up.

"Who was it?" Carol said.

"Some news service. They think Charles is being too modest. People want to honor him."

"Well," Carol said, "he won't stand for it."

"No," Mrs. Connally said. "But I can't help it. I feel so proud of him."

•

He had wandered toward the unfinished houses, braving the open spaces and the quiet, forcing himself to take the steps out of safety, and then he had changed his mind and come back. He had stood in the dull shade of the building and watched cars go by in the street outside Leisure Village; he had watched the guard moving around in his little booth, his breathing on the air like puffs of smoke.

Now, he made his way to the car, got in, and drove out to the interstate and on, toward the place where it had happened to him. He did not think, did not let himself think. He was acting all on impulse, which seemed to gather momentum inside him somehow, so that when he hesitated, just at the exit to the motel, it was only for a second. He drove past the motel and into the parking lot of the convenience store, which was closed, cordoned off. There were fresh-washed places in the concrete and along the sidewalk in front. Two cars were parked there, but the doors were closed and barred. Nothing stirred. Connally stepped over the ribbon and walked up to the jagged window, meeting his own shadow on the glass, so that it was as if he walked out of the lowering afternoon light at his back. Cupping his hands on either side of his face, he peered in. There was broken glass on the floor inside; the place where the body of the nurse had sat propped was a curious lighter color, as if someone had painted over it. Crying now, he walked along the window, marking the ordinary undisturbed racks of merchandise, barely hearing the grit and tiny shards of glass beneath his shoes. It all looked so plain and safe: one could open it and begin to do business. This was abruptly enraging to him. He did not like the feeling. He stared at a row of headache remedies and tried to think of something other than wanting to hurl himself at the remaining sheet of glass. When the wind moved in the little space, cold and searching, getting under his coat, he shivered, and a small sound of alarm rose in his throat. Behind him was the last brightness of the sun, which had burst through the clouds at some point during his drive here, and now the winter afternoon was already beginning to fade, the chilly shadows of trees growing insubstantial as drifts of dust. He wiped his eyes with his sleeves, facing the motel, and then he started up the hill, walking it as he had the night before. When he stepped through the hedge, he saw that the door to the office was open. Arlen's nephew was standing in it, gazing at him.

"I'm closing," the boy called. "I'm glad you came when you did. You're the only guests left."

Connally went over to him, offered his hand. The motion was awkward, and for a second it felt inappropriate. But the boy smiled at him. "Poor old Uncle Arlen." His voice missed a note, and Connally knew he was trying to master himself.

"I'm sorry about it," he said.

"Well." The boy looked off. "At least it was quick."

"I don't think he felt anything," Connally said, seeing in his mind the old man in that ludicrous tangle with Mrs. Wu.

"I'm getting out of the motel business," the boy said. "It's never been anything but a pain in the ass. I'd been trying to talk Arlen into selling the place."

Connally had a moment of wanting to ask him about the

old man: What was he like? What did he want? What did he think he would do next week, the week after? What was he afraid of? It was on the tip of his tongue, and he watched the boy step back into the office and pull his coat off a hat tree.

"Do you mind checking out in the morning?"

"That's what I came to do."

"Now?"

"If you're not going somewhere."

"Hey," the boy said, "how does it feel to be a hero?"

Connally could think of nothing to tell him.

"They were all over me about you — wanting to know where you came from and all like that. They asked to see the register."

"Jesus Christ," Connally said.

"It's true. They're gonna be coming to see you, man. You're gonna be famous. Guy said you jumped the killer and knocked him against the wall so they could get a couple bullets in him. I mean, it's perfect. They've got a dead hero and a live one. They couldn't ask for better."

"I'm not a hero," Connally said.

"Keep talking like that, man. They love that."

And quite suddenly he had taken hold of the boy's coat with both hands and was walking him back into the office. "What're you saying? Make yourself clear."

"Hey," the boy said, struggling with him. "Jesus — what is this?"

"Did you let them see the register?"

"Let go of me."

Connally stepped back. "Tell me," he said.

"Sure I let them see it. Goddam. What is it with you? I'm the one who got an uncle killed. You got out of it."

"I'm sorry," Connally told him. "Christ — look, forgive me."

The boy was brushing his own sleeves with a swiping motion, as if that were where he had been held. "I don't see why you have to be so touchy about it."

"I wasn't a hero," Connally said. "I crawled under a fucking car. Don't they remember that I got on my belly and crawled under a car?"

"I don't care about that," said the boy. "Man, do you think I give a rat's ass about it?"

"I just want to get out of here," Connally muttered.

"Go see a doctor or something, man. You're crazy."

"Right. You're right about that."

The boy opened the register drawer and took money from it. "You're not staying here tonight?"

"No."

"Here." The boy handed him the money.

Connally counted it. Seventy dollars. "Shouldn't it be less?"

"It's a few dollars. I'm selling the place."

"Look," Connally said. "I'm sorry. I mean, I know it wasn't your fault."

"Yeah, well — I'm in this, too, you know. It's been pretty upsetting for me, too. I wasn't that close to Arlen for a lot of reasons, but he was all the family I had, and I didn't especially want him to get shot in the back of the head in the middle of Christmas week. But I guess that's the American way, right?"

Connally said nothing.

"You can drop the room key through this mail slot," the boy told him. "Good luck, man."

Connally watched him drive off. It was getting on toward full dark. He went down to the room and opened it, stood for a moment in the profusion of clothes and bags. It all looked like unhappiness somehow.

When he had packed everything, he remembered that

the car was still down in the convenience store parking lot. He stacked everything in the open motel-room door and made his way across the lot, pushing through the hedge, descending the hill with an obscure sense of having entered some permanent zone of unrest in himself. He was not thinking about what had happened here, now; that was gone. But something else was moving in him, some yearning he couldn't name, which had to do with this place, with its piercing wind and its grit, its sunlight dying on the cinderblock walls, its broken glass and overgrown sidewalk. He couldn't answer it, and he had an intuition that he would never be able to do so. He got into the car and sat staring at what he could see of the dim shapes inside the store. Perhaps it was only that some part of him needed to believe that he could undertake to complete a simple transaction in the store, in order to set it back in its proper place.

The single lighted doorway of the motel startled him until he realized it was his own. He pulled the car to it and got out, looking around, feeling jittery as the dark fell. He heard the sound of traffic out on the interstate, the distant ruckus of the city — horns, engines, music. The wind was steady, and rushed at him. The room smelled of gas. He closed it up, walked to the office, and put the key in the mail slot. Then he turned and made his way back to the car, hurrying slightly, feeling the possibility of someone watching him, the threat of what might be lurking in the deepening shadows of the lot. The slightest stirring of the dimness in the corner of his vision made him quicken his pace. He wanted to think he was imagining things. He got into the car and locked all the doors, then sat for a moment, trying to gather himself. As he was turning the key in the ignition, someone moved across his window, and a sound roared up out of him. In the next moment he was staring at the concerned face of a black man, bundled in a heavy coat, his deepset eyes gazing out from the dark, his lined mouth set in a tight grimace.

"Excuse me," he said.

Connally rolled the window partway down.

"You the motel man?"

"No."

"Where is he?"

"Gone."

"Closed?"

"He said he was closing it."

"You work here?"

"No."

The black man gazed at him out of the shadow of the hood. "You the man."

"No," Connally said.

"Yeah. You the man. You the one that got out."

Connally nodded, without quite acceding to the impulse.

The black man leaned down to look at him. Then he offered his hand through the opening in the window. Connally took the wrinkled, leathery fingers, then let go.

"My wife," the man said. Then he looked down and shook his head. "They —"

"Oh," Connally said, understanding suddenly. "She — that was your —" Again, he saw the image of the dead woman sitting like a dropped doll against the inside of the convenience store counter, her hands in her lap.

"You checking out now?" said the black man, his eyes brimming with tears. "My wife was a nurse, you know. Raised a family and went to school and got a degree."

Connally got out of the car. The other man stood back. For a moment, the two men were unable to say anything. "Do you — can I take you somewhere?"

"I got a car."

"I'm sorry."

"I just had to see the place. The last — whatever was in her eyes the last night and — and I saw you up here, you know. Moving around."

"I'm so sorry," Connally told him.

The other man put his hands in his coat pockets and simply stood staring at the ground.

"Your wife was brave."

"We never liked to be away from each other. Never suffered any separation well."

Connally was silent.

"Thirty-two years, see. You get to a *place*."

"She was defiant," Connally said. "Defiant — and angry."

"Oh, I believe *that*."

"And very brave."

A sound came — a wordless something that was like a breath, with the smallest trace of a voice in it.

"Braver than me," Connally said in the moment of realizing what the other must think, having seen the television reports. "A lot braver."

"Man, I wonder — you know — what happened."

"I didn't see it."

The other nodded, and that sound came again.

"I'm sorry," Connally said. "They took her away from us. No one saw anything."

"It was quick, though."

"Yes."

"Jesus. I just had to look at the place."

"I came back, too."

"Man, I wish you got to saving people sooner." The dark eyes did not quite settle on him. One hand went up to the face and wiped the cheeks, and then the man was walking away.

"I wish so, too," Connally said.

There was the slightest gesture of acceptance — a movement of one arm, like a halfhearted wave. Connally got back into the car and started it. When he looked back, he saw the other car pull out of the end of the drive and go off toward the frontage road beyond the entrance to the interstate. He almost followed it.

He drove back into the city. Everywhere the Christmas lights blazed, and the displays in the storefronts shone. The streets of the city were rush-hour busy, crowded and festive, an unusual number of pedestrians, it seemed, strolling in front of the lighted windows, arm in arm, some of them — couples, parents and children. They all looked like part of a happy migration. The department store on the corner was advertising its after-Christmas sale with a pair of clown-painted mimes, puffy-looking in their padded thermal tights and protected from the wind by a crèche-like arrangement of wood and cardboard, footlighted like a small stage and painted a garish yellow. The mimes bowed and turned and gestured, apparently contending with each other over merchandise, trying to dramatize the idea of thriftiness and getting ready for next Christmas, only 361 shopping days away. In any case, the six-foot-tall letters painted on their backdrop admonished shoppers to save on thousands of gift items by buying them a year early. It seemed to Connally, waiting in the traffic, that all these people basked in the comfortable belief that there would be a next year for them. He understood the essential deranged nature of the wish, the inclination, to get out of the car and sound some sort of alarm; in another time it might have seemed comical to him.

•

He found his mother on the couch, wearing her old flannel robe, a magazine open on her lap. She had combed her wiry hair out and then tied it in two tails; she looked almost girlish, sitting there. Carol had gone to bed. "We added to the salad and made pasta," she told him. "The pasta's in the oven. I'm sure Carol's awake — we both got so worried about you." He looked into the bedroom; Carol lay on her side, asleep in the middle of his mother's bed. He walked over and touched her shoulder, and when she didn't stir he bent down and kissed her cheek.

She opened her eyes and then reached for him, trembling, breathing loud, as if she had been running in her dreams.

"It's all right," he told her.

"I must've been dreaming," she said.

"I'm sorry about what I said, Carol."

She squeezed his hand. "I really was dreaming. I dreamed we had the baby."

Something stirred in his stomach. "Go back to sleep. I just wanted you to know I'm back."

"Where did you go?"

He told her.

"Good," she said. "I didn't want to go back there."

"But, honey — I want to go home."

"New Year's Day."

"That's three days."

"Charles, we have to." She gestured in the direction of the doorway.

"Jesus," he said.

"It'll be all right," she murmured. "She's not going to mention anything again. You should've seen her after you left."

"I've got to get back in there."

"I'll come too."

"No. Sleep. It's fine."

"I think she needs to be with you alone," Carol told him.

He went back into the living room, where his mother sat

staring at her magazine, clearly failing to take in a single sentence.

"Pasta's in the oven," she said.

"I'm not hungry."

"Should I put it away?"

"I'll eat in a little while, maybe." He sat in the chair across from her.

"They called here," she said.

He waited.

"I know you don't want to talk about it. I fended them off."

"Who?"

"Some news people."

"How many?"

"It was just the one call. Some television guy."

"And you fended him off."

"That was what you wanted, right?"

He nodded. He felt vaguely breathless, as if there weren't enough air in the room.

"Carol asleep?"

"She was."

"I bet she's glad you woke her. She was worried about you."

"We'll sleep out here on the sofa," he told her.

"Absolutely not. I'm one person. I sleep out here sometimes anyway. I watch television and fall asleep."

Quite suddenly, this woman in whose presence he had so often felt only confusion and irritability seemed suffused in a glow he couldn't name; for a strange moment he was acutely aware, with a sensation of heat in the bones of his chest, what she was to him, even with her weaknesses and her absences: he remembered the houses they had lived in together, the places she had taken him to in his earliest memories, away from tumult and fright. He was safe again. He sat in the warm light of her lamp and felt it for the first time, felt the days ahead stretching before him, taking on the habits and familiar patterns, the horror receding until it was little more than a story he might tell. It came to him that he could live beyond it.

"Is there something you want to watch?" he said to her.

"Me? No."

"Want to talk?"

She seemed faintly perplexed. "Sure."

"Carol thought the picture of Grand was nice."

"I've always said you can't tell how sick she'd got from that picture. There's a beautiful light in her eyes. That light was there, too. When you looked at her you would swear she knew answers people torture themselves all their lives to find."

Connally saw an image of Winnie Barthley sitting in the sun on the marquee roof, and experienced a momentary little rush of the familiar shame.

"You should've known her when she was younger," his mother said.

"I remember some things."

"Tell me."

"Her laugh."

"Yes." Mrs. Connally sighed appreciatively. "This is nice, isn't it? Quiet."

He said it was.

"You know, everything she did was because she felt such fear all the time."

Connally said nothing.

"I didn't understand it, then. Somehow I just didn't think it was forgivable. But a person afraid all the time must need an awful amount of courage to get through each day."

"Yes," he said.

"And you faced something awful and came through it, didn't you?"

"I didn't die because of the most ridiculous luck."

"Well, but you had something to do with it."

"Let's drop it, all right?"

"You know what she said to me at the end? The last thing she said to me, when they were wheeling her into the intensive care unit?"

"I don't want to talk about her, either, really."

"You went through a lot with her, I know."

"I was with her when it all got bad."

"Well," his mother said, looking away from him, "we couldn't have the best circumstances, I know."

For a moment, neither of them spoke.

"It seems to me," said his mother, "we might've had this talk a long time ago."

"I don't think I knew enough," Connally said.

"I guess I'm to blame for everything," she said.

He shook his head. "I wasn't even curious about who was to blame."

"You're a good son." Her voice broke.

"Grand never did anything to me, anyway," he said. "She just — it got so she didn't know who I was. She thought I was Richard Burton, for Christ's sake. And I don't think she slept five minutes in that last month. Before you came back."

"Well," his mother said, dabbing at her eyes with a napkin, "that's all water under the bridge, now. And anyway, it couldn't be helped." She sniffled and tried to smile. "There were times back then when I didn't think I'd make it. It seemed everything I touched turned to trouble, and all I wanted was to raise a family. Even when he was dying in that — place — I thought we might somehow get through everything and be together. I'd got into the habit of believing it, I guess. Hoping for it." She sighed. "I guess it's why I came back here after you went into the Air Force."

"Well," Connally said.

"I just couldn't stand Virginia anymore, you know. And

he'd left me everything — enough money to live here, any-way. He wasn't a very frugal man, and he never did very well in his business dealings, you know, but he paid his insurance bills. I'm sixty-one years of age and I don't have to do anything but live here. I'm an institution here. I help out in the hospital. Everyone knows me."

"You wrote me about manning the flower shop."

"Oh, well — that was a long time ago. I do much more than that now. I've got those doctors and nurses trusting me with all sorts of things. There's a lot of cancer in the elderly, you know. And I help out with the bad cases."

He said nothing, though she seemed momentarily to be waiting for a response from him.

Finally she said, "Winnie told me God was entering her eyes. Those were the words. Her very last utterance. 'God is entering my eyes.' Isn't that beautiful?"

Connally indicated that he thought it was. He felt very strange, now. There was an almost aggressive urge in him to say something sarcastic. He looked at his own hands, trying to breathe slowly.

"I think that's just so beautiful," his mother said.

They lapsed into quiet. She yawned, turning the pages of the magazine.

"Well," he said.

She said, "Go eat something."

After checking on Carol again, he went and brought in the bags. His mother had made the sofa up and was lying there under the blankets, her hands at her sides, her eyes closed.

"You want me to turn out the light?"

"No, dear. I'm just resting my eyes. Did you get some-thing to eat?"

He wasn't hungry. He took the pasta out of the oven and set it on the counter next to the kitchen sink. Then he turned the television on, and they watched together for a time — a bright movie about a couple struggling through the first year of marriage. In this movie, everyone had clever remarks to make; all the characters were expressive and quite beautiful and completely without dimension, and she seemed tolerantly amused by them, now and again remarking on their clothing and the way they moved or spoke.

The movie ended, and the news came on.

They watched without speaking. About midway through, there was a piece about the quick reaction of the families of the three victims, the surviving members of which were gathering to support one another under the auspices of a new gun-control advocacy group that was starting up in the city. Connally saw, briefly, the black man he had spoken with earlier in the evening — the same stricken face, the same dark, anguishing eyes. The newsman was speaking with a priest who had organized the event. "Do you know that the number of deaths by gunshot wounds in this country approaches the number of deaths we suffered in any year of the Vietnam War?" the priest said with a kind of gruff casualness. "And we go on accepting it. One begins to wonder if this is a culture that respects life as much as it claims to."

"And yet," the reporter said, "you have the instance of the young man shielding Mrs. Wu."

"Yes," the priest said. "I suppose we can hope that's not an exception."

"They're talking about you, honey."

He said nothing.

The reporter went on to say that the gunman who had survived — Mark Hughes — was out of surgery. He would make a fast recovery. Another reporter offered details on his history — petty crimes, theft, shoplifting, breaking and entering, reform schools and work farms, and finally prison, for armed assault, in 1985. Parole, a period of drifting, an armed robbery in St. Petersburg, Florida, in which a bank guard was badly wounded, and an assault on a police officer in Topeka, Kansas, last month. Association with Dwight Fain, wanted for murder in three states, a known killer.

Then a female reporter was talking. "And about the young man who stood up to them, there seems to be some controversy growing. For that story, we go to John Drewry. John?"

The picture shifted to a man in a dark jacket and sweater, with long hair and a rugged face. He held the microphone as if it might try to jump from his hands, and when he spoke his voice was surprisingly high-pitched. "Jane, the young man was apparently here earlier today, and spoke with Seth Waters, who as you know is the bereaved husband of Lena Waters. Mr. Waters tells us that Charles Connally expressed his sorrow that he hadn't acted more quickly to save lives. Something of the feeling of community here, Jane, as Mr. Waters spoke of a complete stranger who happened into this nightmare, and the other people involved, the people in this neighborhood, everyone seems to have felt the need to band together tonight, and to express their concern and their grief."

"I won't say anything," Mrs. Connally said from the sofa, "except that I'm very proud."

"It wasn't like they say it was," Connally told her. "You're just going to have to believe me."

On the screen now, a man was talking about insurance.

"Why do you want to run yourself down, son?"

"You don't understand," he told her. "They're taking it — he took it wrong. Or no — it — the context was wrong. Look, I'd like to try and put it behind me, you know?"

The news was back on; the newscaster had left the subject

of the convenience store murders. Mrs. Connally said, "Turn to the other stations."

"I don't want to watch the news anymore."

"Please, son."

He switched through the channels. There wasn't anything. They had missed whatever the other stations had done.

"A lot of heroes say they don't feel very brave," his mother said quietly.

He got up and moved toward the bedroom door.

"Don't be mad."

"I'm exhausted," he told her.

"Will the television keep you awake?"

"If I'm kept awake," he said, "it won't be the television."

In the bedroom he undressed and lay down, carefully, so as not to wake Carol. The room was not much bigger than a walk-in closet, and though everything was in place, it looked cluttered with his mother's things: embroidered pillows piled one on top of another in the two chairs and lining the dresser top, figurines and wax flowers everywhere, and an ornate wooden jewelry box he'd bought for her when he graduated from high school. The walls were covered with framed photographs, of her with her sisters and her poor mother, of Connally himself at all the stages of growing up, with the sad backdrops of the different houses and places to stay, and he remembered the sense of always making do, somehow. There was even a picture of Winnie Barthley standing by one of the white wicker chairs on top of the theater marquee; Connally got out of bed and stood gazing at it, in a kind of wonder. He did not recall the occasion on which it was taken, though it looked to be from one of those many he took with the gift of his sixteenth birthday, the small Kodak. The picture had to have been taken from his bedroom window, which looked out on the marquee at this angle, with the church and its standing Christ in the square of lush grass in the blurry, blue-green, glowing summer background. All the nights he had lain awake in that room while the marquee buzzed and blinked. And the voices of people below when the theater let out, the laughter of young girls in the soft night, the murmur of assignations. He imagined it all: he was fifteen and sixteen and seventeen, lonely and watchful, worried about himself, alone with a woman who, toward the end, kept up a constant, low muttering on the other side of the wall — a ceaseless, exalted voice, a lunatic rejoicing, going on all night — and he was ashamed of where he lived. But there was something else, too — some quality to the shame that he couldn't express or comprehend at that age, some element of it that seemed to come from too deep inside, as though it had nothing to do with living in three little rooms above a lighted movie theater. There was something almost primal about it, though he wouldn't have used that word — might not have understood it if he had heard it. But the feeling seemed somehow an integral part of nature, what he might have supposed everyone felt if he did not have the contrast of days when for whatever reason he was free of it. Whenever he experienced these occasional, random intervals of respite — as if his spirit, on its own, had simply decided to exult — some part of him knew instinctively that others did not have to contend with the shame, and were not subjected to these shifts in their very ability to stand up in the daylight and speak their names aloud.

Carol stirred behind him.

For a moment, realizing that he had escaped the terror of the convenience store and was alive, he could not believe his luck. And then it was as if his own childhood were somehow a part of what he had escaped. He turned the light out and got into the bed, arranging himself along Carol's sleeping shape. He lay very still, listening to her breathing, reminding himself to savor the tactile, sheltering softness of blanket and bed, the rushing of the wind outside. He thought of safety, and all the people out in the dark lying down to rest — the tremendous trust of removing one's clothes and crawling under sheets.

At some point before he fell asleep, he remembered again, with the slightest touch of anxiety, that Carol was pregnant.

•

They spent the days before New Year's Eve watching old movies and playing cards, and no one talked about the convenience store. The news shows covered the funerals of Mrs. Waters and the off-duty policeman. Only one station mentioned the motel proprietor, whose family had requested that the services be kept private.

"He didn't have any family to speak of," Charles said. "When they say family they mean Eddie, his nephew, I'll bet."

Carol had watched him through the next day, had felt him returning to himself. There were even signs of his old humor coming back. If she noticed a certain withdrawn something in the way he looked at her, she attributed it to the tension of being cooped up inside with his mother, who was charming and who was trying very hard, according to her own avowal, not to be garrulous.

"I just know I'm overstepping," she said on more than one occasion, and the odd thing was that she seemed to be speaking absolutely without irony or sarcasm; she meant to get along. She was glad of their company, glad to sleep on the sofa each night. She'd gone out and bought more groceries the first morning they stayed with her, and she spoke of how much fun it was mothering them. Connally slept a lot, and didn't eat much. But on New Year's Eve they sipped champagne and waited for the ball to drop, standing in that small chapel of a living room while the crowds milled and made their raucous holiday noise on the TV screen. They toasted the new year, and then embraced, and Carol had to fight back tears. Her mother-in-law cried a little, too. Carol discovered that she did not want to return to Virginia so soon. It would be good to continue in this way, being in the home and care of this woman, who by her own half-serious account seemed to be learning for the first time herself what there was to be gained from such nurturing.

After midnight, Mrs. Connally invited a friend over from another apartment — a quiet, courtly old gentleman from Carbondale, Illinois, named Lee Southworth. He had called to wish her a happy new year, and she insisted that he come celebrate with them. Mr. Southworth was eighty-two, thin and pale, with a full head of gray hair, large watery dark eyes, and tufted eyebrows that arched as though he were in a continual state of intellectual surprise. He smiled a lot, showing long white teeth, and now and again he brought a handkerchief out of his shirt pocket and brushed his forehead with it. He wore a neat gray suit with threadbare elbows, and he teased about being overdressed, so Mrs. Connally changed into a gown for the evening; she surprised them all, walking into the small room and making a vivacious turn, modeling it — a lovely aqua-colored cocktail dress with basting across the front and dark bows at the hip. "I haven't worn this thing for more than a year," she said, turning again.

"You look lovely," Carol said.

"Thank you, dear."

"Lovely," Charles said. Carol took his arm. It was almost possible to believe that the horror was behind them.

"Do you like it, Lee?" Mrs. Connally asked.

"I think it's beautiful," said Mr. Southworth, who was so touched by her consideration of him that as he went on to speak about how there weren't many women as thoughtful as Tina Connally, his reedy voice broke. "Well," said Mrs. Connally, "it's just that I know you're sensitive to such things."

Carol stepped between them and offered another toast with the seltzer water she'd switched to after the first sip of champagne. "To friends," she said.

"Friends," said her mother-in-law.

A little later, they sat at the table and played a game of Pictionary — men against the women — laughing at how poorly the drawings came out. Mr. Southworth talked to Charles about having owned a hardware store in Carbondale until he retired. His sons were running it, he said, though he was a little peeved at them for never coming to visit. "Now your mother, here, she's lucky. Not only does she have a son who comes to visit her, she has a bona fide hero into the bargain."

For a moment, no one said anything. Then Carol changed the subject. It surprised her how quickly the damp, chilly feeling in her stomach could return, the cold little balloon of fear that was fluttering under her heart as she asked if anyone wanted more champagne to drink.

"I'm a little tipsy," said Mrs. Connally, "so I'm inclined to say I'll have some."

"Oh, have some," said Mr. Southworth.

"I already have the beginning of a headache."

"This'll ward it off."

Charles said, "I want some."

"Here," said Mr. Southworth, taking the bottle from Carol. "Let me pour the hero some." He poured, and there was just the sound of the liquid in the glass. When he held the bottle toward Mrs. Connally, she said, "Lee."

"Well?" he said.

"All right."

He poured. "Whole time I owned that hardware store, I was afraid of being robbed. And you know that fear is still with me. I'm never more than a few quick steps from a gun. And when I go out on the street here I sometimes have one with me under my coat."

"Lee," Mrs. Connally said.

"It's true."

"I never knew that."

"I've got two thirty-eight caliber revolvers and a small Beretta, Italian model. I carry the Beretta when I go out."

"I think I'm going to go to bed," said Charles. "We have a long trip in the morning."

"This was something," Mr. Southworth said. "Seeing you on television and then getting to meet you." He stood. "I have been fortunate enough to be your mother's friend for almost a year now. And I want you to know my intentions are honorable."

"Oh," said Charles. "Always that."

"I'm a thoroughly nice old boy. You can ask her."

"Thoroughly," Mrs. Connally said.

"To your mother."

They drank. Carol, sipping her seltzer, saw a tremor in her husband's hands. It was late, everyone was tired. She kissed him on the side of the face, then leaned close, reaching her arm around him.

"Look at them," Mr. Southworth said. "Don't they make a picture of youth and beauty?" He held one hand up as if to offer tribute to them. "O Youth. O Beauty."

"I think you've had too much champagne," Mrs. Connally said to him.

"Give us a kiss good night," he said.

"Now, Lee."

"Oh, all right." His tone and his stance reminded Carol of a thwarted little boy. She thought she saw him shuffle one of his narrow feet, looking down. "I guess I have had too much."

Mrs. Connally led him to the door, and Carol walked with Charles into the bedroom.

"He's crocked," Charles whispered.

"He'll hear you."

"Poor guy. I think he's got something going for her."

"I think he's sweet."

"She's *twenty* years younger than he is."

"Charles."

He lay down in his clothes. "It was a good night."

"Yes," she said.

"I don't feel afraid right now."

"No."

"What about you?"

She felt the shiver inside, and said, "No."

"Maybe it's over," he said. "Really over. We're so lucky to be here at all."

She sat down on the edge of the bed and took his hands. Somehow it was important to get him to talk about the baby now, while he felt good. It was as if she might be able to get past everything, the anxiety and the confusion and the trauma, too, to arrive at the version of him that she had believed would want the baby, the family, everything they had planned. "I've been thinking, honey, if we have a girl, let's name her Tina."

He turned slightly away, seemed to consider this, staring at the walls of the room.

"What do you think?"

"Sure," he said.

"Wouldn't that be nice?"

"Yes," he said. "Sure."

"I'm going to go out and have a cup of coffee with Tina."

He sighed. "Don't take too long."

In the living room, Tina Connally was picking up the glasses and the empty bottles. She had already cleared the game off the table. The television was on with the sound turned low. Cars went racing through traffic in an underpass, out of blazing sunlight.

"Can I help?" Carol asked.

"It's about done."

"I'll wash."

"We could leave it. You know I'm tipsy?"

"Are you?" Carol said.

"Lee wants to marry me," Mrs. Connally said. Then she paused, as if thinking through the proposition. "I just might take him up on it, too. He's old for me, of course. But you know Charles's father was, too. By almost twenty years. And I like Lee. He's fun. He comes over here and swears up and down he'll be on his good behavior, and he nearly always has too much to drink. But he's such a sweetheart, even drunk." She paused, seemed to be considering something. "You know, I almost never had any fun with the men I knew. Charles's father and I stopped having fun pretty fast after we were married. Then you know I wasn't interested for a long, long time. There were a few men I allowed to escort me around during the time after Charles left for the Air Force. I made friends with three different men, and two of them turned out to be kind of rough with me, too. I mean, I started wondering if something in me makes it happen, draws it out."

"My first husband was like that," Carol told her.

"Roughed you up?"

"Rough. Yes. I think maybe he just didn't know how to be gentle."

Carol helped her collect the champagne glasses.

"Well," said Tina, "we have to learn how to do a thing as small as brush our teeth, so I guess we have to learn how to be easy with each other, too."

Carol said, "He was like a big infant a lot of the time."

"But they're not infants." Mrs. Connally's tone was definite. "I've been around that kind of thing enough to know. When Charles's father got started, there was something almost second nature about it. It fed on itself like a fever. Something would snap in him and he was gone into it, and you couldn't reach him. You could reach him at other times, doing any other thing. Even when he was mad at you."

Carol wanted to change the subject. "I like Lee," she said.

"Well," said the other woman, "I'm sorry he went on like that about the television and the hero stuff and the guns. I should've found a way to tell him not to mention the trouble, but you know I didn't even think about it. It's been such a lovely few days."

"I wish you'd asked him over earlier."

Mrs. Connally looked perplexed for a moment. "Didn't you find it nice being just us?"

"Oh, yes. I didn't mean to imply anything —"

The older woman went on, almost as if talking to herself. "That's one of the reasons I've hesitated so about Lee, much as I like him. I do so enjoy it when I'm on my own here with nobody to think for or worry about and no troubles except my own."

Carol thought of her own mother, living alone in a little apartment in Point Royal, with her aquarium and her books and her needlepoint, while her father continued to occupy the big house on the other end of Grandville Avenue, the house Carol had grown up in.

"Sometimes I don't like men much," Mrs. Connally said. "But then, I don't have a lot of women friends, either."

Carol said nothing. They were rinsing the glasses now, standing side by side at the sink.

"I'm going to get this dress dirty," Mrs. Connally said.

"Well, I won't have another occasion to wear it — unless I wear it next New Year's."

"You could invite Lee over for a dinner party anytime," Carol told her.

"Lee comes over all the time. I told him to stay away because you all were coming."

"I think you make a nice couple."

"I do get lonely," said the older woman.

•

Midmorning of the following day, they packed everything and said goodbye to Mrs. Connally, who was tearful, hugging them both and begging them to be careful, to call or write. "There's a speeding car coming into every intersection," she said. "Don't forget."

"What?" Carol said.

"She means for us to be careful," Connally told her. "We'll be careful, Ma."

"I went out early this morning and got cold cuts for you — cheese and turkey and some ham and lettuce. It's in the bag there on the front seat."

"You shouldn't have gone to the trouble," Connally told her.

"I put coffee in the thermos, too," she said.

He got in behind the wheel. Carol was arranging herself and her pillows in back; she would try to sleep so she could spell him. He was hung over, and he was thankful about the coffee. Mrs. Connally leaned into the open window and kissed the side of his face, then stood back, shivering, pulling her robe tight.

"You'll catch cold," he said.

"Please be careful."

"Come see us," Carol said from the back seat.

Mrs. Connally wiped tears from her cheek. "I swear I'm

going to miss you so bad I might call Lee and take him up on his offer of marriage."

"That'll bring us back," Connally said.

"You know what I mean."

"He's old enough to be your father," Connally told her.

She was shivering. He saw the bluish cast of the skin around her mouth.

"Go on inside," he said.

Driving away, he watched her in the side-view mirror. She simply stood there, shoulders hunched against the cold. He waved, then made the turn onto the street, going out of sight. Carol had been waving at her through the small spaces between suitcases and blankets in the back window, but Mrs. Connally hadn't seen.

Carol sat crying, holding a napkin to her face.

"We'll come back," he told her. "Or she'll come see us."

"It's just so discouraging to be going back to everything," she said.

He drank most of the coffee before they were out of the city limits. The day was bright and blustery with wind and cold, and it took the car heater a long time to warm up. He felt the cold on his face like the pain of what he'd had to drink. His stomach was sour. When they reached the turnoff to the motel and the convenience store, he made himself keep his eyes on the road straight ahead. He could feel the lining of his stomach, and the whole landscape seemed for the moment suffused in a dreadful wintry light. Carol leaned up and tried to see what she could, but she said nothing. Ahead, the sky was a lowering wall of gray clouds. Some of the traffic coming from the opposite direction was dusted with snow. He thought about the hazards of snow and ice and experienced a little surge of elation — Chicago, and the terrors of the last week, all of it was receding in the distance behind them. With each passing mile he felt as though something were unraveling under his heart, letting loose, relaxing a tight grip; and he shifted in the seat, feeling relieved, wanting to go faster, wanting home. He could breathe.

Carol slept until they were almost out of Indiana. When she woke it was with a small cry, almost like a cough. She sat forward and put her arms on the seatback. "You okay?"

"What were you dreaming?" he said.

"Nothing."

"You can talk about it," he told her.

"No, it's nothing. Really."

"Okay."

They rode on in silence.

"Want the radio?" he said.

"If you do."

"Honey, why don't you tell me about it?"

"I can't remember — really, Charles."

She had dreamed that he was coming after her with something in his hands, something she couldn't see but knew was awful, the story of the dream being that he meant to harm her, and her mind buckled with the chilling sense of some other, elemental force in him, some life she did not know, which was frighteningly familiar to her all the same: a coloration in his way of talk, his stance, reminding her, showing through the fluid, threatening motions — the cold, inimical eyes — of the dreamed man. It was only a nightmare, she told herself, and yet for a moment she was leery of him, reluctant to tell him how he had looked in her sleep.

"Well?" he said.

"I'm still sleepy," she got out.

"You look like you saw a ghost. Must've been some nightmare."

"I don't remember."

They went on without saying much, and Carol wondered if they would just go on avoiding the subject of the convenience store. There was nothing really to say; it was a thing that had happened to him. He drove with both hands on the wheel, thinking whatever he was thinking. It was absurd to feel wary of reminding him. Yet she refrained from asking him to put the radio on, not wanting to take even the minimal chance that what had happened might still be in the news.

•

The roads were better than they had hoped for, and the little snow that fell was only a powder, which blew over the surface of the asphalt like spilled salt. Carol read for a while, and then gazed out the window as the land began to bunch up and grow hilly. There were farms and little lighted towns toward evening. Neither of them felt like having the sandwiches, so they stopped to eat. Then she drove for an hour or so while he tried to sleep. But he had never done well sleeping on the road, and after they stopped to eat again, he took over. They said little to each other, and she thought about how this was the way the trip out had felt.

"I guess I'm not much company," she said.

"I'm not feeling neglected," he told her. "Go on and sleep if you can."

They went on into the night, and she slept again — this time without any nightmare. She woke once and peered through the window at a long, lined, aged face, a tired-looking gas station attendant, counting out change to give her husband. She settled back into the blankets, and it seemed that she had barely closed her eyes when Charles reached back and took ahold of her knee.

"Hey. We're home."

"God," she said, feeling startled at the light in the car. "I slept almost the whole way."

"I think I did too," he said.

They left the unpacking for later, and made their way up to the porch of the house in the gray dawn light — the sun would not fully break through the slowly brightening sheet of featureless clouds in the sky. The house was musty and chilly. He got a fire going, and she opened all the doors to the rooms and started frying bacon.

"Hungry?" she said when he appeared in the doorway.

"Sleepy."

"Eat something before you go to sleep."

"What about all this food my mother made for us?"

"It'll keep. Don't you want something hot?"

"I can't wait for it. I won't be able to stay awake."

"I want to call everybody and tell them we're back."

"Everybody knew we were coming back today."

"Still."

"I'm sorry for everything," he said.

She did not want apologies.

"You think anybody back here got wind of what happened?"

"All the way back here?"

He shook his head. "Fucking television people. It's worse than everybody always said it was. It's a fucking disease."

"Stop talking like that."

He stared at her.

"I don't like that language."

He walked into the other room, the bedroom. She turned the bacon off; abruptly she wasn't hungry at all. She would wrap it up and save it for tomorrow. She found him lying on his side, his hands up to his face.

"Charles?"

"Hmm."

"Just get some sleep."

He said nothing.

In the living room the fire was going, and she let herself

down on the sofa, feeling pins and needles in her feet and along the top of her thighs from being cramped so long in the back seat of the car. She stared at the bright shapes in the flames, wide awake. A moment later, he came in and sat in the chair across from her. "I can't sleep." His eyes were glazed, and he had taken his shirt off.

"Charles," she said. "What do you remember of your father?"

Nothing changed in his face. "Why?"

"I don't know. I thought we might talk. And you've never had much to say about him."

"There's not much to say. He was an older man."

"The way your mother talked about him —"

"What was she talking about him for?"

"Remember what you told me about spending a lot of time with relatives because of your father?"

He gazed at her, and for the smallest instant she felt the clammy horror of her nightmare.

"Do you?" she said, deciding to shoulder it aside.

"I'm a complete blank."

"You said that from the time you were two or three —"

And now he interrupted her. "I know, I know. All right."

"Well, I'm just trying to tell you how it came up."

"I'm more tired than I thought," he said, rising. "I can't concentrate."

"Are you all right?" she wanted to know.

"Not if people keep asking me about it every five minutes."

"Charles," she said. "What in the world —"

"I'm sorry," he said, standing there rubbing the back of his neck. "Look, I'm exhausted. Maybe that's it. I thought when I got back home everything would feel normal again."

"It's got to take a while," she told him.

"I'm going back in and lay down," he said. Then he

seemed to go off for a moment, his hazy eyes not quite seeing her. "About my father, okay? I remember a lot of motion. A lot of heavy motion. And beatings. Ah Jesus. Belts, and his hands pulling me around the room. When I think of what I remember, it's always moving and I'm always screaming in it."

"Oh, Charles."

"A lot of it's gone," he said in a played-out voice.

"Go in and try to sleep," Carol said.

"Goddammit," he said, looking around.

"You're just exhausted," she told him.

He made his way back into the bedroom, and she went after him, stood in the doorway, and asked him if he wanted something warm to drink.

"I'm just going to try and sleep," he said, getting into the bed.

She dialed her mother's number, sat in the kitchen, and looked out the back window at the branch- and leaf-littered yard, listening to the buzz on the other end of the line. Her mother's voice was sleepy, and its softness, its southern music in contrast to Tina Connally's rasp, calmed her. "Honey," Grace said, "I've been up since before sunup. Everybody's so excited. How does it feel to be married to a big hero."

"Oh, God," Carol said. "Not really."

"It was on all the news," said her mother. "Your father is beside himself about it. He was *for* your getting married again, remember? And so this just proves him right. And I'm so excited I guess I don't mind admitting that he was."

"Grace, we don't want — Charles doesn't want anything more about it."

"Well, that's what it looked like from the reports. So don't you worry, now, we'll respect that. That just speaks volumes for the boy."

Carol said nothing.

"No," her mother went on, "you needn't worry about that on my say so."

"Will you call Daddy and tell him we're home? And not to call here today? I'm leaving the phone off the hook."

"Get some sleep," said Grace.

"We just need some time to adjust."

"Well, and you being pregnant and everything."

Charles appeared in the doorway, putting on his coat. "Is that your mother?"

Carol held one hand up. Her mother was talking about the local news people: ". . . didn't think, you know. And I was so proud of him I just couldn't contain myself. But if you're leaving the phone off the hook —"

"Oh, Grace — you didn't."

"They would've wanted to do something anyway, honey. They already had somebody working on it."

"I'm going for a walk," Charles said. "Can't sleep."

"Wait a minute."

"What?" Grace said.

"Charles just came in."

"Oh, let me say hello."

She looked at him, held the phone out. He shook his head. She made a gesture of pleading, holding the handset to her chest, and again he shook his head.

"He just stepped in for a second," she said.

"I understand," said her mother.

"Grace, I'm going to hang up now."

"Can we come over and see you later?"

"We?"

"Your father and I."

Carol said nothing. Since their divorce, the two had kept a vaguely good-humored if periodically antagonistic friendship, and lately it seemed to Carol that they had been seeing more of each other, though both had at various times denied any change or hope of change in the status quo. Yet Carol sometimes wondered what her attitude was supposed to be about these occasions when the two people appeared to be in some sort of harmony of their own. They had decided to go their separate ways before she married Martin (even so, they both strongly counseled her against going through with her own divorce), and neither of them ever spoke to her about their separation with anything approaching regret. Yet they kept in touch. They spoke on the telephone, and Carol's father dropped postcards in the mail to Grace, apprising her of something interesting to do in town or of a new show coming to the theater or even about what was on TV, though he knew perfectly well that she was seldom out of touch with these sorts of things. Sometimes the two of them even spent an evening together, usually in the company of others. And they still bickered like children: on occasion, they had gone weeks without speaking, but they always made it up, and they continued to see each other. For Carol, the fact that her father kept turning up at Grace's apartment, or that there were times when Carol went to visit him only to find Grace standing in the doorway of the house — as if she had never left it — was vaguely embarrassing.

Now, her mother said, "We'll only stop in. Your father has some harebrained surprise he's cooked up. I'm supposed to dress for the outside."

"A date," Carol ventured.

"A harebrained surprise."

"You have to promise not to talk about what happened in Chicago."

"Honey, I'm good at skirting sensitive things. I was married to your father, wasn't I?"

Carol left a pause.

"Is Charles having trouble with it?"

"We're both trying to get over it."

"Both of you. Okay."

"The shock," Carol told her.

"Just make him rest."

•

He had lain near sleep, in the good world of the little converted hunter's cabin that possessed all the rightness and comfort of home, when quite abruptly — as if something in his own being had been affronted at the possibility of healing — he felt the chill of the refrigerator room, breathed the odor of the convenience store, and in one terrible second it was all back, the murders in their absurd, accidental shapes, the shock, the awful minutes of waiting, the huge realization that he would be killed, the panic and the deep cold fright — everything. It brought him bolt upright in the bed, and he came to know that it was not going to be possible simply to walk away from what he had been through.

It made him angry, and when he went in to speak to Carol about it, her placidness and calm, her odd questions about his father, and her obvious nervousness with him fed the anger. He found himself fighting an almost irresistible urge to shout at her. It was as if she thought there was something disgraceful or mortifying about the fact that he had nearly been murdered. She sat there on the couch, pregnant, staring at him, and it was disturbingly annoying. He had removed himself, but there wasn't going to be any sleep, now. When he lay down, he saw the highway, the signs smeared with road dust and grit, the shapes of cars speeding through the dark, the glare of the windshield.

Because she was on the phone with Grace — and because she had tried to make him speak to Grace, whose every word and gesture had in all situations given him her dissatisfaction about Carol's choice of him — he let himself out of the house and walked up to the small park on the other side of Grandville Avenue. The park, as it was called, had once been the playground of one of those old two-story brick elementary schools, which had been renovated into an apartment house. The builders had decided that they would leave part of the old school playground intact — a quarter acre of smooth gravel with a swing set, a sliding board, four seesaws, and a jungle gym ranged around a small birdbath and fountain.

It was to this playground area of the park that Connally walked — or, rather, it was where he found himself a short time after starting out of the house. He was not intending anything. He had thought vaguely of tiring himself out, of removing the strain of being in those closed rooms with Carol while she talked to her mother. The fear had come back, and he was trembling inside, deep. He needed motion, the air outside.

At the park, he sat in one of the swings, resting. It was almost warm here. There wasn't any wind to speak of; the traffic on Grandville Avenue went by, and he watched it for a while. In places, the sun was trying to break through the cloud cover. When he looked back down the street, in the direction of the house, he thought of Carol watching him. He could just see the side windows from where he sat.

And now a young woman came through the trees with a boy dressed in a snowsuit, packed into it so that his arms were sticking out as though blown that way by air. They crossed in front of Connally and strolled over to the sliding board, where she helped the child climb the ladder. Connally watched them, wondering what they must think — a man sitting on a swing in the middle of a park on a winter's day. It seemed to him now that, in the moments just before the shooting began, he had actually felt something like exhilaration — a plain, undistilled sensation of welcome for this disruption of the flow of life. This knowledge filled him with wonder, while it made him sick. He thought of the dead again, the ones who by their own accidents had come to be in one place at that hour of the night.

And Mrs. Wu.

The feeling of wanting to stop her noise, of wishing she would stop.

Across the small expanse of gravel, the woman gazed at him, then looked away. Connally prepared to smile, wanting her to know he was not to be feared. Suppose someone came to this park and harmed her; suppose her life ended suddenly in this barren little park playground, the winter of, say, her twenty-eighth year (Connally was twenty-seven)? The idea fixed him for a moment; it made his stomach flutter, and seemed to leach the oxygen out of the air. He watched the boy go down the slide in his padded snowsuit, and his mind raced with thinking where and how that child would be, what he would love and worry about and know before something happened to him. It was as if Connally himself would be the agency by which the thing would happen, and for a bad minute he knew something of the empty power of the gunman; it went through him like a chill — an eerie sense of the deadness in a soul for which there were only actions following other actions. He knew it must be like that, and now he was again unable to remain still. The sun had come out. He hadn't noticed it. Shadows of clouds were sailing over the matted grass, like something flying toward him.

He stood. The woman was watching him, her long face showing a trace of concern. He almost nodded at her, as if to say she was right to be alert, wary. But she had looked away again, and he started out of the park, feeling frightened, out of breath.

In the house, Carol was watching television.

"Where did you go?" she said.

"I just walked."

"They might stop by."

"I've got to sleep," he said.

She made no answer. In the bedroom, the sheets on the bed had been changed, the blankets were turned back. He got out of his clothes and lay down.

"The phone is off the hook," she called from the other room.

He turned in the bed and covered his head with the blankets. He thought of Chicago, his mother's apartment.

Nowhere was safe.

•

Grace and Theodore drove up in the afternoon, looking like people she barely knew. Her father had got his hair cut short above the ears, and he was wearing blue jeans and one of those military fatigue jackets with the camouflage shades of green and olive drab. Grace was in a parka and hood, and she'd tied her hair up in a bun on top of her head. Without makeup, she looked pale. At fifty-four, she was still lithe and athletic-looking, though her face had deep lines around the eyes and mouth, and her dark hair was brushed with gray. She often teased about which strands had been given her by Carol and which had been the gift of Carol's father. "We're headed out to Skyline Drive," she said now. "Theodore's idea."

"Going on a hike up near the nine-mile post," Theodore said.

"It'll be getting dark in another hour," said Carol.

"This is a short hike. There's a little waterfall I want your mother to see."

"I'm humoring him," Grace said.

"You're bored," said Theodore.

"Charles's sleeping," Carol told them.

"We won't stay. Will we, Grace?"

"We're just glad you're safe, honey."

"I wasn't even there," Carol said. "I was never in any danger."

"We just wanted to put in our good wishes. Grace told me I couldn't say much more than that."

Carol nodded at this, and then felt that something else was required; she could think of nothing.

"He won't sleep tonight, will he?"

"I don't want to disturb him," Carol told them.

They all went out on the porch and stood in the cold, and Carol hugged them, feeling a sudden urge to bundle up and go with them.

"You get inside now," Grace said. "You've got that baby to think about."

"Charles's mother is wonderful," Carol said. "You'd both like her."

"Well, maybe we'll get to meet her sometime," Theodore said. "Now you go on in. It's pneumonia weather out here."

Grace was observing the sky. "Carol's right. We don't have time for this hike."

"Sure we do."

"Ridiculous."

They stepped off the porch and made their way down the walk to where Theodore had parked the Pontiac. He opened the door for Grace and stood back gallantly, bowing at the waist. Carol waved at them from the porch, and when they drove off she went back inside, shivering, experiencing a sense of having been abandoned. The house was too quiet. She stoked the fire and tiptoed into the bedroom, where Charles lay in the dark, a still shape on the bed.

"Charles?" she whispered.

Nothing.

She waited, then murmured, "They're gone."

He stirred. "Oh."

And she had the thought that he must have been awake, that perhaps he was pretending to be sleepy, yawning and stretching, acting woozy, reaching for the light. He could not have known what she meant, otherwise. One of the true-feeling things his mother had said about him during their stay with her was that he had no talent at all for deception. "He'll be a good husband, I can guarantee that. The boy just doesn't have it in him to be devious." In the light, his eyes were clear, and he pulled the blankets back to his chin. "I'm still sleepy. What time is it?"

"After three o'clock."

"Jesus."

"Charles, you don't have to hide from them. I don't expect you to let them worry you about anything."

"Hide from who?"

"You know perfectly well, who."

He sat up and put his feet on the floor, rubbing his eyes with both hands. "Okay."

"Are you all right?"

"Don't keep asking me that," he said. "Please, honey."

"All right." She went into the living room and put the phone back on the hook. It rang almost immediately.

"Mrs. Connally?"

"Yes."

"This is Bill Likens of Channel Fifteen. And I wondered if I might come speak to you and your husband about something the station has in mind."

"No," Carol said, "you may not."

"Are you familiar with our cable show, *American Heroes?*"

"We're not interested."

"Mrs. Connally, how can you say that until you hear what I'm offering?"

"Please leave us alone," she said.

"Can I speak to your husband, please?"

"No, you can't." She broke the connection.

"Who was that?" Charles said from the entrance to the hallway. He had put a clean pair of jeans on, and a sweater. He actually looked refreshed.

"You don't want to know." She put the handset back in its cradle.

"It's all right. Tell me."

"It was Bill Likens of Channel Fifteen."

"It's been on the news back here, then."

"Yes."

"That's what your folks were here for."

The phone rang again. Charles gestured for her to let him get it, and moved into the room. "Hello," he said, and a moment went by while he listened. "Not interested." He hung up.

"Was that Likens?"

"That was Channel Twelve. Anne Trueblood. Ever hear of her?"

"They all seem interchangeable to me," Carol said.

"Ms. Trueblood wants to do a special segment of her nightly program, with other victims of crime."

Again, the phone rang. He picked it up. "What." Then he looked at her and nodded. "Before you get started, Mr. Likens, I think you ought to understand that my wife was doing what I asked. She's expecting, Mr. Likens. She doesn't need the phone ringing all day, and we just want to be left alone, okay? This wasn't a show. There wasn't anything entertaining about it."

Apparently Mr. Likens was saying something.

"That may be," Charles said, then paused again. "That

may well be. I know all about the journalistic aspects of it, Mr. Likens, but that doesn't change a thing, you know? I still don't have anything to say about it." Again, he hung the phone up.

"Grace spoke to one of them," Carol told him. "They got to her before we came home."

He was considering something, shaking his head slightly. He did not look woozy or frightened now, but there was something drawn about his features, as though his skin were being tightened by whatever was going on inside him.

"I never dreamed it would be on the news here," Carol said.

He was silent.

"I'd have called Grace and told her not to say anything to anybody."

"You don't understand," he said. "You think I'm being modest about it."

"No," she said.

"God. Oh, Carol — there was no moment when I exercised any will at all. I was shit-in-your-pants terrified, and I would've done anything. I would've shot Mrs. Wu myself if it would've saved me."

"All right," Carol said. "It's all right now."

"I wish I *was* a hero, like they say. The hero was the black guy and he's dead. And he died by accident, for Christ's sake. In the exact second he was going to save us all the little guy — Hughes — his gun went off. It just went off, Carol. And the shot killed the black guy before he hit the floor. And even so, he got a round off into the other one. Dwight."

"Why don't you tell people that?" she wanted to know. "You could put it to rest."

He was standing there wringing his hands. "I can't go on television and say I'm a coward. Jesus."

"But you're not a coward."

"Have you been listening to me? Didn't you hear what I've been telling you?"

"I know you're not a coward," Carol said. "And I know anyone would be terrified."

"Terrified isn't the word, Carol. I loved the guy for not killing me. I would've done anything for him in the minute it took him to shoot Arlen in the back of the head." He had begun to cry now.

"Oh, Charles — please, don't." She put her arms around him, and he stood there and let her hold him. It felt strange. An odor came up from his body, a stale redolence of the bed and of something else, too. She breathed through her mouth and wondered that what someone felt could cause such changes in the flesh. *My husband is still afraid,* she thought. It was as if a voice spoke inside her. She stepped back from him, her hands on his arms.

"Let's make love," he said in that sorrowful voice. "Can we please make love?"

"I'm so grungy," she told him. "I need a bath."

"After?" he said.

"We'll see."

"I mean, take a bath after. Carol, I need you."

The phone rang again. He picked the whole thing up and hurled it against the wall; it made a tremendous shattering noise, and a piece of it flew off and landed near the hearth.

"Charles," she said in a small, frightened voice, standing back from him.

"You're right," he said through his teeth, "the mood isn't right. You're pregnant."

"Please," she said.

"Don't," he said. "Don't look that way. What're you afraid of? This is me."

"I'm not afraid." Her voice would not obey her. The words came out like a plea.

"Stop it," he said. "I don't mean anything. I'm just — I'm a mess."

"I'm sorry."

"Don't say you're sorry."

"I'm sorry — I mean I won't. I won't say it." She had backed away from him.

"Carol, don't."

"It has nothing to do with my being pregnant," she managed.

"Okay. I know. Whatever you say."

She bent down to pick up the phone. The connection was still intact — a voice spoke in it: "Hello? Hello?"

"Wrong number," she said, and put the handset back in its cradle. Then she walked over to the hearth to pick up the piece that had broken off, a small triangular shard of black plastic. "We can't afford to replace the living room phone," she said, trying to think of what would be normal to say.

He was quiet a moment. Then: "I'm sorry, Carol."

Again she put her arms around him, and when he tried to lead her into the bedroom, she resisted, wanting to take the phone off the hook.

"All right," he said, letting go. "Fuck it." And he went into the bedroom and slammed the door.

"I was going to take the phone off the hook," she said.

Nothing.

•

It occurred to him that he might strike her, and in the next instant he had an image of himself flailing at her, hauling her body around the room. He saw the image of Mrs. Wu's wide hips as she was dragged across the refrigerator room floor. He had felt the huge irritation with Carol at her reluctance to be near him, and then he had the thought, and this image was presented to him, this pathological little mime in his head. It seemed to him now that there was so little keeping anyone from exercising the awful possibilities in every situation. Even as he told himself that this was not an urge to do harm, was only a type of the normal random pictures in the flow of thought, he felt a crawling under his skin — the sudden, hot rush of fright in his neck and jaw, the back of his head, his shoulders. He was holding on, feeling the deep shudder, the climbing panic, witnessing somehow again, almost in the same instant, this worst eventuality possible in himself — the quick, brutal little scene playing itself through in his mind, strangely independent of him now, like the shapes that moved and gestured on a TV screen, as if some uprooted part of his soul were brandishing the thing at him. He was fearful that she might come into the room and say anything — oh, anything else. His heart was beating in the bones of his face.

"Honey?" she said on the other side of the door.

"Leave me alone," he said. "Please. Just for now — stay away."

Silence.

He sat on the bed and put his hands on his knees, listening to her move around in the kitchen. The phone rang again, and she answered it. He could hear her talking, but he couldn't make out the words. And what if he were to do something to harm her, and her baby?

The thought made him come to his feet. He couldn't bring himself to concentrate on the ordinariness of the room — the bed and the night table with its books and papers, the reading lamp, coated with a fine film of dust, and the pictures on the walls, prints of paintings, which he himself had hung — all of it seemed abruptly alien to him, and this awful terror was surging up in his blood, this feeling that something might happen, something might be let loose in the next moment. He breathed, and paced, and when she came to the door he stepped to the bed and took ahold of the headboard, as if to keep from falling.

She opened the door and looked in, and for an instant he did not recognize her. There was something off center about her face, like a line of caricature, an exaggeration he couldn't make out, of one feature or another. He thought of hearts. "It's your mother."

"What?" he said.

"Your mother." She spoke with an edge of impatience.

His mother had wanted to be sure that they arrived safely, hadn't wanted to bother them.

"You're not bothering us." He felt himself tethered to her by the thinnest of threads. It was like all those times in his boyhood: her voice over the telephone. The very similarity of it was frightening to him.

"You don't sound very good," she said.

"That's silly," he told her.

"Well."

He repeated the word. "Silly."

"I don't want to run up the bill."

He held the phone and felt Carol in the room with him, standing close by.

"That Mrs. Wu has been on the television again. She's filling in all the details for everybody. And the gunman who was hurt is being examined by shrinks."

"They said before that he was out of danger."

"I think they ought to electrocute him or something. I think if they do he'll be getting just what he deserves."

"Thanks for calling," Connally told her.

"I know you want to go."

"I haven't got to sleep yet." As he said this, Carol nudged him. "Or it feels that way," he added.

"I said I didn't want to bother you," his mother said.

"You're not bothering anybody."

"Let me talk to Carol again."

He thought of the two women finding things to say about him. "Carol's just stepped out for a few minutes, to get some milk and some stuff for dinner. Oh, and Ma — thanks for the sandwiches and coffee."

"Will you tell Carol to call me when she feels like it?"

"What do you think?" he said. "Of course I will."

"I mean it, Charles. I've taken a liking to her. And I think she has for me, too."

"That's good," he said.

"I miss you, son."

"Me, too."

When he and his mother had hung up, he turned to find Carol staring at him from across the room. "What?"

"Why did you lie to her like that? I would've talked to her. I wouldn't mind talking to her. I like her."

He tried a joke. "Great. The two of you can move in together."

"What is it with you, Charles? That's your mother. I thought you wanted me to like her."

He muttered, "I don't know what I want," and he couldn't look at her.

"This is about the baby, isn't it?"

This sent an irrational surge of rage through him.

"No, it's not about the fucking baby. Jesus, do you think we could talk tonight about something other than your uterus and what it's doing?"

At this, she went into the bedroom and slammed the door. He heard the latch turn, the lock click. *All right,* he thought. Quietly, he put his coat on and stepped out onto the porch. The sky was losing the gold light of late afternoon, and the air was colder. A stray wind kicked up a whorl of dust at the edge of the yard.

Grandville Avenue was a long, tree-lined street that ran

through the center of Point Royal, and today, the day after New Year's, it was crowded with rush-hour traffic, people going home an hour early. He watched the cars for a few minutes, then walked out to the curb and turned to look at the house. In the bedroom window, Carol stood holding the curtains aside, gazing out at him. For perhaps half a minute they stared at each other. Then she closed the curtain and moved out of view. He waited, the cold air biting at his cheeks. The house looked warm, even cozy. The guttering ashes of the fireplace sent a small glow up to the living room windows. This was home; this was what he had wanted so badly to come back to, and had believed would help him out of the anguish he'd felt in that foreign, winter city with its violence. But the violence was everywhere, and he should've known it. He was beginning to sense that he might have done the wrong thing turning away, hurrying from the place where it had all unfolded.

When he looked at the cars inching by him in the road, he thought of finding some authority, someone to tell him a clear thing about it, some categorical fact that could shine back at him like certainty, separating him from what had happened, what could happen.

•

They ate separately the cold cuts Tina had given them, and for a long time after they went to bed, they were both awake, aware of each other lying sleepless in the dark, not speaking. Finally, he turned, seemed restless, sighing.

"Do you have to go to school in the morning?"

"I have an exam," he said. Again, he sighed.

"Should I wake you up when I get up?"

"I'll be up."

"If you're asleep?"

"Yes."

"I can't understand why you're mad at me," she said.

"I'm not mad at you."

They were quiet for a long time, then. At one point, she thought he might've fallen asleep. On the walls of the room, the lights of passing cars moved, making the shadows shift. There was a siren off in the night.

He sat up. She saw his shadow against the dim whiteness at the window, and then the whiteness was gone. "What?" she said.

"Nothing. I can't get comfortable. It's nothing."

"Listen to you. Listen to the tone of your voice."

"Carol, will you please just go to sleep and let me try to sleep."

She lay with her back to him, and then he was getting up, moving around. He pulled his pants on, sitting at the end of the bed. When the lights moved in the room she watched him. He got into his shirt, then stepped into his slippers. In the hall, he turned the light on, stood looking about himself as though he couldn't remember what he'd set out to do.

"What're you doing?" she said, unable to keep the irritation from her voice.

"I'm going to study. Okay? Go back to sleep."

"Who's been to sleep?"

He went into the other bedroom, his study room, and closed the door, then stepped back out and turned off the hall light. Beyond him, the light of the room shone. In a few months, they would make a nursery out of it. He would have nowhere to get off by himself. She could almost read his thoughts now. She saw him glance in at her, and knew he couldn't see much of her in the dark where she lay. It was as if she were hiding from him, from what he might say or do there. She rolled over in the bed, pulling the blankets high on her shoulder, and she heard him close the door. Now it was dark. The traffic rolled by outside, and the dimnesses changed on the wall again. Even if she was awake when he came back to the bed, she would remain where she was, hidden in the pretense of sleep, where she could think and plan and not worry about pleasing him or disturbing his sore places, if that was what they were. She would try not to think about the difference in him now.

•

There was work to go to in the morning, and the idea of picking up the old routines made her want to cry: though work would be a refuge, the job itself — looking into the mouth of decay and atrophy all day — exhausted her. Sometimes lately, given her condition, it sickened her, and Dr. Wilder had allowed her to work the reception desk when he could get help from his wife. Dr. Wilder was a balding, quiet-spoken man with the trace of an English accent and the manner of a rickety old man, though he wasn't fifty yet. He wore a small gray mustache and the suggestion of a goatee at the point of his chin, and he greeted each of his patients with the same formal courtesy, as though each appointment were the central focus of his day. He greeted his receptionist and his dental hygienist this way, too. And each morning, in that tone of courtly solicitation, he would ask three or four general questions concerning the progress of his employees' lives.

This morning, he donned his white coat and then yawned. "I'm actually sleepy at this hour," he said. "Can you imagine? I had family staying through the holiday."

"We went to Chicago," Carol said.

"I'll say you did," the receptionist said.

Dr. Wilder turned to her. "I trust your holiday was good as well?"

"It wasn't sensational or exciting," the receptionist said, looking at Carol. "Didn't you see the news, Dr. Wilder?"

"I don't watch television very much, I'm afraid."

"Carol's husband saved a woman's life on the national news."

The dentist turned his kindly gaze toward Carol. "What's this?"

"It was on the news. It happened in Chicago. And Carol's husband was the hero. He was interviewed and everything."

The dentist looked at Carol. "I missed it."

"Several people were killed," the receptionist said. Her name was Trudy, and she had been hired only last month. She was nineteen, and wore tennis shoes to work, carrying her high-heeled shoes in a bag; her black hair was cut short, not much longer than crew-cut length on the sides, with a long tail at the back, and she wore beads and bracelets and costume jewelry, which rattled when she walked. In her desk she kept a Walkman, and earphones and tapes of old sixties rock groups, which she hooked herself up to when she took her lunch hour. To Carol she had seemed a little arrogant until this morning. Now she took Carol's arm and squeezed, talking about luck and glamour and *The Tonight Show*. "No," she said. "I know. *Nightline*." She held the index finger of her other hand up, as if to emphasize that she had scored a point. "*Nightline*."

"And what is *Nightline*?" the dentist wanted to know.

"It's a news interview show. This is perfect for it."

"I think it's all probably old news now," Carol said.

"They do old news sometimes. I don't understand why you're not more excited."

Carol looked past the receptionist at Dr. Wilder, whose expression was curious, and faintly sympathetic, too. But in the next moment, he said, "Aren't you happy?"

"I'm happy my husband survived it."

"He's a famous figure," said Trudy.

"Well," Carol said, "no."

"He was on. I saw him. He was saying he didn't do anything — you know, real modest-like. And that Jap woman talking about how he stood up and stepped in front of her and everything."

"Well, it's really over now," Carol said.

"We have a full dance card today?" the dentist asked.

"All but the eleven-fifteen slot."

"Can you fill that one?"

"I'll try."

Carol's first client was a man who hadn't been to a dentist in seventeen years, and was proud of it. He sat in her chair and talked about how it usually took wild horses to get him into the hands of doctors or dentists, mostly because he'd simply been too busy doing other things; but he'd had some discomfort on the right side of his mouth, and while he knew it was a wisdom tooth (another dentist had diagnosed this twenty-one years ago, when, after years of neglect of his teeth, he had wound up with only one cavity), he had recently decided he might as well go ahead and get the full treatment.

"I have very strong teeth," he said.

He was also an habitual pipe smoker. When he opened his mouth, the odor of the tobacco — a sweetish, breath-stealing puff of badness, only slightly altered by the minty toothpaste he had used — wafted up into her face, through the mask she had put on.

"Excuse me," she said to him, and went quickly into the little bathroom across the hall. It took a moment to fight off the urge to be sick, and then it took another few moments to steel herself for facing him again. She washed her lips and patted them dry, then arranged herself and stepped out of the room. The dentist was standing in the hallway, one hand on the frame of his office door.

"Are you all right?"

"Fine," she said. And she thought of his polite questions at the beginning of each day. *No, I'm not all right. I left my husband at home this morning without speaking to him, and I don't even understand why we're fighting, since I didn't shoot anybody.*

"You're white as a sheet," the dentist said.

"I'll be all right."

"I'm afraid you'll have to be today. You see, my wife is off on a holiday to New York with friends."

She nodded and went back in to the man in the chair, with his mouth like a terrible hole. He was observing her, showing the slightest nervousness in his expression; his round eyes were dark green and not unkind. Actually, he had a rather good face, strong-featured and circled with blond, clean hair; there was an appealing little crook in his nose. Probably he was careful — even a little vain — about himself in all other ways. His clothes were stylish and well turned (as her mother would put it), and he was just a perfectly nice man with bad teeth. Carol couldn't help seeing his whole life through the prism of that calamity in his mouth.

"This is going to hurt a little," he said, "am I right?"

"A little," she said.

"Those hooks."

She had picked up one of her scalers. "Now just lay back and try to relax."

"Oh, boy," he said, and the something doubtful in his expression made her wish for anything else to do for a job. She told herself to breathe through her mouth, and then she put the light on him. "Lie back, now."

He did as she asked.

His teeth were buried, subsumed, in plaque; it was caked and breaking, like old plaster, on the backs of the lower front, and it had displaced the gums badly all around. At the roots of most of the teeth a brown staining had begun, and the whole mouth was red and swollen and irritated.

"Do you brush?" she managed.

"Every day," he said. He was cheerful, smiling, and it dawned on her with a little jolt to her nerves that he considered himself charming. And he *was* charming, no doubt. She had to remind herself. Oh, how she hated this job! "What's the damage?" he asked.

"There's quite a lot of work to do. It might take a couple of visits."

"A couple?"

"Yes, sir."

He put his head back. "Let's get started."

But she couldn't do it. She sat forward, breathing through her mouth, and when the blood started to flow she had to excuse herself again.

"I guess it's pretty bad," he told her, choking on the blood.

"Rinse," she said to him, indicating the little bowl, and she may have uttered an epithet; she wasn't sure. She thought the word "shit" might've escaped her. She looked at him and attempted a smile through the mask, but in a moment it became necessary to go back to the little bathroom, where she began spitting into the toilet, trying very hard not to think about anything. Trudy came in and stood with her back to the door. "Dr. Wilder's on the phone, looking for a hygienist."

"I can't help that."

"You don't want to get fired."

"He won't fire me," Carol said.

"No," said the receptionist, "he'll fire me. Can't you get out there and tough things out? I mean, I know you're pregnant and all, but — Jesus."

"This is not a reaction you tough out," Carol said, pushing past her.

Out in the hall, Dr. Wilder was explaining to the patient that his hygienist was pregnant. "Morning sickness," he said.

"I hope it's not the flu," said the patient. "For *her* sake. The flu can be really rough when you're pregnant."

"It's not the flu," Carol said. Everyone was so kind, and wished to think the best of everyone else.

"Well, I'm bleeding and I'd just as soon stop."

"I've already started," Carol said.

"Can you continue?" Dr. Wilder asked her.

"I can try."

"There's a girl."

The man lay back with his head in the little kidney-shaped cushions, and she worked on him, trying to concentrate only on the packed corroded surfaces of the teeth, which *were* strong, and free of cavities, for all the neglect they had suffered. When she had finished the first part of the work, Dr. Wilder came in to look at him, and suggested another visit, to finish up.

"That's fine with me," said the man. "This hurts more than I thought it would. And I thought it would hurt a lot."

"There's just so much buildup," Carol told him.

"Well, seventeen years. Must be like excavating a ruin."

There were five other patients in the waiting room when she went to call the next one. Her heart sank. Dr. Wilder was standing in the entrance of his office again. "I can't get anyone."

"I know," she told him.

"Will you be all right?"

"Excuse me," she said, heading into the bathroom again. There she took deep breaths and tried to empty her mind of all images, but then she was coughing and spitting into the sink, and in one spasm she felt something in her lower abdomen. She got herself into a stall and closed the door, feeling the something move down, like a kind of draining. When she looked into her panties there was blood.

"Oh, no," she said. "Oh, Jesus. Oh, God."

Trudy had come in again, and was on the other side of the stall door. "Hey?" she said.

Carol was crying. "Oh, please. Call someone. I'm — oh, I'm bleeding." The door opened and closed. Carol stood trembling in the stall, holding on, crying quietly. "Please," she murmured. "Oh, please."

The dentist was calm, even reassuring. He got her to one of the chairs and kept her quiet until the ambulance arrived. "Lots of women spot a little during pregnancy," he said.

"But it hurts," she said.

"There, there." He touched her forehead. "It may not be anything to worry about."

"It's a lot of blood, Doctor."

"You're going to be all right."

"No," Carol said, seeing him in a blur of tears. "I'm losing my baby, now. Aren't I?"

"You're going to be fine," Dr. Wilder told her.

When the medics arrived they took her pulse and listened to her heart. Then they cleared the room and examined the bleeding. They were very young: they didn't look old enough to shave, but both wore beards, trimmed close. They might've been brothers. The one who examined her was burly and a bit darker than his companion, with ash-colored hair and a way of blinking when he talked, as if he meant everything as a friendly secret among them. He asked if she could stand, and went on to say that the bleeding was not dangerous to her.

"Am I losing my baby?" she asked.

"Well, we can't say no to that," he told her. "But it could be that you're not. This could just be an episode, you know."

"I feel it draining out of me," she said, crying.

The young man took her fingers and massaged them. "We'll take you in the gurney. Okay?"

"Oh," Carol said. "Oh, God."

"Tell me your name."

Carol looked at him. There was that dimly conspiratorial look on his face.

"You're fine," he said. "Tell me your name."

She did so.

"All right, Carol. We're just going to give you a nice and comfortable ride to the hospital. We'll contact your doctor on the way, and everybody'll be waiting for us."

She nodded.

"There's a girl," Dr. Wilder said, standing in the doorway of his office.

•

Connally walked up Grandville Avenue to the school in its open green meadow. On his way, he looked at the windows of the houses lining the street — the doors left open, the unlocked gates and entrances. It was a chilly, sunny day, and small children were playing on the lawns, bundled in padded coats, wrapped to the chin in bright scarves. No one seemed to be watching them. At the college, he went straight to the lecture room, though he was ten minutes early for the exam. The room was empty. He sat in a desk near the back wall and waited. When a young woman he didn't recognize entered, he said, "I can't remember what I studied." He wanted to get her talking; he had a sensation of heading himself toward some normal procession of minutes in the day, righting himself, getting back to his own memory of himself.

The girl nodded at him and took her seat. She was very young, with long, carefully disordered blond hair and too much makeup. She sat with her legs crossed, swinging one booted foot and staring at it. Now and then she popped the gum in her mouth. Finally she turned and looked at him. "You in the three o'clock class?"

He nodded.

"I thought so. I'm in the eleven."

Two other people came in, a couple, very moony about each other, and Connally recognized them as being from his own class. They seated themselves in front of the room and held hands across the aisle. She had the same wild, consciously disordered hairstyle, and she was also chewing gum. Her fingernails were a strange lavender color, and very long. He was big and innocent-looking, with wide empty blue eyes and a soft, whiskerless, unlined face. They stared into each other's rapt expressions, and nothing about them, Connally supposed, seemed remotely fit to stand up to the slightest trouble or pain. It had been hard enough coming to school, being older than the other students; it had felt retrograde and foolish, and Connally had tried not to think about it in that way.

He opened his book and stared at a diagram of marine life at different depths. His hands shook. Others were coming into the room. He watched them for a moment, watched their nervous fidgeting. Finally he was unable to remain in the seat, and he made his way to the front of the room, to the door, out into the gathering crowd in the hallway. Another exam, across the way, had already begun. A man was giving instructions, writing on the blackboard. Twenty or so students waited, sitting with their hands folded in front of them like children.

Outside, it had begun to cloud over, and a chilly breeze was blowing from the north. The trees swayed and the bare branches clicked. He paused in the doorway of the building, trying to decide what he could do — his mind was in a kind of suspension, as if he were awaiting the outcome of something. But nothing came to him. He was inexplicably quiet inside. A little later, seeing his history professor ambling across the square, he stepped back from the door, then hurried into the men's room on the left side of the foyer. The high, wide windows in there were open, and the cold came in. Connally looked at himself in the mirror, thinking of murderers. His heart raced; it occurred to him that he was not going to make it. And then the professor entered. The professor's name was Ansel Williamson. He was an imposing man, tall and balding, with a long, square jaw and thick, bloodless lips. A senior professor of the college faculty, he had authored a book about the Roosevelts and the Kennedys that had been in print now for almost ten years. To his students, he was a stern, dour-looking crank with the air of someone playing a part — he seemed quite aware of the anxiety he caused them, and derived obvious pleasure out of playing the part to the hilt. Connally stood by the window, regarding him while he washed his hands.

"So," the older man said, "how does it feel to be a hero on television?"

Connally said, "I didn't ask for it."

"It was thrust upon you."

"I never wanted anything like it."

The older man pulled two towels from the dispenser, then faced him. "Were you by chance hiding from someone in here, Mr. Connally?"

"No."

"I saw you duck back into the building."

"I forgot something."

"Did you want to talk to me?"

"I don't feel like talking to anybody right now."

"You look like you've seen a ghost."

Connally said nothing.

"I have people in Chicago, you know. I had no idea we shared the heartland in that way."

"My mother lives there," Connally told him. "I never lived there."

"It's my mother who lives there, too, with my sister."

This seemed to require no response.

"Are you feeling all right, young man?"

"I'm fine."

"You're shaking."

"I'm all right."

"I wonder, will you be up to taking your history exam tomorrow? Perhaps you should put it off a while. We could arrange something, I'm sure."

"I'm not taking the history exam," Connally told him.

Professor Williamson gazed at him. "You're doing well so far, I believe. I'm not surprised this has put you under some stress."

Connally returned his gaze.

"I can see it has done that."

"People won't let it rest," Connally said.

"No."

"I can't concentrate."

"Do you want an incomplete grade?"

"I don't think I want to be in college anymore."

"Well, then I guess that's it, isn't it?"

There wasn't anything left to say.

"Perhaps you ought to see someone . . ."

Connally felt cornered, thinking of the killings. It blew through him like a freezing wind. The older man's face wore a tolerant, fatherly expression.

"You know, I thought you'd be the sort that stuck his chest out. I mean, you looked so humble and aware of how it plays on television."

"It wasn't a show," Connally told him.

"Of course it wasn't. I was talking about your sense of history."

Connally could think of no answer to this, either.

"No," the older man said, "that's not really fair. That's — glib. You don't need that now, do you?"

"I don't know what I need," Connally said.

"Well, there *are* support groups for victims. And people who specialize in it in the psychiatric community."

"Thank you."

"If I can be of any help . . ."

"No."

"You don't look good, young man."

"I'll be all right."

Professor Williamson shook his head slightly, then opened the door and was gone. The door swung shut. Connally didn't move for a few moments, expecting him to come back. But the halls, the building, grew quiet.

He went out into the quad and sat on a slatted bench in the shafts of sun that shone through the creases in the cloud cover. The wind had stopped. Students he knew walked by him, nodding and going on: not everyone had seen the newscasts. Having come here at all, he felt that he had accomplished something, some definite thing. It was oddly liberating. But then everything grew confused again, and he was sitting there staring at the two-hundred-year-old façade of the college's main building, with its bright windows and its gargoyles lining the roof.

He walked three miles to the Point Royal Hospital Mental Health Center. The chill in the air, and the exertion of walking in it, calmed him a little; several times he thought of turning around, going on with the rest of his life. But the weeks and months ahead seemed blotted somehow. He could not imagine a time when his own thoughts might belong to him.

The mental health center was in a renovated mansion set back among tall old trees and bordered by a grass field beyond the new, red brick towers of Point Royal Hospital. A flagstone walk wound across the field and emptied into a cement patio in front of the building, whose porch was stacked with boxes and chairs, one on top of the other — a thicket of chair legs and bent cardboard shapes, bursting with papers. As Connally stepped up onto the porch, the front door opened, and a man backed out of the place carrying a box of books.

"Excuse me," he said.

And then a woman was standing in the doorway. "Can I help you?" She smiled.

Connally watched the man move along the porch, apparently looking for a place to put the box. The man was heavy, with big shoulders, and he wore his long dark hair in a ponytail.

"We're moving into our new quarters this week," the woman said. Her eyes were lined with wrinkles, and when she smiled at him the wrinkles deepened. She had a sweater tied at her waist, and her glasses were on a small black strand dangling over her white silk blouse like a necklace. Now she took them up and put them on, then gazed at Connally. "Do you wish to speak with someone?"

He nodded.

"Do you have an appointment?"

"No."

"Come in," she said, and stepped back for him to go past her. Inside, there was more confusion — boxes and papers and supplies everywhere, and more piled furniture. The walls showed faded places where pictures and plaques had hung, and the curtains were gone from the windows along the left wall. A skinny boy in jeans and sweatshirt was standing on a chair, taking the curtains on the right wall down. In one corner, a desk and chair stood, and the woman led Connally there. They passed a hallway stacked its whole length with more boxes and chairs.

"Make yourself comfortable," the woman said.

Connally sat down. His stomach was churning; he had a moment of feeling dizzy, out of control. "Are you a doctor?" he said.

She smiled again. "No."

"I was wondering if I could talk to a doctor."

"Did you want counseling?"

Connally looked around at the boy standing on the chair, and then the woman said something he didn't quite hear. "Pardon?"

"I said it's perfectly all right."

He was at a loss.

She gestured toward the boy. "He's deaf."

Connally nodded at her; the information seemed pointless to him.

She opened a lower drawer of the desk and brought out a printed form. "Well, if you'll just fill this out. And I'll go see if one of the counselors can see you."

"I need to see a doctor," Connally said. And he almost went on: *I don't want to hurt anyone. I'm so frightened I might hurt someone.*

Again she smiled. "Fill that out, please."

The form was a standardized information sheet. The questions asked for details of his medical history, and then there was a list of hundreds of symptoms and conditions, with boxes in a column to the right: YES or NO. He looked at the list: anxiety, sleeplessness, panic, violent mood swings, inability to concentrate, blurred vision, nausea, rages. He stopped reading. At the top of the form were lines for him to put his name and address and phone number. He wrote his name. He could hear the voice of one of the doctors in an office near the entrance to the hallway. The doctor spoke very calmly, almost soothingly: "I'm sure we can get you started on regular visits before very long. The first thing we ask for, though, is a complete medical examination. If you've had one recently, we can see about getting the doctor to release the results. That way we can hold the evaluation process down to the neurological tests. It saves time and money, too. But we want to rule out all the physiological possibilities first."

The woman came back to the desk and stood behind it. "Someone can see you now," she said. "If you want to, you can finish that when you come out."

"A doctor?" Connally said.

"We have counselors," she said. "They're the first step."

"I can't see a doctor?"

"Is this an emergency?"

"I just thought I could talk to a doctor."

"Our counselors are very well trained. You'll be in good hands." She stepped to the entrance of the hallway and held one hand out, as if to show it to him. He thought of the stylized movements of women in television advertisements; there was something faintly commercial in the way she stood there waiting for him to make his way back to the suite of offices. She stepped in behind him and said, "Third door on your right."

The door was ajar. When he hesitated, she came to his side and knocked once, peremptorily, then pushed the door open, revealing a man seated behind a big, cluttered desk with his hands folded across his stomach. Behind him was a window looking out at the back of a shopping center. The ground was dotted with refuse.

"Come in," the man said, sitting forward.

Connally took the chair on the other side of the desk.

"Do you have your form?"

"No."

"Well." The man leaned back in the chair. "We're all a little less formal while we go through this move. I'm Joe."

"Joe," Connally said.

"You're Joe too."

"No."

"Okay," he said with something like barely controlled frustration. "I'm Joe, how do you do. And you're?"

"Charles."

"Charles. Good. What seems to be the trouble, Charles?"

"I was in a robbery," Connally said. "People were hurt." And as the words left his lips, he knew he would not be able to say more about it.

The man had written something on a pad of paper under his hands. "Yes," he said.

Connally was trembling — he could feel it starting in his jaw and along his spine. Abruptly he was afraid of letting the other man see how badly he was shaken. He stood. "I'm sorry, really. There's nothing — I'd be wasting your time."

"Why don't you let me decide that."

"No, thanks anyway," Connally said. "It's something I can work out myself." He did not wait for the man to say more. And when he passed through the outer office, the woman wasn't there. The deaf boy sat with his feet up on her desk, eating a sandwich. Outside, several people were loading boxes onto the back of a truck, the driver of which was polishing the side-view mirror with a handkerchief. The street was bustling with traffic, and noisy with engines and horns, and everybody was preoccupied with something; Connally felt as though he were slipping through them unseen, as though they would stop him if they knew enough.

He went home, straightened the bed, then got in under the blanket. When the phone rang he lay with the blankets over his ears, breathing into the palms of his hands. He slept little, but when a dream began, he woke with a start. This happened two or three times. Outside, the surf sound of traffic increased. It was getting toward the middle of the day.

Not long after one o'clock, he heard the sound of footsteps on the porch. He got up and went to the door, pulled the curtain aside, and looked out: a face he did not recognize, a slender, young, boy-smooth face without a hint of complexity in it. He opened the door a crack. "What?"

"Mr. Connally?"

"What is it?"

"I'm with the *Point Royal Gazette,* and I'm doing an article on what happened to you in Chicago. Believe it or not, I've already talked with Mrs. Wu —"

"I don't have anything to say," Connally told him.

"Mr. Connally, I know you're reluctant to talk about it, but I thought if I helped you we could just put it to rest for good. We could say it in a way that'll make everybody stop bothering you."

"You're bothering me."

"It won't take a minute, sir. Really. I really want to help."

Connally stepped back and let him in. He'd taken his shoes and shirt off, and he went back into the bedroom to put the shirt on. When he came back, he found the young man staring at one of the pictures above the mantel — Carol in a black bikini, standing in the bright sun of Virginia Beach, trying to keep her hair out of her face, the ocean merging with the sky in the blue distances behind her.

"Lovely," he said when he saw Connally. He seemed a little sheepish, as if he had not meant to be found looking at things in that way, like someone snooping.

"Sit down," Connally told him.

The other did so with a kind of alacrity, as if glad to get past the embarrassment of being caught. He opened his jacket and brought out a small notepad and pencil, and then sat waiting for Connally to speak.

"What do you want me to say?"

"I'm sorry. I thought you'd just want to talk."

"I don't believe all the interest in it," Connally told him.

"Just a minute," the other said, writing laboriously in the notepad and murmuring, ". . . don't believe . . ."

"Wait," Connally said. "Who the hell do you work for, anyway?"

"I thought I told you. The *Point Royal Gazette*."

Connally stared at him.

"All right," he said, "it's the *Ledger*."

The *Ledger* was the college newspaper. Connally sat back and regarded the other man. "The *Ledger*, huh?"

"But we can sell the piece to other papers. I'm sure of it."

"Sell it."

"They pay for pieces of general interest. I'll give you complete control over everything that's in it. I mean — well, they always do some editing and all, but you can control what they see first. It can be your statement about it."

"There's not going to be anybody interested in statements," Connally told him. "It's not like this is world history."

"You never know," the other said. "There's a lot of curiosity at school. You're a sort of celebrity, you know."

"Well, all right," Connally told him, making up his mind. "Okay, here's what happened. These two guys walked into the place with guns blazing — am I going too fast?"

"— guns . . . blaze," the younger man said. "I've devised my own system of shorthand."

"Okay. So they came in shooting, and I managed to get one of them with a — with the cash register drawer. You ever feel one of those? I mean, how heavy they are?"

The other man had stopped writing.

"Well?" Connally said.

"The cash register drawer?"

"Come to think of it," Connally told him, "maybe it was the coffee machine. I just grabbed whatever was handy. Just to get in their way."

"The — the coffee machine?"

"Come to think of it, it was the safe."

"You're putting me on, right?"

"I'm telling you what happened."

The other man stared at him.

"You don't believe me?" Connally strove for outrage.

"The news reports didn't say anything about —"

"You want the story or not, man?"

"Yes."

But there wasn't any point in it, nor any kindness, running this young, credulous man's flag up. "Please leave," Connally told him. "Now."

"All right, I'll listen."

"No, you don't understand. It's bullshit. All right? I was bullshitting you. It's all bullshit."

The man stood and began very carefully putting his notepad and pencil away. "You don't look like any hero to me, you know. You look like somebody who's afraid," he muttered. "That's what you look like."

"You ever seen anybody shot?" Connally asked him, hearing the tremor in his voice.

"You can't threaten me," said the other.

"Jesus," Connally said, "I'm not threatening you."

"Try to help somebody —"

Connally followed him out onto the porch and partway down the cold sidewalk. "I'm not threatening you," he said. By the time they reached the curb, the man was running.

"Don't you touch me." He had fear in his eyes.

Connally watched him drive away, and then was surprised to find Carol's father pulling in. Theodore got out slow, favoring his arthritic hip. Connally went back up onto the porch and waited for him.

"You answered your phone yet?" Theodore called.

"I just got here."

Theodore looked at him from the walk, then approached. He wore a gray suit with no tie, and a brown hat cocked at an angle; it looked as though he had been jostled in a crowd and hadn't got himself straightened yet. His step was cautious, rickety. He was a man whose every physical gesture carried the signs of what his dreams had been the night before: when he was confident of himself and his night had been restful and dreamless, his step was light — he seemed strong, years younger, even graceful — but when he suffered nightmares, when the nights went on and were slow, agitated with fright and despair, he walked like this, with a halting, aged limp. "You don't look like you just got anywhere, son."

"What is it?" Connally asked him.

"Your wife is in the hospital. She's had a little bleeding episode." Theodore held one hand up. "Oh, she's all right. But Lord, boy. We've been trying to call you all afternoon."

"I'll get dressed," Connally said.

"Don't bother with that. Grace is bringing her home." The older man looked off, down the street. "I guess they stopped to get something for her to read." He made his way up onto the porch, then held the door for Connally, who went inside, seeing as though with his father-in-law's eyes the cramped living room of the house.

"She's going to have to lay low for a time," said Theodore, "but everything's on course."

Connally excused himself and went into the bedroom to put his shoes on and button his shirt. In the other room, the older man coughed, then cleared his throat. When the phone rang, he answered it.

"Hello?"

Connally waited.

"Just a minute, please."

Connally went in to him, and took the handset when he held it out. It was Detective Sergeant Donovan calling from Chicago.

"Yes," Connally said.

"Well, sir, you know we're going to need you to come out here and testify against this guy."

For an instant, the idea of traveling back there felt like a means of escape.

"We'll pay your expenses, of course."

"Yes, sir," Connally told him. "I told you all I know."

"Got to tell a jury that, too, though."

"Yes, sir."

"That's the way it works."

"When?"

"Oh, it'll be a while. I just wanted to make sure we kept in touch."

Connally was silent.

"How you holding up?"

"Fine, sir."

"Hell of a thing," Sergeant Donovan said, "id'n it?"

"Yes, sir."

"Well, I guess that's all. Oh, you might be interested to know that they put together a real nice benefit for that police officer's family, and there's been a behest of some money in his name. Every year now the department'll give out a memorial medal — you know, for bravery in the performance of duty."

"That's good," Connally said, and felt that he had failed to say enough.

"Well, I thought you'd want to know."

"Thank you, sir."

"Sorry for the intrusion."

Connally hung the phone up. Theodore stared at him with those old, pained eyes. "I take it that was about Chicago. And that I'm not supposed to say anything."

"You can say whatever you want," Connally told him.

"That's not what I hear."

For a moment, neither of them spoke.

Connally said, "Is this — this bleeding episode Carol had. Is it because of what happened in Chicago?"

"The doctor says it could be — wants her to rest."

Connally sat down in the easy chair across from him and rested his elbows on his knees; it seemed cruelly out of balance just sitting here when everything in his life was in such doubt. But he couldn't move, couldn't think or speak. He was fighting a kind of numbness, an absence of recognizable feelings, of a sensibility he had taken for granted.

For a harrowing moment something in him acknowledged his own increasing sense that the most ordinary actions now felt dimly pathological. He rubbed his eyes and tried not to see any of the images that now rushed through his mind, like forces racing into a vacuum: the nurse in her terrible propped stillness; the uneven trails of blood on the dirty concrete; the oriental woman's wide hips as she crawled across the floor. The thought of heading back to Chicago to testify had had a tranquilizing effect, and then he remembered the relief he'd felt heading *out* of Chicago, going home.

Home, this little place, these rooms of his dread and his uneasiness with the woman who had begun, today, to be in danger of losing a baby he hadn't wanted — this chilly little room where he could sit facing his worried, anxious father-in-law and have these entirely selfish thoughts.

"Was that *Nightline* on the phone?"

"That was the Chicago police."

"Ah," Theodore said, nodding.

A moment later, he said, "But — the news people — they have been calling you."

"Some of them called."

"I think that's quite something."

"Ted, can you tell me what happened today?"

The older man sighed. "I don't know much about it myself. Grace called me a couple hours ago and wanted me to try and get you. Well, I tried and I tried, and finally I went over to the hospital. They were just checking her out. Grace and I both tried you again from the hospital. And then I just came on ahead."

"What did the doctors say?"

"Oh, you know. She has to stay down a few days. Grace did this, too, when she was pregnant with Carol. Bled for a week — we thought she'd lost the baby. But then she went in for a look a couple of weeks later, and damned if she wasn't still pregnant." The older man seemed more animated now, sitting with his hat pushed back slightly and his hands folded under his chin. His skinny legs were crossed at the knee, and his slacks had bunched up on the white, hairless calf.

Connally remembered that when he wasn't on other tranquilizing drugs, he often drank bourbon to calm himself.

"Would you like something to drink?"

"No thanks."

They were quiet.

"So the Chicago police called."

Connally nodded.

"I guess they're grateful to you."

"They want me to go back there and testify."

"Oh, of course. Then it'll still be in the news, there."

Connally said nothing.

"A man doesn't have to feel brave," Theodore said. "In fact, if he does feel brave maybe he's a fool."

It's past that, Connally wanted to tell him. Can't you see that I am afraid I might hurt your daughter? *Oh, God. I wish I could go back to before.* He stood, moved to the windows, and looked out. He was close to screaming; there was a scream struggling up his throat. Everything was slipping away in him, and he had to get out, get away. He stared at the street. It was almost dusk. "Where are they?" He did not recognize his own voice.

"Should be along any minute."

How wonderful to be worried only about harming one's self. He couldn't think. Behind him, reflected in the window, sitting with white calf exposed, swinging the crossed leg slightly, his father-in-law yawned.

"It's going to be all right, you know."

Connally watched the headlights come, watched them turn into the drive. Carol got out and looked over the roof of the car at him as he stepped out on the porch.

"I'm okay," she called to him.

He felt sick to his stomach. He went to the edge of the porch and waited for her. Behind him, Theodore coughed, shuffling in the doorway. "Just a matter of laying low for a few days. That's just what her mother did."

"It could have been serious," said Grace, getting out on the driver's side and hurrying around to help Carol totter up the walk to the house. Connally had come partway down the stairs.

"Honey, you don't have a coat on," Carol said. She reached for him, put her arms around his neck. "We'll be all right," she breathed. "It's going to be all right."

He helped her into the house and on through the living room. Grace followed them. "She's got to stay down," Grace said, "and that means complete bed rest until this stops."

"It's going to be fine," Carol said.

"I'm going to stay a few days and help out."

"Isn't that nice, Charles? You don't have to worry about school getting interrupted."

Grace was helping her out of her clothes, looking with obvious disapproval at the unmade bed. She muttered, "Change those sheets . . ."

"We don't have anything clean," said Connally.

"Lord."

Carol got into the bed and her mother put the blankets up to her chin. "I feel like a little girl."

Connally stood back, waiting to be told what to do. In the other room, Theodore coughed again.

"We'll take good care of you," Grace said. "This baby'll do just fine."

"You know, Mom had the same thing when she was pregnant with me," Carol said, giving Charles a look that seemed almost heartbroken. He turned away slightly, smoothed the blanket at the edge of the bed.

"Well?" Grace said to him. "Don't just stand there. Give the girl a kiss. She was brave today. You're not the only hero around here."

Connally stooped to kiss his wife on the forehead. She put her hands around his neck again, and murmured in his ear, "I love you."

"I love you, too," he said, shivering inside. *Oh, I do. Help me.*

"Now, I think she should sleep some," Grace said.

"I don't want to sleep."

"I'll make something to eat," Grace said. Then, to Connally: "You'll have to show me where everything is."

"He'll be out in a little while," said Carol.

When they were alone, she held her arms out for him again. He sat down and buried his face in the folds of her robe. He could hear her heartbeat. She caressed the back of his head, then murmured something he didn't hear.

"What?" he said.

"I know part of you might be a little disappointed. It's natural."

He couldn't speak.

"When I thought I was losing this baby, Charles, it — it was the worst thing I've ever felt in my life. Please, I know you'll feel something of what I feel about it."

"Jesus Christ," he said. "How can you think I'd be *glad*."

"I didn't say *you*. I said *part* of you. And it's perfectly natural. It's a perfectly natural thing."

"I'm not even thinking about the baby," he told her.

She waited.

"I'm — I'm thinking of you."

"Darling," she said.

"No." He stood. "It's something else. Something's happening to me."

She was simply lying there, waiting for him to go on.

"I have to go back there," he said.

She uttered a small, bitter syllable of comprehension.

"They called. They want me to testify at the guy's trial."

"When? What about school?"

"He said it would be a while."

"Well, when? Spring break? Summer?"

"He didn't say."

She moved on the bed, turning, pulling her legs up. "I can't have this, Charles. Let's talk about it later."

"I'm sorry," he told her.

"I have to sleep now — please."

"Carol."

She was silent.

He turned the light off, closed the door. Then he opened it again. "I love you," he said. But it felt hollow in his mouth, and he couldn't bring himself to wait for her to respond. In the living room, Grace and Theodore were sitting on opposite sides of the couch, like two strangers in a doctor's waiting room. Theodore had opened a magazine and was paging through it.

"Let me make something to eat and then Theodore will get out of our hair," Grace said.

"I can make something," Connally told her.

"Just show me where you keep everything."

When he returned to the living room, Theodore was building a fire. "Chilly in here," he said. He was still wearing the hat.

Connally sat on the sofa, but then couldn't keep still. The room seemed to be contracting. He had to move to keep from crying out.

"I guess you have studying to do," Theodore said.

"Yes."

In the hall, he came face to face with his mother-in-law. "Hey," Grace said, leaning up to kiss him on the cheek, "I'm just going to say one thing: we're proud of you."

He patted her shoulder, then moved to the door of the room. Here was the refuge of his desk and papers, the room's look of days when he was attached to his own life, and happy. He hadn't known how happy. He closed himself inside and sat at the desk. None of the books on the shelves would tell him how to behave now, in this terrible fear. He didn't know where to look. But he was convinced that something in him had been set loose by what happened in the convenience store, and it was floating around in his soul, dark, interested only in its own nourishment.

•

When her mother brought something to eat — broiled whitefish fillets and a baked potato — Carol sat up and tried to oblige her, but she lacked an appetite, felt vaguely nauseous. "I did, too, when it happened to me," Grace told her, sitting down on the edge of the bed. Since her divorce, Grace had made efforts to change her appearance: she'd lost weight, and she wore younger clothes. For a time her hair had undergone a series of color alterations and styles, and Carol knew that lately she had begun smoking again, though she never had a cigarette where anyone would see her. But the small apartment she kept in Point Royal smelled of tobacco, and the odor of it was in her clothes. She chewed gum constantly, and kept a small container of breath mints in her purse. Carol had seen her spray her tongue with Binaca. Grace had a fear of being thought unladylike, and when Carol had flirted with the idea of smoking as a teenager, her mother expressed horror at what others would think of her, a girl smoking a cigarette, like any boy in the street. Carol and Charles, who smoked sparingly, had joked about her habit when they were alone, calling Grace "Huck" and teasing about being thankful it wasn't gin she was taking on the sly.

Now the smell of the tobacco was making Carol feel ill. She sat there with the tray on her lap. "Where's Charles?"

Her mother looked over her shoulder, gesturing toward the closed door across the hall.

"He has exams," Carol explained.

"I don't get it. Where's all the bravery?"

She knew her mother had meant this as a joke, that she was imagining Charles to be the proverbial nervous father, and even so it was impossible to control her voice, or her anger. "Oh God, I swear I don't want to talk about it ever again, Mama. Please."

Grace was silent, sitting with her hands folded in her lap.

"I didn't mean to jump," Carol told her.

"You've had a bad day."

"It's all bad days lately," Carol said, trying not to cry.

"Poor thing," Grace said, patting her arm. "Nobody

thinks of what the wife goes through in a terrible thing like that. Such trauma. You poor dear."

There was no telling her; Carol didn't know how to begin.

"Come on," Grace said. "At least try some of the potato."

"I can't."

Grace forked a little of it into her own mouth. "It's good."

"Please take it away," Carol said.

The older woman rose, carrying the tray. "Is there anything else I can do?"

"Don't be hurt," Carol told her.

"I just asked."

"Relax. Watch some television."

"Your father's reading," said Grace. "You know how it is."

It was an old argument between Carol's parents that through the twenty-odd years of marriage they could never agree on how they would amuse themselves, were always coming up against their own momentary wishes: both liked to read, both liked movies and music and television game shows, both had much the same taste, and a good deal of the same attitudes and opinions. Yet in any given week of their marriage, there were few coinciding impulses: when he felt like reading, she felt like television; when he felt like listening to music, she felt like talking; when he felt like talking, she wanted to read. They liked each other, they even approved of each other, yet they bickered all the time, and they were not affectionate with each other. They lavished affection on Carol, who, growing up in that house, had assumed their way of speech and manner with each other was the way parents generally were. She could remember a time when she was eleven or twelve years old, being stunned to see a school friend's parents kiss each other. She had been trying to struggle into a heavy coat for the walk home, and the friend's father had arrived from his job in the city. The two people stood embracing in the open doorway and the cold came in, and Carol's friend complained. "Every time he gets home, we freeze," she said.

Carol stood with her winter coat half on and watched in amazement. And she never saw the girl in the same way again, never felt the same interest in her that she had begun with. It was indeed difficult to keep from thinking of her as having something she was not smart enough to appreciate; there seemed something vulgar about such a person. It was years later before she came to realize that the girl had simply been fortunate, had lived all her young life in the so breathable atmosphere and clarity of love, had learned to expect it, and assumed others had it.

Carol had come to know this because she'd believed she had that kind of love with Charles. She had told him about the couple standing in the chilly open doorway of that long-ago house. In a way, she had confided in him about it, feeling shy and even a little fearful that he might not see how she meant it to seem, because, as she discovered telling it to him, she had carried the image with her over the years, and something in her own hunger for affection, for that nourishing air and light, was contained in it, like a fragile, crouched thing inside a shell.

"So that's what you want me to do?" Charles said, smiling. "When I come home from school, wait in the open door for you and then the two of us can heat the outside?"

"Don't tease," she said.

"I think it's a lovely idea," he said. "I really wasn't teasing a bit."

"I'm serious. I can't explain it. But when I think of us, that couple comes to mind."

"Braving the cold."

"Charles."

"I'm serious," he said.

"You make me feel embarrassed to tell you."

Now his face was almost grave. "When I was a kid, one of the houses I lived in was my mother's brother's and his family. They were like that. Like this couple you saw in the doorway. They took showers together in the middle of the day. My mother would be working, or off with my father, and they'd get me to watch their kids while they went upstairs and fooled around. They were in their late fifties — they got married late. And they still made whoopy about every damn day. At least I heard the shower going every day, and them talking in it. I didn't get much experience of married love, either, remember."

"I think my parents love each other," Carol told him. "I just don't think they ever learned to show it."

"You know how to show it," he said.

That time — when was it? a year ago, two years — oh, she had nestled in his arms. And when was it, really? How long ago had any of it been? It seemed to her now that every good thing she could remember was in another life, somewhere else.

•

Her mother had packed only a few things, and in the morning she went over to her apartment and filled two suitcases with clothes and books and makeup. "It's just that I feel so naked without my belongings," she said to Carol. "I won't be here a minute longer than you need me."

She stayed almost two months. Theodore had promised to have her apartment painted, and it was decided that since Grace would be absent from it for a while, this was the time. The painters created delays of their own — some of the plasterboard on the walls had buckled over the years and needed to be replaced, and there were leaks in the ceiling upstairs that would have to be dealt with — and so Grace remained with Carol and her husband. She had Theodore bring her small portable television over, which she put in the bedroom for Carol. It sat on Carol's tall dresser, and now Grace spent time in the bedroom with her, sitting on the bed or even lying on Charles's side, watching the afternoon programs.

The bleeding stopped after a few days, but then started again a week later. Carol lay in bed, sometimes with the door closed — Grace wanting to encourage her to sleep — hearing the movements on the other side of the door: Charles going in and out of his study room. When Charles looked in on her, he seemed almost shy. The new semester began, and he went off to school each day and stayed away into the evening hours. Friends called — Carol's from her old job at the department store, two of Charles's from his time in the Air Force. They wanted to know how Charles was doing, and several of them had seen the news reports. Word had got around. The cleric who had married them, Nancy Halstead, who was now pastor of a church in the country, called to say she would be glad to listen to anything Carol wanted to say about what happened in Chicago, having learned of the whole thing from a parishioner. "You must be so relieved," she said. "Such a close call. I mean, it must've been terrifying."

"I wasn't there," Carol said.

"Tell me, what exactly happened?"

"Oh," Carol said, "it's a long story."

"Well — and you're still on Grandville Avenue?"

"That's right."

"Good," the woman said. "Do you have my number?"

"I think so."

"I'll try to stop by in the next week or two."

Carol thanked her, with a trapped sense of the other woman's tendency not to hear refusal, to leave a person little room in which to demur or resist. The problem with her, Charles had said once, was that she heard only what seemed to fit her idea of whatever she should be doing to help. Well, Charles hadn't been entirely right: Nancy Halstead was compensating for something, and it made her fairly obtuse at times. Lying in bed, Carol felt all the more helpless, an invalid, at the mercy of people with charitable intentions. The room looked like a sickroom. She sat up, then stood up. Her mother was in the kitchen making something; there was the sound of running water, the small clatter of dishes. She tried to stand and, feeling another little gush, lay down again. Her back ached. She cried for a spell, and then her mother walked in with a tray of hot chocolate and tea.

"Are you all right?" she said.

"I'm sick of laying here."

"It's *lying* here, I think."

"Oh, for God's sake."

"Sit up. Can you sit up?"

"Where's Charles?" Carol demanded. "Where does he go all day?"

"I think I make him uncomfortable."

"No," Carol said, "*I* do."

"I think he's trying very hard," Grace said.

Carol sulked. Her mother poured the hot chocolate and gave her a cup. She blew across the top of it, then put it down on her nightstand.

"I was watching a show," her mother said, turning the television on. "Do you mind?"

They watched *Days of Our Lives.* Carol dozed, then jerked awake. She had almost entered a dream of the hospital, the baby coming. Her mother sat on the end of the bed, sipping her tea. There was something about Grace's face when she concentrated; she looked almost simple-minded. It was her large, round eyes, of course, and the long dark lashes.

"Mother," Carol said.

"Go back to sleep. I'll turn it down."

That evening, after a quiet dinner and more television, Charles came in. Claiming exhaustion, he got out of his clothes and into pajamas and a robe.

"Where do you go all day?" Carol asked him.

"The library," he said. "It's easier to study there."

Grace coughed in the other room.

Carol whispered, "Is it because she's here?"

He shook his head, but he didn't seem to be listening.

"She wants to be helpful."

"Don't worry about it," he said.

Grace prepared the meals now. In the evenings, Carol left her bed to sit with them, wearing her robe and slippers. There wasn't much talk. They ate what Grace had prepared, and then Charles cleared everything away. More and more often they ate with the sound of the television in the living room, and in the late nights Carol woke to the flicker of the portable, Charles lying in bed watching it with the volume turned down to almost nothing: *The Tonight Show*, late movies, scenes of violence and conflict.

"Can't you sleep?" Carol would ask him.

"Am I keeping you awake?"

"I'm worried about you. You're not getting enough rest."

"Is it keeping you awake?"

"It's not keeping me awake."

She lay wondering at how difficult it had become to say anything at all to him; it seemed that something between them was broken, something neither of them could speak of, and it was as if every word they uttered were an attempt to mask it somehow, or at least not to confront it.

"Does Grace being here — does that make it worse?" she asked him.

"What?" he said. "No."

"What did I say?"

"I heard you."

"And it doesn't bother you?"

He said nothing.

"I'll ask her to leave, Charles."

Now he glanced over at her. "No." He had spoken with something like alarm. "No," he said, a little less forcefully. "I want her to stay. She should stay."

A moment later, she said, "Charles, what is it? Is it Chicago?"

"I don't know what you're talking about," he answered.

"You do, too. For God's sake."

"I'm trying to watch this," he said. "I didn't hear you."

She turned from him, lay with her hands clasped along the side of her face, breathing the odor of talcum and soap. Behind her the television chattered in its pocket of muted sound, the colors shifting on the window across the room.

Mornings, she tried to think about going to work. But the spotting continued. Grace made breakfast on a tray for her and the two of them watched television. Grace's habits were taking over, it seemed. She had always liked the quiz shows, liked to play along. She sat on the end of the bed and ate her own breakfast, talking at the television in a calm, confiding voice, as if she were teaching Carol about it. "That bid was way too high," she would say, watching *The Price Is Right*. "Watch. He's gone way over. You never bid in double figures for one of these small cars."

Charles usually left for school well before his classes, and he simply stayed away. Once in a while he called during the day, and to Carol he always sounded guilty, vaguely sullen with it, though she heard contrition in the way he said her name. Because Grace was there it was hard to speak to him directly about anything, and she knew it would be hard to do so anyway. Yet she kept wanting to ask him: What is it? What's the matter?

There were no more calls from news people or magazines, and the furor seemed to have died down. His mother called to say she had spoken to someone with a Chicago station, but that she had given him nothing. She asked Carol how he was when Carol got on to speak to her. Charles was sitting across from Carol, who was on the sofa.

"Fine," Carol said.

"Is he still planning to come back out here?"

"I don't know," Carol told her, looking at her husband.

"Give me the phone," he said.

"He hasn't talked to you about it, has he?" said his mother through the static of a bad connection.

"No," Carol said.

"What's she saying?" he wanted to know.

Carol gestured for him to be quiet.

"I don't know what's got into him."

"Pardon?" Carol said.

"Will you let me have the phone?" Charles said.

"He wants the phone back," said Carol.

"Well," said Tina Connally, "maybe you can get from him what he thinks he'll accomplish by coming back here. But I want you to know, I told him I thought he should stay right there."

"Yes," Carol said. "Thank you."

"Now, I've got to go, sweetie. Lee's here, and he's taking me out to the movies."

"Bye," Carol said, giving Charles the handset.

He put it to his ear, then put it back in its cradle. "She hung up."

"Charles," she said, "I'm going to have this baby if I can."

He stood suddenly, as if he would stalk away. But then he

stopped and gazed at her. "Have I said anything about the baby?"

"Tina says you're talking about going out there?"

"There's going to be a trial," he said in a tone of utter exasperation.

"Is that what she's talking about?"

"What do you think?"

Grace entered the room, having come from the kitchen. "What're you two squabbling about?" she said.

"We need to be alone for a few minutes," Carol said.

"No," said Charles. "It's all okay. There's nothing wrong. I've got to go study."

"Charles."

But he had already left the room. Grace waited a moment, then sat down next to her where she lay on the sofa.

"I hate this," Carol said.

"I stayed down for almost four months," said her mother.

Carol looked at her. "I wasn't talking about the spotting."

"Of course not," Grace said, moving her hands lightly over the V of the neckline in the sweater she wore. There were dark freckles in the skin, and the single miniature shimmer of a diamond on a pendant. "You mean — my staying here."

"No," Carol told her. "I'm glad you're here. I wouldn't have anyone to talk to if you weren't here."

"Perhaps you could both talk better if I wasn't around."

"I don't think so," Carol said.

Her mother touched her wrist. "Do you want to talk to me about it?"

They heard Charles in the other room, opening the hall closet. He came through in his coat.

"Where are you going?" Grace said. "Dinner's about to be ready."

"There's something I've got to do at school," he said, bending down to brush Carol's forehead with his lips.

She reached for but missed his hand. He had stood back and shoved it into the pocket of his coat, opening the door with the other, heading out.

"Do you want me to hold dinner for you?" Grace said.

"I'll get something at school," he said, already out on the porch. The door closed on the cold air, and the two women said nothing for a time, feeling the difference in the room, the sense of something lifting.

"That," Carol told her. "That's what I hate."

Neither of them could eat. Carol apologized, asked the other woman to leave the mess, then went into the bedroom and lay down. For a while she heard Grace in the kitchen, and then Grace came and stood in the doorway. "Maybe I should go."

"I asked you not to clean up," Carol said.

"It wasn't much. Did you hear me?"

"Yes."

"Well?"

"I don't want you to go."

"Yes, honey, but isn't this the old conflict, the mother-in-law on whom no love is lost, coming to stay?"

"It isn't you being here. I don't know what it is. It's Chicago. It's people shooting each other in the head. It's me having this baby. It's not you."

"I've been getting complaints from your father."

Carol waited.

"He wants to become more involved."

"I'm on my back in bed all day."

"He just wants to help. He feels he's missing all this good time we're having."

Carol was silent.

"Well, and I'd be lying if I said I wasn't glad of the time, honey. And so he feels left out. He wanted me to go see a movie with him tonight and of course I said no."

"Go see a movie with him," Carol said. "I don't need around-the-clock care."

"I want the time with *you*. Sometimes he forgets we're divorced, and I have to remind him of it."

Carol said nothing to this.

"You'd think we'd gone back to the days when we were dating or something," said her mother. "I swear, you'd think a man would get tired of believing his own fantasy all the time."

It dawned on Carol that the older woman was trying, in her way, to allow room for talk of Charles. "Daddy's still in love with you," she said.

"No, I think he depended on me so long, he just can't let go. But, from a certain distance, he can be okay."

"He still loves you," Carol said, wanting to cry.

"Well," her mother said, patting her wrist, "you try to go on to sleep."

"You don't want to watch television?"

"I can watch it in the living room. I'm afraid I told your father he could come watch it with me tonight."

"Oh," Carol said.

"When he gets here he'll want to come in and say hello, of course. If you're not asleep."

"I'd love to see him."

Her mother shut the door. It was quiet. She lay crying quietly in the lamplight. A while later, she heard the sound of the television, and then an array of confusing noises: a car horn, and the front door opening and closing, murmurings.

Finally her father knocked on her door and opened it. "Awake?"

"Yes."

"Can you come up to the window?"

"Why?" She felt a stirring of fright, even with the happy, boyish expression on his face.

"I parked it under the streetlight."

"What, Daddy?"

"Take a look-see."

She turned around in the bed and, reaching behind the lamp, opened the curtain at the window there. Under the cone of light from the streetlamp was a light-colored pickup truck.

"This one's a little fancy, but it's the same idea. It has a tape player and all the works — power steering, brakes, windows. The whole works. Drives just like a luxury car."

"What color is it?" Carol asked.

"Baby blue, of course. I traded in the Pontiac. When you're ready, I'll take you into town in it."

"A pickup truck?"

"Wait'll you ride in it, sweetie." Something had gone out of his voice.

"Well?" Grace said from the door. "Isn't it cute? After all these years."

Carol lay back down. They were both standing at the foot of the bed, staring at her. "What?" she said.

"She doesn't remember," said her father.

"Sure she does." Grace came around and sat on the edge of the bed. "She just needs to be reminded."

Carol was silent.

And now Theodore left the room.

"When you were a little girl he drove a pickup around. Baby blue. You wanted to go with him all the time, all the time. And riding in that old thing was the biggest thing to you. You don't remember?"

It seemed now that she did remember. "I'm sorry," she said.

"Don't be silly," said Grace. But Grace was near tears. "Your father is just such a sentimental character, honey."

"Daddy?" Carol called.

He came to the door. Grace stood and moved to the foot of the bed, and Carol held out her arms. He came and leaned down into her embrace.

"I do remember," Carol said.

"I rented it," he told her. "I didn't really trade the Pontiac. But you know, I like it so much I might buy it." He was wiping his eyes.

"It's all right," Carol said to him. "I'm going to have a baby. A nice healthy grandchild for you both."

"Talk about nervous fathers," Grace said. "You should've seen Theodore."

"Well," Theodore said, rising. "You rest now. Doctor's orders."

"He just doesn't want to miss the start of the movie," said Grace.

"For God sakes, Grace. Sometimes — you amaze me."

"I was just teasing," Grace said.

"Making jocular with the heavy artillery," said Theodore, "like always."

"I am sleepy," Carol told them.

They went out of the room muttering at each other, and Grace closed the door quietly.

Carol turned the light off and tried to sleep in the sound of the movie they watched — pounding drums, laughter, voices raised in alarm. She couldn't drift off, and then she woke and knew that she had been asleep. It was late. She had come up from a dream of rain to the sound of Charles in the room. She heard his belt buckle, the rustle of clothes. When he sat down on his side of the bed, a sigh came from him, almost like a moan. The light of the portable TV startled her.

"Oh, no, Charles — please."

He turned it off and lay down. She listened to him breathe for a few minutes.

"Were they here when you came back?" she whispered.

"Who?"

"I guess not."

"Who're you talking about, Carol?"

"Mom and Dad."

"No."

Again, there was just the agitated breathing, as if he were exerting himself.

"Do you want to talk?" she said.

•

He had ceased to go to classes, and for a while spent much of each day in the little alcove at the back of the old student lounge, avoiding people he knew, throwing darts, or playing video games — at several of which he had become good enough to play for more than an hour on one coin. People came and went from the lounge, but it stayed empty a lot of the time, and so he had it to himself. Concentrating on the games, his mind eased a little. He had developed ways to kill time. It was just staying away from the house, with Grace there and with Carol in the tangle of bedsheets, helpless. He saw none of his professors, and when people he recognized came in he made his way out the side, down a small flight of stairs, and through a Tiffany-glass-framed exit door into an alley. Sometimes he just ducked into the little walls of the video machine and simply pretended not to see. Mostly, people left him alone. If there was any curiosity about the convenience store and being on the news, Connally hadn't heard it.

Finally he stopped going to the campus altogether.

He had begun using the money from his last student loan — fall semester's tuition. And he was looking for work.

He went into record stores and shops and pharmacies, filling out applications. Apparently no employer needed anyone. People looked at him and told him this. When he filled out the forms, his hands shook; he knew he looked ragged, nervous, and sleepless. He couldn't quite hear what was said to him in the interviews. When they asked him what he was presently doing, he said, "I've been in school."

One man said, "You're not in school now?"

"No," Connally said.

This was in the elevated office of a department store. Below them, people browsed amid aisles of merchandise and small groups of manikins, which all appeared to be communing only with each other in some mute, proud dismissal.

"Did you graduate or something?"

"Not yet," Connally said.

"You quit?" The man was Connally's age, and wore a three-piece suit. He kept a small trim beard, which he stroked now with the fat fingers of one hand.

"I wanted to look for work," Connally said.

"You look familiar. Have I seen you before?"

He decided the best thing was to tell the truth. "I was in that holdup in Chicago. Those shootings. People made more out of it than it was."

"Shootings," the man said, sitting back slightly, staring at him. "You — you're not — I don't —"

"I didn't really do anything," Connally told him.

The man simply stared.

"Television," Connally said.

"I — look, I don't understand. You're here to apply for a job."

"Right."

"You took part in a holdup?"

"I was *in* a holdup. They said I saved this woman's life."

"Oh."

"It was on television."

"I don't watch television."

Connally said nothing.

"You just looked familiar, that's all."

"Of course," Connally said, trying to seem calm. "I have one of those faces." His own voice sounded strange to him now.

"Well, we don't have a thing open," the man said, getting jittery.

"I'm not in school now," Connally said.

One afternoon, he walked the four miles across the superhighway and bypass, on around a new shopping mall and office park, which had been built on the fallow grass field of a wrecked farm, to stand alone on Mission Street across from the old movie theater, which was a Toyota dealership now, though the façade was still intact, the marquee still jutting out over the sidewalk. A man sat in what had been Connally's bedroom window, with a visor on his head and dark bands around his sleeves — the picture of someone keeping books — and Connally remembered the room as it was when he'd lived there: the cutout magazine photos of sports celebrities (Muhammad Ali, Johnny Bench, and Hank Aaron) on the walls; the radio with its gridded plastic front cracked, sitting atop the dresser; the bed with its four posts notched for the bunk that wasn't there; and the plants his grandmother kept in the sunlight of the window.

He stared at the window where he had lived, and then he thought about asking to be let inside, feeling as if he might find some harmless facet of himself there. But he knew he would find nothing. A man sat in a room, adding figures. Lights shone in the finish of cars.

All the other buildings on the street had been torn down to make room for a parking lot and a computer store. Even the old church had been reduced, its yard paved over for the garden court of a mini-mall. The chapel looked huddled in the shade of willows, its doors opening on a sidewalk now, its windows closed to the perpetual sound of an escalator.

He remembered Winnie Barthley and himself, seated in wicker chairs on the roof of the marquee: a summer afternoon in his eighteenth year.

"God is great," his grandmother said, "God is good." She was holding a piece of bread and a glass of milk. "Well?" she said to him.

And he repeated it, humoring her.

She had ceased to recognize him weeks before. But he would always recall her in that moment, sitting out on the marquee for one of the last times, the final traces of the struggling identity gone, quite happy now, offering him the bread and repeating, "God is great, God is good."

"Yes," he said to her.

"A fine young man," she said. And then she sat contentedly staring at the cars below, the colors in the sky.

The whole passage had been a kind of game she made him play, a spiritual hide-and-seek, for there had been glimmers of lucidity, and she had sometimes been able to tell him he was looking in the wrong places for her. And they'd had such lovely times, times when she laughed at what he said, or listened to him, or reached over and patted his wrist. Perhaps all he knew of love, he knew from her. And how valiantly she had fought to keep from disappearing into the clouds that had begun gathering in her mind before Charles ever came to her.

•

Now, when he returned home in the late afternoon or early evening, making up lies about where he had been, he felt a separation from the others. Several times he tried to find the words with which to tell Carol the truth, but something in her worried gaze stopped him. He told himself he would work everything out, accomplish something, find a job, and then tell her. It would be easier if he was already hired somewhere.

Grace kept up a steady stream of talk. Sometimes Theodore was there too, sitting with his pant legs drawn up over the top of his socks, looking vaguely beset, and the talk among the three family members — mother, father, daughter — could go on for a long time without requiring anything from Connally at all. He went into his study room, pretending to work, or watched the little portable TV in bed.

After the first month of Grace's stay, in the aftermath of failing again to find a job, he had called his mother from a telephone booth. "I'm sick," he told her.

"Poor baby."

"No," he said, "you don't understand." But he couldn't find the words to tell her, either.

"Charles?" she said.

"I miss Grand," he said. "I thought if I could talk to her."

"Is that to hurt me?"

"No," he said. "Don't you miss her?"

"Of course. But she couldn't have told you anything."

"Look," he said, "I know my father did things to me when I was small. I know he hurt me. I remember him hurting me. And I've heard you talk about it and Grandmother talked about it, too. I need to talk to somebody about it."

"Well, I don't understand that at all."

"I don't remember all of it."

"Charles, please stop this."

"No, I want you to tell me."

"There isn't anything to tell."

"He did things to me. I remember bad things. I want you to tell me what they were."

"I will not discuss all this over the telephone, Charles."

"Just tell me something. I'm asking you to tell me something."

"Charles, now stop this. I'm going to hang up if you say another word about it."

"I have to come there again."

"Come where? What're you talking about?"

"I'm coming to Chicago."

"Now?"

"What if I came back?"

"Why would you do that? Charles, what in the world." She made a throat-clearing sound. "I won't stand to have you talk like this."

"I need to get to the bottom of it all."

"Son, now you're not thinking straight. Your father has nothing to do with any of this."

"Never mind," he said.

"Talk to Carol about it," his mother said. "She's your wife. She's the one who can help you. There's no sense spending all this money on the telephone company. Besides, what's done is done. It's all past now — over and done with. Your father's been in the ground almost ten years."

"He's right here," Charles said under his breath.

"What?"

"Nothing."

"Son, why don't you talk to your wife about it? Tell Carol what you're thinking."

"What am I thinking?" he said.

"You know — coming out here. All of it."

"All right," he said, "I will." And for a moment he was resolved to do so. Only a little more than a month ago he had felt confident enough in her company to tell her his feelings about the pregnancy. They had always been able to talk; they had always been so relaxed together. He had never been so much at ease with anyone.

Now it was hard to look at her or speak to her, as if some invisible barrier had risen in his mind and he could no longer see her as herself. The image of the nurse, the dead stare of her dark, smooth face, kept recurring to him. All of it was possible. It had happened. It was waiting to happen, everywhere.

•

"Well?" Carol said, lying in the dark at his side. "Do you?"

"Do I what?"

"Want to talk."

"I think I'm losing my mind," he said.

"That makes two of us."

"I'm afraid I'm going to hurt someone."

She was silent.

He breathed. "I think I need to go back."

"Fine," she said. "Go."

"I have to get to the end of it," he said.

"Do you feel like you should've been killed? Is that it? You feel wrong because you got out of it alive?"

"I don't know, Carol."

"Well, what?"

"I can't see anything without — without it. It — everything's colored by it. Everything. And it feels like it's going to be this way all the rest of my life. I can't imagine getting out of it, getting where I don't think of it every minute."

"Why don't you see someone? There're doctors you could talk to, you know. Or you could see the counselor or somebody over at school. It's anxiety, Charles. It's natural, for what happened to you."

"No," he said. "Not and feel this way. Like it's in me now

and is waiting to come out, whether I want it to or not."

"Then see a doctor."

"My grandmother went to the doctors, Carol. They put her on medications. She went crazy in stages, and they just hurried it along."

"You know that's not the truth," she said.

"That's how it feels. And anyway, we can't afford it."

"You had a terrible thing happen," she told him. "Stand up to it."

"That's why I think I have to go back there," he said.

"You're wallowing in it."

"No. I swear I'm trying to get out of it."

"Well, then stop circling it in your mind."

"You don't understand," he said. "I have to do this myself."

"Because you're the hero?" she said. "Is that it?"

"Right," he muttered. "Jesus."

"Nancy Halstead called," she told him.

"Oh," he said, and felt a surge of something bitter in his heart. "I get it. You're thinking of leaving me. I mean, that's who you went to when you were leaving Martin." His own words seemed to come from someone other than himself.

She said nothing.

"No," he said. "I didn't mean that."

"I can't believe you could think such a thing," she said.

"I didn't mean it, Carol. Please." He left a pause. "What did you and Nancy talk about?"

"I was going to tell you she might come by."

"Fuck." He got out of the bed, felt the chilly floor on the soles of his feet. "You told her we have a problem. Right?" It dawned on him that he had raised his voice.

"Be quiet," Carol said. "You'll wake Grace."

"Fuck Grace." He could feel his own heartbeat in the cords of his neck.

Carol turned in the bed and pulled the blanket up over her shoulder.

"Look at me," he said.

"Stay or go," she murmured. "Just do it quietly."

"Did you ask her to come here?"

She looked at him. "She invited herself. Now stop it. You're scaring me, Charles."

They both paused at the sound of the knock on the bedroom door. "Is everything all right?" Grace's quavering, sleep-drugged voice from the other side.

"Go back to sleep," Carol said.

They were quiet; they heard the older woman run water in the bathroom. She coughed, going by the door.

Carol sat up, ran her hands through her hair. "Nancy invited herself over. There wasn't anything I could say."

He got back into the bed.

"What will you do about your classes if you go back to Chicago?"

She would actually accede to his going. But now he felt the threat of what she might do when she knew he had stopped going to classes. He said, "I haven't thought it all out."

"You can't miss them, can you?"

"I said I haven't thought it all out." Now he couldn't keep the irritation out of his voice.

"Charles," she said, "will you tell me what I did?"

"It's not you," he told her. "And it's not the baby, okay?"

"But it's like you blame me for *something*. I mean, you were mad at me when you went out that night at the motel. Is that it?"

"You didn't push me out the door," he said.

"Well, but is that it?"

"I'm not mad at you and I don't blame you for anything." He lay down. It was hard to keep still for the beating of his heart. When she snuggled close, he breathed the bedridden odor of her hair.

"Maybe I hope Nancy Halstead does stop by."

He couldn't remain still. Sitting up, he put his hands to his face and rubbed the clammy skin there. "Jesus God," he said.

"All right," Carol said behind him. "I just meant — she does counseling, that's all."

"I don't need any counseling from her. Jesus, Carol — Nancy Halstead. I mean, did you ever notice how deeply clichéd the woman is? I mean, come on."

"She can be a sympathetic listener."

"She was good for you — you were beaten down and discouraged. But Nancy Halstead."

"Well, I just mean you should talk to someone."

"I did."

She was quiet.

"I can't just say it out to a stranger."

"Say it to me."

"I'm afraid I'm going to do something bad. I'm afraid I'm going to hurt somebody."

"You're the most gentle man I've ever seen," she said.

"I wish it never happened," he said. "Ah — God. I'm — I can't think straight. This is — this is horrible. It won't go away. It keeps — coming at me and coming at me."

"See a psychologist," she said.

"We don't have the money."

"What about the public health office?"

"I don't need any psychologists."

"The hero," she said.

"You can think what you want. I'm doing my very best, and it's not enough anymore."

"I'm just trying to get from one day to the next," she said.

"Yeah," he said. "Try it when you've had a gun held to

your head. When you've watched four people get shot to death."

She was quiet.

"I didn't mean that, either," he said. "That wasn't fair and it wasn't exactly the truth, either."

A moment later, he lay back down. They were side by side now, both gazing at the ceiling.

"Can you say what you're frightened of?" she said. "That's supposed to help."

"Everything," he said.

She said, "That narrows it down."

"I wish it was a joke."

"I'm just trying to make you relax."

They were both quiet. There was the sound of traffic outside, sirens in the distance.

"What will you do if you go back?"

He sighed. "I don't know. Talk to people about it."

"What people? Who?"

"The oriental woman. Maybe the nurse's husband — Seth Waters."

"He isn't going to want to see you. He's got his life to live, and he's not going to want it all called up again. Besides, what can he tell you? He wasn't there."

"I've got to do something." He felt a little turn of his stomach. "I'm afraid something's going to happen."

"What, Charles? What's going to happen?"

"You'll have to understand," he said. "This — this thing — it started something in me, and I'm scared all the time now."

"So am I," she said, and he could hear the tears in her voice.

He put his arms around her and held her, trying not to think. Her skin was cool, and he thought of death.

"Can't we be all right?" she murmured.

He patted her shoulder and was quiet, unable to utter one single sound.

•

In the mail the following morning was a letter:

Dear Sir
*   I got your address from the lawyer. I was sorry for what happened. I didn't mean to hurt anybody. It happened overtop of me, against my will and consent. I didn't mean for the gun to go off. And then the man was shot and I was in it. It's not my fault. I was sorry about the other man. He got me unable to think. I went to school. I had a job, too. I'm sorry for everything I was very confused scared and mad. I'm contrite and have remorse as well. I didn't know what I was doing.*

                                                            Mark Hughes

Connally read it alone on the porch, standing in the bright sun out of wind, feeling the heat, the trace of spring in the warm windless light. Some part of him shivered anyway, and his heart beat in his face and neck. *It all happened overtop of me.*

Inside, Carol and her mother were sitting at the dining room table, drinking herb tea. Grace had brought out her silver tea set; it shone in the light from the window. Everything was vivid — twice as bright, twice as loud. Connally went into the bedroom and read the letter again.

"Honey?" Carol said from the door.

He turned. She'd spilled some of the tea; there was a small stain on the lapel of her blouse. Imperfections made him morbidly nervous now. "What?" he said.

"What was in the mail?"

He gave her the letter. She stood there reading it, and then gave it back to him.

"I'm going back," he said. "I'm taking the car. Grace is staying here a while longer anyway."

"All right."

"I have to, Carol."

She said nothing.

"Carol."

"I can't help feeling you're running away from me."

"No," he said.

"Because I'm having the baby."

"For Christ's sake," he said. "No. You couldn't be more wrong."

"That's what it feels like."

"Did you read this?" He held the letter up.

"I read it."

"I'm doing the best I can," he told her. "I don't know what else to do."

•

The next afternoon, Nancy Halstead drove up. Grace and Carol were seated on the porch, crocheting in the unseasonably warm February sun. Grace had been trying to distract the younger woman, talking about her recent trip to the mountains with Theodore — how she and Theodore had bought a bushel of apples and then argued about what to do with them all the way back to Point Royal. Nancy Halstead pulled up in a small red foreign car and got out, waving, her hair done in a bright tangle framing her face. She was not attractive, and she knew it. She spent a lot of time making herself up, and if at first glance there was something glamorous about her, one saw almost immediately that it was clothes and hairstyling, not the features — her skin was acnescarred, and there was a colorlessness about her eyes. Today she wore a burgundy skirt and a flowery blouse, and she'd tied a cream-white sweater over her shoulders. Carol remembered with a sour little turn of her mind that the minister's image of herself was jaunty, as if she were imagining herself on the set of one of those movies in which lithe girls come flouncing home from tennis. She strolled lightly up the walk, grasping the drooping sleeves of the sweater as a man might hold the straps of suspenders.

"I hope I'm not intruding," she said, smiling, clearly confident that she would be welcomed.

Carol introduced her to Grace, who stood and then seemed unsure as to whether or not she should remain standing. "I remember, from the wedding," Nancy said.

"Yes, the wedding," Grace said, not meeting the other woman's eyes. "I was wearing black."

"That's right," Nancy said, missing the joke. "How nice. Yes, it seems an age ago, doesn't it."

"Not to me." Grace smiled tolerantly at her. "You know how people say it seems like yesterday?"

"Right," Nancy said.

"Well, to me it feels like *earlier today.*"

"I know what you mean."

"Let's go inside," Carol said. "I'll fix something to drink."

"Oh, don't go to any trouble," said Nancy Halstead.

It struck Carol as they entered the house that the cleric was ushering her in, as though it were not where she, Carol, happened to live. This annoyed her a little, and she offered the other woman the chair opposite the couch. Grace had already gone through to the kitchen. Carol followed her there.

"I'll make lemonade, honey. You go back and talk to your guest."

Carol shrugged, as if to indicate that she had no idea what she should say.

"You look a little pale," Nancy told her as she reentered the living room.

"I've been spotting."

"Oh, are you pregnant?"

Carol thought she had said so in their first conversation. She let herself down on the couch and folded her legs under her.

"Isn't that nice," the other said.

Carol was at a loss.

"That's a nice flagstone fireplace."

"This was a hunting cabin once."

"Isn't that nice."

Grace brought the lemonade in, and as she set the tray down one of the glasses overturned. There was a general commotion as they all moved to clean up the mess. At some point during this difficulty, Grace called the other woman Mrs. Halstead.

"Please, everyone calls me Nancy."

"I was going to name Carol Nancy," Grace told her.

"Isn't that nice."

"I really was."

"That's a very nice thing to know."

When they were all seated again, there seemed nothing left to say. Nancy Halstead gazed at the fireplace, the books on the shelves flanking it — Carol's novels and art books, Charles's biographies, histories, and anthologies.

"So, the conquering hero's not at home," Nancy said.

"Charles left for Chicago early this morning," said Grace. And it was clear enough by her tone that she did not approve.

The other woman seemed slightly troubled. "That's a long drive, isn't it?"

Grace looked at Carol, who felt it necessary to make some excuse. "He had to see his mother, and there are details about the trial, you know." It was exactly what she had said to Grace earlier.

"Well. Duty calls," Nancy said.

"He thought, what with my spotting and all, it was best that he go alone," Carol told her.

"Well, that's nice."

"He's doing very well in school," said Grace. And before the other woman could speak, she added, "We think that's nice, too."

"Yes," said Nancy, "very nice." A moment later, she said, "I'll bet he's ecstatic about the baby."

"Just wild," said Grace.

"First child and all. Being a father."

"It's very nice," Grace said.

Nancy cleared her throat. "This — thing that happened. It must have been just awful."

Carol and her mother looked at each other. It was as if each were waiting for the other to speak.

"Well, you'll both have that new baby to think about, soon enough. It's the future, and you just have to set your sights on it. You know what I say about the past."

"I don't think I do," Grace said with a kind of amused cheerfulness.

"The past is a canceled check." The other woman spoke with the confidence of someone who is accustomed to being listened to. Yet there was a certain earnestness about it, too.

"Oh, well, of course," Grace said.

"A canceled check," Nancy repeated. But now the tone was faintly condescending.

"Isn't that nice," said Grace.

Again, they were all searching for something to say. The minister looked at the room, admired the fireplace again. They talked about being pregnant in the summer, and about the tall oaks and black locusts outside, the shade the leaves would provide.

"Well." Nancy breathed a little satisfied sigh.

Carol watched her finish the lemonade. "Would you care for more?"

"No, thanks. I have to go soon."

Yet Carol had the feeling that she might wait until time for dinner. The light came brightly through the windows, and for a spell they watched the dust rising in it.

"I'd better get something out of the freezer," Grace said, getting to her feet with some effort.

"I really have to go," Nancy said.

"Well, it was really nice," said Grace, nodding at her, then heading out of the room.

Nancy sat there, regarding Carol.

"It's so pretty out," Carol said.

And the other woman leaned forward slightly. "Mother staying with you?"

Carol simply returned her gaze.

"I sense something wrong. Some tension."

"Everything's fine," Carol told her.

"You're certain there's nothing I can do."

"No," Carol said, "we're fine."

The other woman stared for another few seconds, then sat back. "Well, if you're sure." She stood. "Stay down."

But Carol had come to her feet.

"You know my number."

"Yes."

"I expect to hear from you anyway."

"Right," Carol said.

Nancy kissed her on the cheek, then called to Grace. "It was nice meeting you again."

There was no response from the kitchen.

"Grace is a little hard of hearing," Carol said. She watched the other woman go down the walk and get into her car. Nancy didn't look back until the car was in gear. She waved, pulling away, and Carol waved back, thinking of Charles as he pulled away in the morning, remembering now as she did in the morning the end of her marriage to Martin — the dead, windless, hot summer afternoon almost six years ago when she walked out of the apartment at Point Royal Mews and crossed the traffic circle there, thinking of the little church as just one of several cool public buildings one could enter and remain in for a time.

Then, she had been feeling crowded, beset from all sides, breathless, as if the rows of high-rise apartments on either side of her were thwarting the jet stream, keeping all the new breezes from crossing the face of the planet, as if weather had stopped, no wind playing in the tops of the still trees, nothing moving the lifeless clouds along. A gray haze lay over everything, an appalling drift of gases and photo-chemical droplets. That summer, everywhere she turned Martin was there; he had been put on graveyard shift in the mechanical platoon at the Marine base. He slept all morning, and in the afternoons he drank beer and watched television. When he went out, there were always mysterious hints and innuendoes and indications — when there were not direct admonishments — that she was to mind the apartment and keep her curiosity down: he was involved in something classified, he would say, and his face took on the frowning, willful expression of a belligerent child, a child being cruel. The facts of the matter were that he was a boy, a case of arrested emotional development, someone completely unprepared for the responsibility of living with another person — at least a person other than his mother. And perhaps he *was* having an affair. By that time it didn't really matter. He was unable to feel much passion for her, but he needed her, even liked her. "I love you like family," he said. "I'm just not too sexy." He would put his uniform on and go out the door, and she would be glad of the time alone. He almost never touched her in the last months. But it seemed he was always there, and his assumptions about her were suffocating: she was continually experiencing the feeling, when she was with him, that she had to gasp for breath. And so she walked out of the square of high rises and crossed the traffic circle, to the church in its grassy lot, that building which looked so spacious and airy — with the high, open places in the façade and the pretty stained-glass windows whose colors seemed brighter and more vivid than the faded colors of the trees and sky. Letting herself in, she breathed the cool, cedar-smelling fragrance of the place, the dark wooden doors protesting slightly as she opened them. She sat in the back, in the last pew, and it wasn't long before Nancy Halstead walked in. Carol watched her do something at the altar, then turn, facing her. They looked at each other for a minute, and finally Nancy approached.

"Hot out," she said.

"Very."

Nancy introduced herself.

Carol said her own name, and to her amazement began to cry.

This was what Nancy Halstead had that caused her to feel free to question the fact that Grace was staying in the house — this moment when Carol, depleted and more desperate than she knew, had let down and asked for help. Even in the happier time of planning for and then going through with the marriage to Charles, there had been a proprietary note in Nancy's voice when she spoke to them — and especially when she spoke to Carol, as though Carol were no more capable of taking care of herself than a child would be. And the fact that Carol often wanted to be a child again, and nestle safely in someone's arms, did not finally signify: she was not a child. Having been raised in a quiet house with two very complicated people, she had got herself married early, had suffered for the mistake through a long two years, and had got herself free of it substantially on her own. She had supported herself, had lived alone, and it was through her will and determination that her amiable, also fairly immature, new husband (the immaturity had been Grace's objection) was in college, and it was because of the job she had worked every dissatisfying day of the last two years that he could remain there. She didn't know what it was about her that made people feel it was necessary to guide her or protect her. She herself had not finished college, as Nancy Halstead had, but she knew things, too, and she had known in the first minutes of Nancy's visit that the woman had nothing for her this time, and would have nothing.

She wished it were otherwise.

And even so, she had a fugitive sense of affection for the woman, for her sincere desire to be helpful, and for what must be some dim awareness — Carol thought she had seen it in the other woman's eyes — of just how impoverished her capacity for the free play of conversation was.

Grace had gone into the kitchen and merely waited until Nancy was gone. She came out as Carol closed the door, and gave a simpering smile. "Isn't that *nice*," she said. "And isn't *that* nice. And *isn't* that nice."

"Okay," said Carol. "I knew when you disappeared."

"Was I rude?"

"I don't think it was noticed if you were."

"That woman's a fool."

"She's just trying to help."

Grace muttered, "Canceled check. My God."

A moment later, she said, "Shall we call Theodore and ask him over tonight?"

"I don't know," Carol said, feeling abruptly desolate.

Grace looked at her.

"I don't have a clue, Mother."

They cleared away the lemonade, and then Carol had to go back to the bedroom. Grace said she ought to try to sleep some. She even kissed her forehead and tucked the blankets at her shoulders.

"Lord," Carol said. "I'm all right."

But she felt rickety inside, and when her mother closed the door quietly, the little metal latch clicking to, she lay crying into her fingers, with an overwhelming and forlorn sense of having been cast adrift. But she would not call to her mother. She sat up in the bed and wiped her eyes with a napkin; there was the baby to think about, yet it seemed impossible to be anything but afraid, now. What had taken place in Chicago was still happening; it was only part of what was on the way. She wept in the helplessness of feeling this, and feeling, too, that she would be powerless to stop it, whatever it might finally be.

•

The clearest sequential memory Charles had of his father involved a car trip and a walk across a railway bridge. Charles was unsure when or how the railway bridge figured into it, and at some point his mother also appeared: he had an image of her standing with her back to him, facing his father and talking. Pleading. A tone came into her voice that he recognized, and that always made him want to remove himself from her. For years he had been acting on it without thought, as automatically as a parasympathetic change. The car trip took place during his stay with one of the relatives — his great-uncle, Winnie Barthley's brother, in Charlottesville: a big gray Gothic-looking old house with an enormous ornate porch, leaded windows, a parlor with red velvet couches and lace doilies, and shining wood. The brother's name was Evan, a massive frighteningly gruff man with a bushy red mustache and a full head of dark red hair. The mustache came down over his lips, and when he coughed it blew out like a piece of cloth. He'd had five of his own children; four of them were grown, and the youngest, a girl, was Connally's age. The big man would stand the two children side by side and then crouch down with all his bulk on the floor of the parlor, facing them like a big breathing wall, and blow the end of his mustache out with a huge chuffing sound. The girl would laugh with her whole being, begging him to stop, and Connally remembered being terrified of this, afraid even to cry. He heard an element of fright in the girl's voice, too, because the sound she made seemed to express his own fear somehow, with its high-pitched squeal.

Connally's mother had put him on the train south from Point Royal with an older cousin, who had delivered him at the doorstep of the big house. He no longer remembered the cousin as part of the journey — the cousin had gone on to duty in the Army in Georgia. Connally had been shown pictures of him, and had even seen him during several of his mother's various sojourns away from his father, but he could not imagine him or see any trace of him in his memory of the train, the ride south, and the street with the big old house on it. The cousin was a friendly, quiet man with a thin, reedy voice that always seemed to be straining, and whenever he saw Connally he reminded him of their having once traveled together. Each time, Connally would try to remember. He wanted to have it as a part of his history; he had begun to hoard things, for fear of having them taken away.

On a sunny day near the end of July, his father pulled up in front of the house in a brilliantly polished black car with tail fins. Connally was playing in the red dust in the shade of the porch, and when the car tires crackled in the gravel of the drive, he looked up. The figure in the car waved to him.

"Hey."

The boy stood.

"You a big boy?"

He nodded. He knew it was his father; he was almost six years old and hadn't seen him for a long while, and he knew.

"Come here."

Connally walked across the little expanse of grass and stood at the passenger-side window, looking in. He saw the new wood-grain finish of the dashboard, the radio with its dim dials, the ashtray stuffed to overflowing with smoked cigarettes. He saw his father's face — the eyes glazed over by something. He remembered, many years later, that the eyes gleamed unnaturally.

"Get in."

The boy obeyed, and found the door too heavy to pull closed. His father got out and walked around the car and shut him in. He sat there staring at the dash, feeling small in the big space of the seat, his heart beating in his throat. With him, like something cold under the skin, was the hard knowledge that you did not refuse this man, who now got in and shifted gears, looking at the house a moment.

"Want to know where we're going?"

Connally nodded at him.

"You're not scared, are you?"

Again he nodded.

"Scared?"

"No."

"A big old boy like you?"

Connally simply looked at him.

"What's there for a big old boy like you to be scared of?" his father said.

"I'm not," Connally told him.

"Nothing to be afraid of, right?"

The boy sat against the door and watched him, feeling trapped.

"Absolutely nothing to be afraid of."

Then his father was watching the road, concentrating on the driving. He had both hands on the wheel, and Connally looked at the bones of the knuckles.

"Here we are," his father said after a time. He stopped the car, got out, and walked around to let the boy out. Connally took his offered hand, shivering.

"Calm down, will you? What the hell are you shaking for?"

It took the boy a moment to realize that an answer was expected.

"I'm not shaking."

"What do you call it, then?"

He was searching desperately for something to say, and the hand that held his hand squeezed, almost gently, until it began to hurt.

"Well?"

"I don't know," he said.

"You don't know. A man has to know a thing like that. Can't you tell me?"

The boy kept his head down. "No."

"But you're not scared."

He shook his head.

The hand let go. "Come on with me, then."

They crossed a wide asphalt lot and entered a terminal of some kind, walked through to a platform, then on up the platform a ways. To their right was a railroad track going off into the distance, where the blue shadows of mountains seemed to crowd upon one another. They kept walking.

"This is where I saw my first train, kid," his father said. "Close up."

They had entered a small walking bridge that ran parallel to the tracks. In the middle of it they stopped.

"Now," his father said.

Connally looked through the metal links of the fence and waited with his father for the train. He looked at his father's brown shoes; there were swirling lines in the leather of the toes. The shoes were shined very bright; he could see his face in them.

"Goddam train's always late," his father said with a new friendliness in his voice. He put his hand on the boy's shoulder, then took it away. The train was coming. It rumbled past in the smell of metal and electricity, the wheels making a wonderful clattering sound. The wind shook. Connally held on to the fence and peered into the windows of the cars as they passed. People were reading, or sleeping, or eating. There were tables and chairs, and doilies on the arms of the chairs, and it looked to him like a moving living room.

"There it is," his father shouted over the noise. "Big son of a bitch, huh?" Then he knelt down and held the boy by his arms. "You take this with you, okay? I ain't always a bastard. I was a kid once, like anybody else. And I got the shit knocked out of me, too. It didn't start with me. It goes way back from me. Understand?"

The boy nodded.

"Are we straight on that?"

Connally said "Yes," feeling that he would cry, fighting it with everything in himself for fear of what it would cause the other to say or do next. He did not cry, finally, and his father stood, scratched the back of his neck, looking down the track at the retreating train. "Okay," he said, "let's go back."

The return seemed faster, and then he was getting out of the car, hurrying across the grass, and his mother was there. She looked him over, touched his face with her fingers, held his head back slightly to examine his throat, and pressed the muscles of his arms and hips and legs, as if looking for something he might have tried to conceal. His father was a tall shadow on the sidewalk, and then his mother was standing with her back to him, talking. There was the pleading note in her voice. "I can't do it anymore, Billy." Perhaps that was what she had said. He could no longer trust that part of his memory.

•

He drove all day, feeling an increasing sense of something lifting inside him. The roads were swept with the stains of salt bordered by mounds of melting snow, brown heaps with cuts of pure white, surprising vivid stripes where a car had pushed through or torn past. The sun shone over the fields and the stands of naked trees, the wide valleys below the mountains. He went fast, and the day stretched before him. In Ohio he stopped to eat. The restaurant was crowded and noisy. He sat at a table near the door and watched a family of seven struggle to keep a baby girl happy. The baby was in a high chair provided by the restaurant, and she kept standing in it, trying to climb out of it. The little straps designed to restrain her were of no use; she squirmed out of them, or put up a fuss trying to. He watched this and for a little space there was no pressure, no sense of events closing in on him. He felt almost benevolent. The waitress brought his sandwich and he ate it quickly, surprised at his own appetite, nearly happy with the sense of mission.

He had taken a hundred dollars from the student loan money, and when he paid for the meal, handing over a five dollar bill and telling the waitress to keep the change, he had a bad moment of remembering that he was squandering the money for school, money Carol had worked to make in a job she had grown to hate. It was money neither of them had, and with a baby on the way. As he walked out to the car, the climbing sense of his own selfishness felt as if it might choke him. He stopped and leaned on a newspaper vending machine, catching his breath. He thought he might be sick. People came past him, but he heard only the sound of the trucks and cars roaring by on the interstate.

In the car, he started the engine, put the heater on, then pulled around to the gasoline island and filled the tank. The mere action of his hands, the automatic feel of it, was vaguely palliative. When he paid the attendant, he remarked on the chilly sun.

"Hope the weather holds," the attendant said. "I don't want no more snow."

The attendant was a young man with a shadow of whiskers on his cheeks and bad teeth, a perfectly decent young man working a job. As he counted out change, Connally noticed that he wore a wedding band. There were kindnesses that people could assume about each other, and yet he had felt outside it all, had felt that it was all impossible for him, and as the attendant handed him his change, smiling at him, Connally wanted to ask him point-blank: Have you ever thought of murder?

The question went through him like a chill.

He thanked the attendant and got back into the car, feeling himself trapped again, circled by the scenes of blood and the aloneness, the fright.

He drove on into the lowering sun, and for a long time there was just the rushing sound of the air at the shut windows, the small rattling of the dashboard.

It was well past dark when he approached the exit to the convenience store. He didn't stop, though he could see light over the hill where he knew it was. The owners had no doubt reopened it. He felt nothing — he had expected some change, some badness — except a faint shortness of breath. He drove on, concentrating on the road ahead.

Chicago was a dazzle of lights and tall shadows. The lights shone on the sky, a wide glow, from miles away. He drove to his mother's. She didn't come down to greet him, and he made his way to her through the security guard and past the lobby to the bank of elevators. Her door was closed, though she knew by now that he was in the building. He knocked and waited, then knocked again. She opened the door in a bathrobe, the nightgown with its frilled collar spilling out of the top of it. Her hair was brushed straight back, and stood up a little from her scalp. She put her arms around him, and he smelled alcohol. "Lee's here," she murmured, and he thought he heard something pained in her tone. He looked at her, saw that she was smiling at him, and decided that he had been mistaken.

Lee Southworth was sitting at the small dining table with a bottle of brandy between his long-fingered, violet hands. He gave Connally a firm handshake, half standing. He wore a brown bathrobe over a shirt and tie. It appeared to Connally that he had arrived in the middle of an occasion.

"You're sleeping in my room," his mother told him. "I'm going to be up later than you."

Connally looked at the old man, who nodded, pouring more of the brandy.

"All right?" his mother said.

Connally turned and started into the bedroom.

"Make yourself at home, dear."

In the bedroom, he put his bag on the floor by the bed and stared at the pictures again. He wouldn't be able to sleep. The bed was turned down, the pillow smelling fresh. In the other room, Lee Southworth laughed. Connally sat on the bed and tried to clear his mind. He had to call Carol, to tell her he had arrived, was safe.

Safe.

He picked up the phone on the nightstand and dialed the number. Grace answered.

"It's me," Connally said.

"Oh, just a minute."

He waited.

"Hello."

"I'm here," he said.

"Anything else?" she said.

"What?"

"I said, 'Anything else?' "

"I don't understand."

"Is there anything else you want to tell me?"

"Honey, I said I was sorry I had to do this."

"Are you?"

He said nothing.

"How sorry are you, Charles?"

"Look, what is it?"

"We heard from the school today."

He was silent.

"What were you going to do, Charles? Just let me keep going to work pregnant, paying for nothing —" She broke off.

"Carol —"

She was crying.

"Honey —"

"I won't talk about this over the phone," she managed. But then she was crying again.

He sat listening to it. *Oh, baby, please.*

"I don't know what I'm going to do," she said. "I wish I did. I don't even have a car now."

"Grace is staying with you," he said.

She hung up.

He dialed the number again, and it rang for a long time. Finally Grace answered.

"Please put her on, Grace."

"She won't talk right now," Grace said.

"Grace, please."

"I have no control over this, Charles. She's in her room and she's closed the door. And if you ask me, I can't say I blame her."

"No, I can't either," he said. "Please. I thought I'd get better and go back. I — I didn't know how to tell her."

"You have a lot of thinking to do," Grace told him. "And it's not getting done while we talk."

"Grace," he said. But she had hung up, too.

His mother opened the door. "Are you separating?" she said. "Is that it?"

"No," he said.

"Lee's passed out."

It took Connally a moment to realize that she meant him to do something about it. In the living room, Mr. Southworth sat slumped across the couch, his face aglow, a happy man sound asleep.

"It's getting to be an every-night thing," Connally's mother said.

"Why do you put up with it?"

"Oh, I don't mind it. He's sweet. He never goes too far any other way. He's just a — friend."

"What do you want me to do with him?"

"I need you to carry him to his own apartment."

Connally stared at her. "What do you do when I'm not here?"

"I let him sleep on the couch, of course."

"I'm not carrying him anywhere," Connally said. "I'll sleep on the floor. Really. You go into the bedroom."

His mother gave him an apologetic look. "I didn't think he'd pass out like this." She lifted the sleeping man's feet and pulled him around so that he was lying along the couch. Then she put a blanket over him. Mr. Southworth snored, and made a tiny blowing sound.

"You're sure you don't mind?" Connally's mother said.

"I don't mind," he told her.

"Do you want to talk?"

He thought he saw dread in her eyes. "Not right now," he said.

She gave forth an audible sigh of relief. "There's really nothing else to say, anyway. It's no good to dwell on the past." She had busied herself with the several woolen comforters and pillows of the couch, was fashioning a bed for him on the floor. He stood and watched.

"Do you need to use the bathroom?" she said.

He took his overnight bag in and washed his face, cleaned his teeth. When he came out, she was in the bedroom, the door closed. Lee Southworth lay inert on the couch, making no sound at all. Connally arranged himself on the floor, his back to the room. Before him was the window over the kitchen sink, with its view of the starry sky, the glow of the city. He couldn't sleep. Now and again he heard his mother moving around in the bedroom, and he thought of nights in his boyhood, sleeping in blankets on floors, or curled up on sofas, in the living rooms of other families — his mother's sisters, his great-uncle, even his mother's employer. And finally the little apartment over the movie theater, which, he remembered now, had seemed like a luxury in the first days: a place with a room he could sleep in, all his own.

It occurred to him that he had never felt any of this as being particularly important until now; it had never caused him to consider that he had been through very much as a child. For a long time when he thought of it, he had only the sense of the recentness of it all, and a certain pride, that his growing up had come faster than it does for most people. He was perfectly aware that people had been through the same, or worse. None of it had left much of a mark on him, or caused him any trouble that he was aware of. He knew intellectually that this was only a construction of his mind, but it seemed to him that he had lived quite happily in a kind of sweet ignorance before he walked into the convenience store, and he could not explain how everything inside him — hope and memory and the wish to be gentle — should feel so wholly different now, as though what had transpired in those terrible minutes in the middle of a night in Christmas week had somehow mixed with it all, and altered the chemistry that was himself, emptying some poison into him.

He could not get out of the circle of his own thoughts.

Out in the night, sirens sounded, and perhaps the sharp reports he heard in the distance were gunshots. The sirens grew louder, and at last he got up and went to the window to see. Below, cars moved by; the street looked peaceful. Lights in the other buildings glowed through shut curtains. But the sirens kept sounding, and he lay back down, beginning to be afraid of being here, of going out in those streets alone. It seemed logical, like a story, that he would come all the way back only to find himself under the control of another gunman. And now there were more reports in the distance: impossible to imagine that it could be anything but gunfire . . .

He sat up in the dark. "Jesus Christ," he murmured. The bright numbers on his mother's wall clock changed with a little faltering click. He watched the minutes pass.

And then Lee Southworth began to dream, the dream causing him to speak aloud, like someone in delirium. "Not that one, *that* one, right — put it down."

Connally regarded his shape in the dimness.

"I'll be along in a minute."

"Hey?" Connally said.

The other man didn't seem to be breathing, but then he stirred slightly, and spoke again. "I sell tools, too."

"Mr. Southworth?"

The old man sat up slowly, into the moon-like light from

the window, the light of streetlamps, and with a kind of puzzlement rubbed his hands through his hair and over his face. Then he stared off, clearing his throat and making a small sound like a groan.

"Mr. Southworth."

He looked at Connally, then seemed to peer at him. "Oh."

"You fell asleep."

"I passed out."

Connally said nothing.

"Oh, my head." The old man lay back down, then struggled back to a sitting position. "Lord."

Connally abruptly realized the strangeness of the situation. He looked at the room — his mother's crowded decor, with its dark wood and carved surfaces, and the statue in its little grotto in the wall. Outside, the city struggled toward rest, and the sirens sounded. He had come all this way, leaving everything. That after-Christmas morning he and Carol had set out seemed an age ago now, and yet here he was again, as though he had never left. In the vast dark and sparkle of the city, people were going on with their lives in the aftermath of violence. And surely someone else's life was at this moment entering the heart of fright. In his own fear, like an element of it, he felt the strong urge to begin — head out and find his own companions in the awful ritual: find Mrs. Wu and the killer, Hughes. Especially Hughes.

"I'm thirsty," Mr. Southworth said.

Connally wondered if this was meant as a request. He remained where he was.

"What time is it?"

"I don't know. Late."

"When did you get here?"

"You were awake when I got here."

"I *seemed* awake."

Connally made no response to this.

"Where's Tina?"

"She went to bed."

"I'm thirsty."

This annoyed the younger man. "You know where the faucet is," he said.

"What brings you back?"

"I wonder if I might borrow that Beretta of yours," Connally said on an impulse. His heart jumped in his chest. But then it seemed right: he was going out in the streets of this city where he had suffered such terror. It came to him that he wanted the benefit of being armed.

The old man gazed at him.

"I have to go out later."

"And you want protection."

"Protection, yes."

"Maybe I'll go with you."

"No," Connally said. "Never mind."

"Man ought not to go out alone."

"You go out with my mother?"

"We usually stay around home."

"You carry the Beretta when you do go out?"

Mr. Southworth touched the right side of his chest. "Right here."

"And you don't think you can let me carry it?"

The other man seemed not to have heard him. "Nice lady, your mother. Very tolerant."

"Because she lets you sleep on the sofa?"

"Well, that's where I wake up most nights."

Connally lay on his back and stared at the subtly shifting light on the ceiling, and for a while he listened to the other man sighing and coughing, clearing his throat — a heavy, liquid sound. "Thirsty."

"I have to go back to where it happened."

"Between you and me, son, I don't really have any bullets for the thing."

"What about your other guns?"

"I don't have other guns. That was just talk."

"Okay," Connally said.

"I guess I worry too much what people think of me, you know, and I wanted you to — well, you know. It was New Year's and we were all talking." He coughed, cleared his throat again — that sound.

"I understand," Connally said. It now seemed important that he fall asleep. He closed his eyes and knew he wouldn't be able to.

With a great creaking and groaning, Mr. Southworth stood and made his way along the wall to the kitchen area. There was the sound of cabinets opening and closing, the clink of glass. He ran the water, then swallowed loudly. It seemed to go on and on. But then he was making some sound in the back of his throat, and Connally realized it was later — Mr. Southworth had come back to the couch again, was asleep, sending up the disturbed, almost desperate sound of his snoring.

Morning came slow. Mrs. Connally walked through at first light and made herself some tea. She wore the same robe, and her hair was standing on end, like a fright wig. When she saw her son gazing at her she made a gesture of polite alarm, hurrying to tamp down her hair, pulling the robe tight around her throat.

"I thought you were asleep," she said.

"I'm up."

She stepped over to the table and sat down, tucking the robe between her knees. Then she looked over at Mr. Southworth. "Poor Lee."

"Why poor Lee?"

She shrugged. "I don't know. Look at him. He wants to marry me. Can you imagine it?"

Connally turned slightly and regarded the old man, who lay on his back with his mouth wide open. The sound he made with each breath was like a small cry for help.

"He comes in and swears he's just staying for a minute. And almost every night he sleeps on the sofa. I don't have the heart to send him away."

"Are you going to marry him?"

"I like things the way they are," she said.

Connally lay back. He was experiencing another rush of the strangeness of being where he was. He thought about the Beretta.

His mother went on talking about Mr. Southworth: "Last night, I told him you were coming and that I was planning on giving you the bedroom, and he said that was a perfectly good plan, and when I said it meant he couldn't stay, he said of course not, because he was only staying a minute. He was only going to have one drink. And look at him."

"Why don't you make him leave?" Connally said.

"I told you, I haven't got the heart."

He stared at her, and remembered his grandmother sitting in the dry bathtub, in the garish light of the tiny bathroom of the apartment above the movie theater, tying her wiry hair back with a ribbon and calling him Richard Burton. He was seventeen years old, and his mother had been saying she would be home any day, anytime, for almost three years.

"What?" she said now.

"Does he eat down here, too?"

"We order out sometimes."

A moment later, she said, "Why did you look at me like that?"

"I was thinking about Grand."

"Stop dredging." She sipped the tea, and kept her eyes from him.

He sat up, pulled a shirt from his travel bag. "I'm going to be gone most of the day."

"Where?" she said.

"I got a letter from Hughes."

She frowned.

"The one who killed everybody, Ma."

"My God, what did it say?"

"It's an apology. He's sorry and he couldn't help it."

"Do you have it?"

"It's in my coat."

She stood and went to the closet. He watched her, hearing the deep, troubled sound of Mr. Southworth's snoring. She opened the letter and read it, then put it back and closed the closet door.

"Gives me the chills," she said. "What're you going to do?"

"I don't know," he said. And he truly didn't.

"You're not going to tell me what you were thinking about Grand, either, are you?"

"I was just remembering her, that's all."

"I guess I know what you think about that," she said.

He waited, knew he should say something to relieve her, and couldn't bring himself to move.

"Well, no matter what you think, you weren't old enough to really know."

"I was just remembering her," he said.

"Things were different back then. You don't know."

"We got past all that," he said, "long ago."

"That's exactly right."

He nodded, realizing with a little tremor in his blood that he had wanted to tell her everything he had been through over the past weeks, and discovering at the same time that he could resist the urge. "All right," he said.

"I've been paying for my mistakes. All these years."

In the past, always, he had somehow kept from making the gesture or saying the thing that would acknowledge remarks like this. What had gone on between them was backdrop, and since nothing would change any part of it, he had never felt the necessity of admitting it into their talk.

Now he murmured, "I don't know what you expect me to say."

"I want you to listen to me," she said, putting the cup of tea down with a sudden little clatter. "I don't have any way of appreciating what happened to you in that store, but it's over with now, and the time has come to get on with the rest of your life. You've got a baby coming and a wife to think about."

He gazed at her, and knew that she was thinking of the hollowness of these words in the light of their specific history.

"No," she said, as if he'd spoken this out loud. "I'm the one who *can* tell you. I'm the one who knows."

He thought she might begin to cry.

"All right," he said. "Tell me this. I have a memory of being dragged around a room."

She stared.

"I remember whippings, with his belt. I couldn't have been more than four years old."

He left a pause, then: "He hit you, didn't he? He hit me, too. What else did he do to me?"

"I'm not going to talk about this."

"You have to." He had almost shouted.

"Stop this, son."

"Just give me five minutes, Ma. Five minutes of something besides this fake pleasantness you always put up."

After a hesitation, she said, "I didn't know that was how you felt. If I'm such a figure of scorn, I —"

He stood, holding the blanket around his middle. He was aware that he loomed over her. "I want to know what happened. You know what else I remember? I remember lying in a bed with people around — strangers. And a pain in my middle, like death. I want you to think about it and then tell me what that was."

She seemed braced, as though he might begin to rain blows down on her. He knelt beside her and waited, and she seemed to be trying to think, or remember.

"It's been too long," she said finally.

"Tell me this one thing. You can do that."

There was a space in which she seemed to mutter and then breathe. It was as if she were deciding. "He'd go crazy," she said, beginning to cry.

"Tell me," he said.

"I just did tell you."

"That isn't all of it, goddammit."

Again she was going over something in her mind. Her face seemed about to collapse on itself, and her eyes swam. "Why are you doing this, Charles?"

"Just tell me."

"He was set in his ways. You have to understand. And — and I got the two of you apart."

"*Before* you got us apart, he pulled my arm out of the socket. He broke my nose. He hit me with a cane."

"I didn't know," she said. "I wasn't in a position."

"What else?"

"Beatings. With the fists."

"I don't mean that. I remember that, all right."

She put her head down on her folded hands and then looked at him. "He caused internal bleeding. You had a seizure."

"What else?" he said.

"There's nothing else."

"Oh, yes there is."

She stared at him.

"I want you to tell me how you could let it happen."

She said nothing.

"Please." He was almost crying. "Tell me that, Ma. How you could let it happen?"

"There were times he was wonderful with you." She took a sharp breath, almost a sob. "He loved you, son. He just didn't know how to do it. And that was what had been done to him. You have to understand that he couldn't help himself."

"No," Connally said. "Goddammit, don't tell me that."

"I took you away from him for good when I knew it wouldn't stop — that he couldn't stop it."

Again he stood, loomed over her. "Well, what told you it wouldn't stop? What convinced you, for Christ's sake?"

"Stop this," she said.

Abruptly, looking into her face with its beset, stricken expression, he felt wrong. He touched her shoulder, then let his hand drop to his side.

"I'm — I've always been so frightened of loneliness," she said. "I don't know what else I could've done. I didn't want to make him any angrier, you see." She shook her head, glanced at her son, and then fixed her eyes on the table. "No. I was afraid he wouldn't love me anymore. You see, I was alone so awfully much, growing up." Her voice broke. "Winnie didn't like many people and we were always moving, and I mean I just — I never had boyfriends or dates or anything like that." She sat straighter in the chair, and when she spoke again it was as if she were offering a form of resolution. "I was very, very skinny. And shy. You know — awkward and not very much to look at, and I didn't learn how to be with people, really. And, with your father I — I thought I could make it all come out right some way. I was in love — and I liked being in love. I needed to be in love." She gave forth a little sobbing sound and then seemed to gather herself. "The first time he hit you, I — oh, honey, I never felt such terror."

"How old was I?" he said.

Now she was looking at her hands, worrying the cloth of her robe. "I don't remember."

"Tell me, Ma."

"Oh, my baby." She began to cry. "My little baby, you — you had an ear infection and you were crying, you kept crying, and he — he thought it was a tantrum." She put her hands to her eyes and sobbed, trying to repress the sound of it. When she could speak again she gave him a pleading look, then murmured, "I have carried the picture of your face, that child's face that kept turning to me and then back to him while he hurt you."

"Tell me," Connally said, fighting back his own tears.

She reached up and touched the side of his head, her fingers closing on his ear as if to shield it. "He slapped you, here."

Connally took her wrist, and she moved to put her hand in his.

"Honey, I screamed at him. And he hit you again — the other side. And he kept hitting you, all over. Your legs, your back. He just went into it, and when I tried to stop him he hit me in the stomach and knocked me down. But he couldn't have been more contrite after it was over — you never saw anyone feel worse, like a little sad boy. He put his head in my lap and cried." She took her hand away and touched the corners of her eyes, sniffling. "I wanted so badly to believe it would be all right."

On the sofa, Lee Southworth coughed, sputtered, then turned into the cushions and said a name.

"I was a baby," Connally said to his mother. "How old was I? Was I a year old?"

She sobbed. "Eight months. You had pulled yourself up to standing in the crib. You were standing there crying, and we were yelling at you, and then he started hitting."

"Yelling at me. You, too?"

"I thought if I could make you stop, he wouldn't be so mad and he'd — he wouldn't hurt you."

"Jesus Christ," Connally said. He was finding it difficult to exhale. He pulled the blanket around himself. "Oh, God," he managed.

"You're a sweet, gentle boy," she said. "You always were."

He didn't return her look.

"Always, the most tender-hearted and sensitive boy," she said. "And, honey, you have to know that when he was himself and things were all right, the two of you were wonderful together — laughing and chasing around the house. Beautiful together, and he took such delight in you. He really did. Those times were awfully sweet, and when it was like that I just couldn't believe it would ever be bad again. And you missed him, too, after I finally took you away. You asked about him all the time in this sad little voice. It used to break my heart."

He couldn't speak. He sensed that she was waiting for him to respond; he was thinking of his father's shiny brown shoes with the swirls in them, wingtips. He felt his own heartbeat in his throat and face.

"And, you know," his mother said, "in those days it wasn't as easy for a woman to go out on her own. I mean, really — when you look at it, what else could I have done?"

"Nothing," he said, shuffling away from her. "Maybe I just wish you had done something about it sooner than you did, that's all."

"Well," she said. "You don't know how it was. You weren't —" She stopped.

"I wasn't there?"

"Don't be ridiculous."

"No, that's what you were about to say."

She had her hands down in her lap, and she was looking at them again.

"You were about to say I wasn't there."

"I don't want to talk about it anymore. It's obvious you hate me, and you hate everything I did."

"No," he said, low. "I hate what you didn't do."

"I did my best."

"It wasn't good enough."

"You're being unfair."

"No," he said. "I'm just telling the truth. For the first time in our lives, Ma. The unadorned facts of the matter. You had a baby and you weren't up to it, and you let him do those things to me and then you farmed me out to people because, as you put it, you were in love."

"No," she said.

"You liked being in love. Isn't that what you said? You liked being in love. No, you *needed* to be in love."

"I was a girl. He was a lot older than I was. I never intended to do a thing wrong. What are you doing this for? What do you want me to say?"

He moved back to her side and knelt there. "No, you don't understand. Don't say anything. You don't have to say a thing. Just listen, okay? And I'll tell you. Okay? You ready? I have these awful images now, Ma. And my God, it's not just the shootings I see. The shootings — hell, they're just the key that opened the little door in my head. That little door that leads into the terrible dark, way at the heart of me, way at the heart of the sum total of what I am and what I learned from Mommy and Daddy, and there in that little place I can see myself hitting Carol. I can see myself dragging her body around a room, Ma."

"Stop it," his mother said in a broken voice. "Oh, please. I won't have it."

He stood, and in the next few seconds he was just watching her try to compose herself. He felt almost dispassionate about it, though his heart was beating fast.

"I never dreamed you could hate me so much," she said.

He sighed. "I don't hate you. Jesus — I love you. I wanted you home with me all those years, and I didn't even care where we lived. I would've been happy in a cave as long as you were there and nobody was hitting me."

"Oh, my baby." She reached for him, put her arms around his waist.

He patted her shoulder, feeling confused and sick.

"You got in a fight in school once," she said. "You were ten or eleven. Do you remember?"

"Chester Fromm."

"Well, I don't remember the boy's name." She sat back, brought a napkin out of her robe, and wiped her eyes. "But you beat him in this fight. You got your arm around his neck — you showed me, standing in Great-uncle Evan's living room that time — how you got him in this hold and wouldn't let go until he quit."

"I remember," Connally said.

"You cried telling it to me, don't you remember? You felt so bad for the whole thing. A little two-minute squabble on the playground between boys."

"Yes," he said.

"That's you," his mother said. "That's the boy I raised."

He was quiet.

She muttered, "I guess I shouldn't say 'raised' exactly."

"It's a word," he said. "It'll do."

"You know what I meant."

"Yes."

"And you didn't say that to hurt me, I know that, too."

"I don't want anybody hurt," he said. "Jesus, I wish no one had got hurt." His voice broke.

"Don't, son."

"I'm afraid of myself," he said. "My own mind scares me."

"You're a wonderful, brave, sweet young man."

"I feel dead, deep down."

"No," she said.

And now Mr. Southworth moved, emitted a little whimper, and sat up.

They watched him come to.

"Well," Connally's mother said, all cheerfulness and charm through her tears. She lifted the cup of tea. "Ready for some hot tea?"

"Good Lord," said Mr. Southworth. "I must have overstayed my welcome again."

Connally got into his jeans and started out of the room. "I have to get going."

"Where you headed?" Mr. Southworth said miserably. "You just got here."

"I have some business to attend to."

"He won't listen to me," his mother said in that voice that was all light and music.

"Is everything all right, Tina?"

"Why, it's just fine," Connally's mother said.

But then the old man seemed to shift awake. He struggled to his feet and began putting his shirt on.

"You can stay for something to eat," Mrs. Connally said.

He had started buttoning his shirt, and then he reached for Connally's arm. "Come here, son."

"Where are you going?" Mrs. Connally said.

"We'll be just a minute, Tina."

Connally followed him out into the hall, where he punched the elevator switch, and then finished fastening the buttons of his shirt.

"What," Connally said.

"Little secret between the two of us men," Mr. Southworth said. There was something awkwardly familiar and ingratiating about the way he leaned toward Connally to murmur these words. "Between men," he went on, "some things are assumed territory."

The elevator opened, and they got on.

Connally understood everything, and yet something in him wanted to get the old man to say it out. "The Beretta," he said.

Mr. Southworth's conspiratorial nod embarrassed him, and he looked away. "Don't tell your mother."

"No," Connally said.

"I shouldn't do this."

"I thought you didn't have any bullets."

The old man smiled. "More talk. Believe me, it's always loaded."

Connally stared at him.

"I don't like to tell people it is, see."

The elevator door opened on the old man's floor and he led the way down the hall, which was thickly carpeted, with an almost overpowering redolence of soap and cleanser. In the quiet, their footsteps made a soft whispering sound, and from somewhere music came, guitars and drums. Mr. Southworth's door was at the end of the hall. When he opened it, the odor of alcohol met them.

"Poured myself some wine, here, and then never drank it," he said. "Wait here."

Connally remained in the doorway, gazing at the disorder of the room — clothes strewn everywhere, books and magazines stacked on the chairs and the sofa, bottles ranked along the dresser top against the left wall. A bright window made everything appear shadowed, and there were stains in the carpet. The walls were bare.

Mr. Southworth came padding back with the small black pistol in his hands. It lay on its side in his palms, like an offering. "Here she is," he said.

Connally held out his hands and let the other man put it in his palms.

"Let me show you the safety."

"I see it."

"If you should have to use it, you want it here." Mr. Southworth moved the little lever.

"I see."

He moved it back, then took a step away. "You're not going to rob a bank, are you?"

"Right," Connally said, smiling.

"Safety on?"

He looked at the lever. "On."

"You're set."

He put the pistol in the pocket of his jeans.

"You can see it there," Mr. Southworth said.

"I won't keep it there."

Mrs. Connally was in the bathroom running water when they returned. Connally let Southworth put the Beretta in his coat while he dressed, and when his mother came out, she looked them both over.

"Well?" she said.

"Between the boys," said Mr. Southworth in that ingratiating tone; he was milking it for all it was worth.

"What're you two into?"

"Now, that's for us to worry about." He put one arm over Connally's shoulder and squeezed; he was obviously happy to be referred to with Connally as "you two."

"Charles, I think you should call home," Tina Connally said in exactly the tone of motherly command he knew from other times, and he remembered it with the same sense that it was forced somehow, a brave lie on her part, assuming authority she did not have.

"Well?" she said, staring at him. It was almost a challenge.

"I better get back upstairs," Lee Southworth said.

"Don't leave on my account," said Connally.

He used the telephone in her bedroom again, standing by the rumpled bed and waiting for the connection to go through. Grace answered.

"Please put her on, Grace."

"I don't think anything's changed," Grace said, "from last night."

He waited.

"I'm here," Carol said in a tight little voice.

"Honey," he said, "I'm sorry about it all."

There was just the static of long distance.

"Carol?"

"I'm here."

"I should've told you."

"I don't understand," she said.

"I just needed to talk to these other people who were involved," he told her. "I can't explain it."

She said nothing.

"Can't you try to understand, Carol?"

And then he knew she was crying. "I can't believe you'd — why you would lie to me like that."

"I didn't lie. I just didn't tell you."

She sobbed.

"Carol, please."

"What are we going to do now?" she said, crying. There was a note of panic in her voice that made him wince.

"It'll be all right," he said. "Please." In his heart, he knew that his coming here had been a kind of fleeing from her, even for the sense that he must somehow get to the root of the thing: he had felt that he must get away, that if he remained with her in the little converted hunting cabin, he might lose his mind. He was losing his mind. The thought rose in him like a judgment, an inner verdict. A man standing in a room talking on the phone, haunted with images of murder. *I am losing my mind.*

"Charles?" she said.

"Oh, Jesus." He couldn't breathe.

"I'm scared." Her voice was small as a whimper on the other end of the line.

"I have to go," he said.

She was silent.

"I'll call you later. I have to go."

Grace's voice came now. "We'll be waiting, since that's all we can do."

•

Sergeant Donovan's office turned out to be in a suburban setting, back from the road among trees and with four tall flagpoles in front. The building was fronted with aluminum and glass, and there were several police vehicles parked in the lot. Connally made his way along the walk, seeing out of the corner of his eye his own reflection melting into and out of the glass frames. Through the spaces of tree branch and shrub, the land opened out onto a vast dump, with crowds of sea gulls ministering to it. A steady, balmy wind was blowing, and the sky was the color of galvanized metal. Inside the building a receptionist greeted him, a woman in uniform with a pistol high on her hip.

"Can I see Detective Sergeant Donovan," he said to her.

"Hey," she said, as if she recognized him. "Sign here."

"Is he in?"

"Not yet."

He signed the sheet of paper she put before him.

"He'll be here any minute," she said. "Why don't you have a seat."

He walked over to the padded bench against the wall and sat down, thinking that if he were someone who had come here to harm Sergeant Donovan, there was apparently not much in the routines of this place that would discourage or deter him. He felt the small solidness of the Beretta in the bottom of his coat pocket, remembering, in all the movies he had seen, the old clichés where the outlaw points the pistol through the cloth of a coat. The whole country loved murder, and entertained such avid curiosity about it — all the books, all the mystery stories and the movies and the television programs. You could make a body count any night of the week, and none of it was like the real thing — the sheer inanimate weight of the dead, the lightless stare, and the blood. He remembered that there had been so much blood. The pressure building inside him seemed to shift now, and he almost gagged. Rocking slightly back and forth on the chair, waiting, he looked over at the woman behind the desk, at her badge shining in the light from the door. Her round face was puffy, all chin, her uniform collar looking as if it might choke her. She had apparently forgotten him, was reading from a sheaf of papers in a folder, and then she looked up to catch him staring at her. Smiling, she opened one of the desk drawers and brought out a handkerchief, with which she brushed the wings of her nose. Connally looked away from her, letting his gaze wander over the plaques and framed photographs on the opposite wall. One of the photographs was of Sergeant Donovan — a thinner, younger version of him. Connally stared at it, and then the detective walked in, looking exactly as he had the night of the shootings: the same gray suit, the same tie, the same weary countenance. Connally stood as the woman behind the desk indicated him to the big man, who turned and regarded him with an air of the impatience a man has who is too busy for unexpected details. He walked over and shook Connally's hand. He smelled of bay rum, and faintly of tobacco. It seemed to Connally now that all his senses were too finely attuned to things: Donovan wheezed slightly when he breathed, and his movements made a whispering in the suit he wore. Everything divided and was distinct: sounds, odors, the texture of the air with its cool pockets and tropical drafts from the heaters.

"What can I do for you?" Donovan said.

"I wanted to talk to you."

Donovan studied him.

"The — the convenience store," Connally said, feeling breathless.

"Oh, right." Donovan rubbed the back of his wide neck. "Man, I'm not awake yet. What're you doing here now? We don't have a trial date yet."

"I won't take long."

The other man sighed, motioned for him to follow. They went through a set of double doors into a hallway, on either side of which were other doors. Connally heard voices, the clatter of a typewriter, laughter. Donovan's office was a surprisingly clean and orderly little cubicle at the end of the hall. There was one window behind the desk, overlooking a sloping grassy lawn with evergreen trees and a creekbed. Beyond the trees on the other side, the gray hills of the dump were visible.

"Have a seat," Donovan said, indicating a straight-back chair on the other side of the desk. The desk was clean, with two pencils lying beside a legal notepad like the one Donovan had held the first time Connally saw him. Against the wall was a table with a coffee machine on it, and an ashtray. Donovan turned the machine on and lighted a cigarette, then took his place behind the desk. The chair he sat in squeaked, and he leaned back in it, regarding Connally with calm interest.

"I wondered if I could see the other people involved."

"The trial's not going to be for a while, you know. They're

still evaluating the kid, and of course he's still recovering. He'll be in a wheelchair the rest of his life."

"Did you say they're still evaluating him?"

Donovan made a circular motion at his ear with one finger. "It's an accepted defense these days, you know. In fact, the lawyer's already setting the groundwork. I suppose you got a letter of apology, too."

Connally changed the subject. "If I could just have where I might go to see them —"

Donovan regarded him from the casual pose of sitting back in the chair, with one foot on the edge of the desk.

"Mrs. Wu. And — and Hughes."

Now he sat forward, opened the middle drawer, and took out a pencil.

"Is the store open again?" Connally asked him.

"Far as I know."

"Is Mrs. Wu still —"

Donovan shook his head. He appeared to be doodling on the legal pad. "She don't want to talk to nobody, son. She's like you were."

"Can I just have where — where I can find her?"

"I'd have to go downstairs and get the file."

Connally waited.

The other man breathed a sigh. "Look, after her little bit for the news people she was pretty clear about wanting to get all this behind her. I think I ought to find out if she minds anybody having her address."

"I'm not just anybody, sir."

Donovan seemed to consider this a moment. "No, I guess you're not."

"Does this Mark Hughes — does he have a family?"

"No," Donovan said. "Not a soul. But you know the other one? Fain? No kidding — mother, father. Brothers and sisters, too. The youngest of seven. Model kid all through school. Got his diploma and set off on a life of cold-blooded crime like somebody trying to fulfill an old ambition."

"Did he come from Chicago?"

Donovan wrote something on the pad and then tore the paper out of it. He looked at Connally. "Son, you're shaking like a leaf."

"I'm a little chilly."

"Never enough heat in these sealed buildings," Donovan said. "Or too much." His tone was kind.

"Mr. Donovan, I think I just need to put things in some kind of order for myself."

"I understand — all the hoopla, a thing like that can get lost." The big man folded the sheet of paper and handed it across the desk. "Here's your information."

Connally looked at it, a written address under Mrs. Wu's scribbled name, and the letterhead of the Cicero Detention Center.

Donovan clasped his hands on the desk in front of him, and when he spoke now there was a brittleness in his voice. "I don't expect to be getting any calls from people about this. If they don't want to talk to you, you'll respect that, right?"

"Yes, sir," Connally said, feeling that this had been the right thing, and wishing Carol could understand it. He was very close to tears.

"You're not here for anything else, are you?" Donovan said.

"Anything else?" said Connally.

"Well, the newspapers — the hero stuff."

"No."

"It's an angle, you know. The hero comes back to talk with the one he saved, and the one he got." Donovan's tone was now faintly sarcastic.

"No," Connally told him. "But I want to talk to Hughes, too. He did write me."

"I don't know if that'll be possible, son."

"Just to talk to him," Connally said.

"You did get a letter, huh?"

Connally nodded, feeling a sudden, sharp urge to laugh. "He said he went to school and had a job."

"Well, it's no secret where he is, so I'm not breaking any rules giving you that. And I suppose if you went there and asked to see him like any visitor."

"He said it all happened against his will."

Donovan shook his head, staring down at his hands. "You wonder how people get through the days sometimes."

This seemed not to require an answer.

"You write him back?" Donovan asked.

"No."

"Me neither, of course."

Presently he said, "Wonder who else he's writing." Then with something like a sputter: "Some damn lawyer's ploy."

"I just got the apology day before yesterday," Connally said.

The other man stood laboriously, lifting the weight of himself and moving with a lurching motion around the desk. He hiked the loose belt of his pants. "Well?" he said.

Connally came to his feet. "You've been helpful."

"Just remember what I said about not making a fuss for anybody."

"I will."

"You all right, now?"

"Yes, sir," Connally told him.

Donovan shook hands. "Hell of a thing," he said, "id'n it?"

•

That morning, over her mother's objections and protests, Carol got herself dressed and drove to the college. She took Grace's car. It was a bright, cold, cloudless day, the sun blazing everywhere like the principle of happiness and health. She hadn't quite formulated to herself what she would do there, beyond trying to talk with Connally's professors to see how bad the damage was. She thought she might explain, and that something might be arranged for his return. Yet as she pulled into the parking lot beyond the School of Government, her resolve began to weaken: she felt woozy and frail; her heart fluttered and raced. She had a coppery taste in her mouth, and she was afraid she might be sick.

She parked the car and sat staring at the patterns of brick in the building, the skinny trees in the quad. The campus looked abandoned. One woman was making her slow way across the quad — an Arab wrapped in dark robes, everything veiled but her eyes. Along the crest of the far hill, two young men tossed a basketball back and forth, trotting side by side in the direction of the field house.

Carol got out of the car and headed toward the building, pausing at the edge of the street that traversed that side of the quad. A bus was approaching. The driver slowed, stopped in the high-pitched chuffing sound of hydraulic brakes, waiting for her to cross, smiling kindly. She stepped out, landed wrong, something faltering in her left ankle, and then she was down on all fours, trying to rise, while the bus driver, a young man with bony rough-feeling hands and a badly scarred face, held her arms and lifted. She was afraid she might've passed out, didn't remember seeing him get off the bus. She said, "Oh, thank you," as he supported her. He strained, held on, talking kindly to her about tricky curbs. Somehow, she managed to stand. A crowd of passengers had shouldered forward to gaze at her out of the windshield of the bus. The driver stood back, still holding her lightly by one elbow.

"You okay?"

"Fine," Carol said, wanting only to be out of his sight and hearing. She couldn't stop the rasping sound of her own breathing.

"You're sure?"

"Yes, thank you." She was dizzy. When she turned from him she almost fell again, and he reached for her. "I'm all right. I'll be all right."

"You're bleeding."

She looked at him.

"Your elbow."

"Oh," Carol said, still trying to turn away. She walked a few paces in the street, then stopped.

"Here." He held out a handkerchief.

"I have one," she told him. "Thank you."

"Can I call somebody for you?"

"I'm fine," she said. Her ankle hurt. She couldn't quite get up the curb on the other side of the street. He hurried to her.

"Maybe you ought to sit down," he said.

"Thank you," she said to him.

They stood there. He was holding her by her good elbow. The other was swollen and bleeding slightly. She touched a handkerchief to it, gingerly dabbing the blood.

"I bet that stings."

Carol said, "It's just a scrape."

"Are you okay, now?"

She nodded. His hand left her other elbow, and she felt herself waver slightly. But she stood straight. "Thank you," she said again.

"No problem." He was backing away slowly, as though through some effort he had balanced her there and thought she might begin to fall.

When he pulled the bus away he waved, and she waved back. The passengers all stared out the windows. Carol made herself return the stares. Then she was standing alone at the edge of the street, holding a handkerchief to her barked elbow. She turned and went on, and the fear surged under her heart that she had harmed something deep, where the baby was. It hurt. Everything hurt.

Inside the School of Government, the hallway was crowded. Apparently a class had just been dismissed. People rushed along in surprising myriad forms of casual and showy dress — everyone looking so colorful and confident, shouldering tote bags and knapsacks or carrying books. These people were all set in their lives; they had purpose, and they were doing something they wanted to do. Carol felt momentarily invisible. She got to the side of the hallway and then edged along it, trying to stay out of everyone's way, still holding her elbow.

The History Department was on the second floor. She knew where it was, and she had been putting the thought of it away from herself, simply proceeding, drawing herself on. Now she stood at the base of the stairs and uttered a sigh of exhaustion.

"Are you all right?"

She turned to see a man she recognized immediately as Connally's history professor, Dr. Williamson. She looked into his heavy-lidded eyes and tried to speak.

"You've hurt yourself."

"Professor Williamson?"

He nodded.

"I need to talk to you."

"My office is down the hall, here," he said. "You don't have to climb the stairs."

He led her to a smoked-glass door at the end of the hall, turned a key in the knob, and opened it into a small octagonal book-lined room with a spiral staircase at its center leading up to another, more brightly lighted room, also lined with books. "We don't have to climb those stairs either," he said, offering her a chair. She eased into it, feeling the sore places in her knees and along her lower leg, from where she had hit the asphalt. Mostly, though, it was her elbow that hurt.

"That's a nasty abrasion," he said.

"If I could have something to wash it with."

He went out. She waited there, her stomach roiling. The room smelled musty, and for a moment she felt dizzy again. It had been a mistake to come here, and yet she couldn't bring herself to move. When he came back, he had a wet paper towel and some medicated cream he'd got from one of the secretaries in the History Department. She put the wet towel on the wound, and its coolness was startling; it took all the heat out of the sting.

"Thank you," she said.

"I'm sorry, nobody had any Band-Aids." He moved behind the desk and sat down. He was wearing jeans, she noticed; his shirt was open at the collar, the sleeves folded up his forearms. His sparse hair had been pushed back as if with both hands, and it stood up in a fuzzy crown. "I have some iced tea here."

"Yes, please."

It was all so polite. He brought the thermos of tea out of the cabinet at his side and poured two glasses. The room was very quiet, and the liquid made its convivial little sound being poured. Carol thought of him in his ordered existence, bringing tea in a thermos to school. She took the glass he offered, and drank from it, unable to believe the dryness in her mouth and throat. She emptied the glass.

"More?"

She nodded.

He poured some from his glass into hers.

"No," she said, "really." And she tried to pull away, causing him to spill some of what he had. Quietly, he put his glass down and crossed the room, opened a drawer in the roll-top desk there, and brought out a small terry-cloth rag.

"I'm sorry," she said.

"No harm done." He bent down and wiped away the spilled tea. When he had returned to the desk he folded his hands under his chin and regarded her. "I'm certain you're not in any of my classes. And yet I know you."

"I'm Charles Connally's — wife."

He said nothing.

"Connally."

Now he frowned, considering. "All right."

"He's sick," Carol said, and began to cry. She couldn't stop it, and yet he just sat there, as if waiting for her to do just that.

Finally he stirred. "I'm —" he began. "I'm sorry, I don't have anything." He stood again. He was apparently looking for something she could wipe her eyes with — he picked up the rag with which he had removed the spilled tea, looked at it, shook his head slightly, then put it down — but he was also clearly trying to find something to keep himself from having to face her in her distress. She understood this in some wordless, mortified corner of her mind and was trying, for his sake, to stop the tears. She opened her purse and brought out a napkin and showed it to him.

"There," he said, standing over her. "There now."

"I wondered if you could let my husband have some time."

Obviously the professor was made very nervous by this show of emotion. When he sat down he fingered the papers before him, then leaned back in the chair, not looking at her.

"Charles Connally," Carol said, then held the napkin to her nose.

"Isn't he — your husband is the one who was on television. The murders."

She nodded.

"Terrible thing."

"It's made him sick," Carol said. The sound of these words on her own lips frightened her.

"He was the hero, wasn't he?"

She said nothing.

"I saw him here at the beginning of the exam period."

"I know when he gets back on his feet —" Carol began. Professor Williamson gazed at her. "Where is he now?"

"Chicago."

The other was waiting for her to go on.

"He needed to talk to the ones — you know —"

"Well," the professor said. "We don't really have any provisions for a case like this, you know. I mean, even if someone was in the hospital, we'd have to drop him from a course — unless some effort is made, or some arrangement, you know. And I'm afraid it would have to be something the student himself would arrange. Could you have him call me?"

"No. He won't — you don't understand."

"It has to come from him, you see."

"Can't you let me take his work home?" She heard the note of desperation in her voice. She thought he might've cowered slightly away from her.

"Lacking any will to proceed on his part, I don't know what good that would do."

"I know he wants to teach."

"Have him call me," the professor said.

•

Mrs. Wu lived in an apartment complex off the interstate, two exits east of the convenience store. Her apartment was on the third floor of the first building, facing a small courtyard. Connally rang her doorbell, but no one answered. He waited for a time, experiencing a strange sense of anticipation, as if this were an appointed meeting and she was late. Finally he was on the stairs, heading down into the courtyard. The sun had broken through clouds to the east, and was reflecting like liquid fire on the cars out in the parking lot. Everything seemed blinding, a part of this brightness. He put his hands to his eyes, thinking of broken bones, bruises, beatings. He could remember whirling in a white room, something tearing in his arm, and he recalled the sense of dread and awe at the protuberances of bone in his father's fists.

She had allowed it all to happen.

Now, armed, far from the stresses of home, he was beginning to feel some lessening of the tension inside.

In the courtyard was a stone bench. He sat there and waited. Though small sheets of ice remained in the pools of shade, the air was almost warm when the wind was still. Before him, partly obscured by a small stand of bare saplings, was a bus stop where two women sat on another bench. It took Connally a moment to realize that one of them was Mrs. Wu. She was talking animatedly to the other woman, someone older, wearing a dark burgundy dress under a black coat and possessing the same brilliantly black, straight hair. Mrs. Wu was in a gray, featureless, robe-like parka. Connally stared at her a while, then got up and walked over to stand facing her at the curb a few feet away. She went on talking, fast, in that language that sounded like singing, and at last she looked at him, her round face registering only irritation and wariness.

"Excuse me," he said, approaching slowly.

And now she recognized him. "Oh," she said, standing, reaching for him. "Oh, Mistah Connarr-ee. Mistah Connarr-ee. Oh."

For some reason, he found it astonishing that she knew his name. He let her take his fingers into her cool, rough-feeling hands, and she led him to the still-seated older woman, who kept nodding and smiling, looking back and forth between them as if she weren't certain who to seek explanation from. The two women had an enthusiastic exchange in the other language, Mrs. Wu gesturing at him, still holding on to him with one hand. She held tight. Connally stood smiling at them.

"Velly blave," Mrs. Wu said, nodding at him.

He said, "Not really," and it sounded ridiculous, entirely false. A fake modesty built on a prodigious lie. "No," he said. "Christ."

It became apparent that Mrs. Wu had missed his distress, and wanted him to accompany her back into the complex. He went along, being pulled like a child. Mrs. Wu's friend bustled at his side, chattering, smiling, and in another moment Connally realized that this was Mrs. Wu's mother, or mother-in-law. The relation wasn't clear, though when they arrived at Mrs. Wu's door she took some trouble to explain. Connally kept nodding, trying to catch what he could. Oddly, she seemed somehow less able to speak English.

In the apartment, the older woman began immediately to prepare refreshments while Mrs. Wu led him through to the living room. It was a surprisingly spacious room, bordered with plants and with the ornamentations one associates with exotic places or scenes from movies about the Orient: a Buddha sat amid scented candles on one table, and there were miniature trees and jeweled statuary and paintings of royal processions, a kind of silent entourage, around him. The air was redolent of spices, fragrances he couldn't place. He walked into the middle of all this and thought of civilizations older than Greece or Rome. He was, after all, someone who had been interested in history.

Mrs. Wu gestured for him to sit down, and he chose a red velvet love seat between two dark end tables, on each of which stood a slender statuette — porcelain girls with demure, small red mouths and delicately drawn lines for eyes. Sitting there, he had an abrupt sensation of having entered another time. Mrs. Wu had gone into the kitchen, and seemed to be arguing with her relative. The two women were moving about as if in a great hurry. He looked at the statuary, the many tropical plants and potted trees, the paintings; he noted the drawings of emperors and great processions in the wallpaper. An odor of ginger and sesame oil came to him — something being put together in the kitchen, something exquisite.

Mrs. Wu came back with a tray of tea things and poured him a steaming cup of herb tea. He thanked her, wondering how he would begin; it was clear that his presence was making her nervous. She sat in the wing chair opposite him and pantomimed drinking the tea. He sipped it, tasted a subtle orange flavor, and something else, too. He smiled. "Good."

She clasped her hands together under her moon-like face and smiled back. "Good."

"Very good," Connally said.

She stood. "Nice." Then she turned to leave him there.

"You're working at another store," he said.

She stopped and regarded him, then nodded slowly. "Yes."

"I wanted to talk to you," Connally said.

She waited.

"I wanted to ask you some things. And tell you something, too."

Now she seemed puzzled. She came toward him slightly, wringing her hands, staring at him as if she thought he might suddenly begin shouting at her. And then he had an urge to do just that — to stand and say at the top of his voice the thing he was quickly beginning to know he did think about it all, sitting there holding the saucer with its little tea cup rattling in his trembling hands, the idea blossoming in him that until this moment she had been doing better than he, that she had somehow made a kind of truce with her own memory of what had taken place, and managed to put it behind her: she had found a refuge, an unbreachable inner harbor. It dawned on Connally with a bitter, wordless self-deprecation that while he had experienced this terrible sloughing off of all the things mooring him to his own life, she had simply drawn about herself the safety of her ancient traditions.

When she took another step toward him, smiling now, yet seeming almost wary, he felt patronized, as if to her he were nothing more than a man with his own frightening, barbarous land to live in — a man obviously unhinged, requiring caution along with the ageless courtesy.

"Do you think about it?" he said, putting the tea cup down.

"You rike eat?"

"No," he said. "I need you to tell me if you think about things. What happened. You think about it, right? It feels like it's not over yet. Tell me."

Her gaze seemed to go past him.

"I keep seeing it in my head," he told her, his anger gone. They had both been through this awful thing. And all of it was showing in her face now.

"No look," she said. "Work."

"Did you know any of them?"

This seemed not to have made an impression on her.

"The people who were shot."

"Dlink tea." Her voice was firm. "You dlink."

"You knew the old guy — the one who ran the motel."

She said nothing.

"Right? Arlen. You knew him."

"You dlink." She seemed about to cry now, and Connally went through a tottering moment of wanting to embrace her. He thought of her as a child, thought of the ghost of the child she'd once been, that cowering, frightened thing she was carrying around with her through the damages and the irremediable complications of the world, thousands of miles from anything like home, having to grope daily for some foothold amid the treacherous syllables of the strange, other language, and having been subjected to such violence — why shouldn't she cling to all the familiar trappings?

"I'm sorry," he said. "Please."

"Dlink tea," she persisted. There was something almost impatient in her voice.

He lifted the cup and put it to his lips, and she watched him with all the proprietary interest of a teacher observing an exercise. "Fine," he said. "Thank you."

She nodded, and kept watching.

"You don't want to talk about it," he said.

"No."

"I need to talk about it."

"Velly bad. Dlink up."

"You must've seen some of them before."

She simply stared at him.

"The motel owner."

"Yes," she said.

"You knew him."

"Know his face, yes."

"And the others?"

She shrugged. "Many faces. Each night many faces." She moved to the small cabinet along the far wall and, opening the top drawer, brought out a piece of paper. Then she turned, and with a reaching motion, as though she were afraid to get too close, handed it to him.

Dear Madam
  I got your address from the policeman. I was sorry for
what happened. I didn't mean to hurt anybody. It happened
against my will and consent. I am an ordinary man. I went to
school. I had a job. I'm sorry for everything. I have remorse.
It was too confused. I am sorry.

Mark Hughes

He returned it to her, and she went back to the cabinet
and put it in the drawer again, closing the drawer quietly as
if it contained something delicate. When she sat down across
from him once more, the other woman started into the
room, carrying a tray full of food. Mrs. Wu said something
to her in the language, and then the two of them had what
looked like a bickering exchange, at the end of which the
older woman turned around with the tray still in her hands
and, muttering to herself, left them there alone.

"I have one, too," Connally said.

"You have retta?"

"A letter, yes."

"Velly sad boy."

"Yes."

"Sick." She held one hand up and touched her heart.
"Here."

"Do you feel scared, still?" Connally asked her.

She simply looked at him.

"Scared."

"Velly scared."

"I wanted to talk about that."

She waited.

"I don't even know what I'm after," Connally said. "I
thought if I could talk to you —"

"You velly blave."

"No. I wish it was true."

"You save me."

"No," he said, rising. "That's also what I came to tell you. I didn't — I'm not responsible."

She kept an expression of polite interest on her face, and then she touched her eyes. "No sreep."

"Pardon?" The word on his lips sounded almost pathetically polite, utterly inappropriate, as if he had complimented her on her dress or her hair.

"Eyes. No sleep." She pronounced it carefully.

"Right," he said.

She leaned forward slightly. "Me, too."

It took him a moment to understand. "Nightmares?" he said.

"Bad dleams with eyes wide open."

"You can't sleep?"

She shook her head.

"Nightmares," Connally said.

"Eyes open," she said.

It seemed to him now that they were friends, that they had known each other for years. He could tell her everything. "I got scared I might hurt my wife," he said. "I'm afraid it's inside me, like a disease. Things happened — when I was little."

She appeared to be trying to encourage him to go on, to tell her more. But there was nothing else he could think of to say.

He simply repeated himself. "When I was little."

And now she reached over and put her cool hand on his wrist. "You come here this far."

"No," he said, fighting tears. "I'm sorry. I can't stop thinking about it."

"You still blave boy."

"I didn't set out to save you," he told her. "It was an accident." His voice faltered on the last word.

Her expression now was of a sort of bemused tolerance.

"Do you understand?" he said.

"Yes."

For a moment, neither of them spoke.

"Thank you," Connally said.

She called to the other woman, who came hurrying back in with the food: small strips of fish in garlic sauce and a bowl of steamed dumplings. He demurred, apologized and thanked them both, and Mrs. Wu walked with him out into the hall, her arms folded, her kind eyes looking into his. Twice she reached over and touched the back of his hand. "Bettah forget," she told him.

"Do you understand that I was trying to save myself?" he said.

"No think," Mrs. Wu said. "No damn good."

They parted at the stairs, with Mrs. Wu indicating that he could come back if he wished, and even as she waved and smiled he knew there could be no situation in which she could be really glad to see him.

Outside, the wind had picked up; it was colder. He got into the car and drove to the Cicero Detention Center, though he was beginning to know that the answers he wanted were not outside himself, his own history. Something in Mrs. Wu's refusal to dwell on the events in the convenience store seemed vaguely practical rather than temperamental: she appeared to have come to a decision as to the importance of the thing, its place in the flow of her life; if she was still having nightmares about it, she would not allow it into the rooms of her deeper self.

Now he entered the foyer of the detention center — which looked like an art gallery — a large, open area with lights hanging from thin cables in a high ceiling, and paintings on the walls in little splashes of light. The front desk was in one corner opposite the doorway, and behind it two men in uniform sat talking about football.

"Excuse me," Connally said.

One of the men looked at him, and seemed to be considering the face.

"I'd like to see the prisoner Mark Hughes."

"So would a lot of other people," the man said.

Connally waited for him to explain, but he simply stared. "Is Mark Hughes being held here?"

"He is."

"What do I have to do to see him?"

"You a relative?"

"No."

"A reporter?"

"I'm the one who got him caught."

The two men exchanged glances. "You can put in a request to see him. If you're not a doctor or with the police department, it's really just a matter of whether or not he wants to see you."

"All right," Connally said.

The others hesitated a moment, and then one of them, the younger of the two, went to a cabinet behind the counter and, reaching in among the stacks of pencil boxes and manila envelopes, brought out the form.

"How soon will I know if I can see him?"

"Fill it out and we'll take it upstairs," the younger one said.

As Connally wrote his name on the form, he said, "How is he doing?"

"Doing?" the older policeman asked.

"He's healing up nice," said the other. "He even gets out of bed twice a day now."

The form simply asked for name and address and phone number. Connally remembered that he would have to go back out to the car to hide the Beretta; certainly they would search him. He handed the form over to the older policeman, who stared at it a moment and then said, "You're a long way from home."

"I'm staying with my mother."

He handed the form back. "Put that address down, too."

Connally did so. And then the younger officer carried the form up the stairs behind the counter.

"I'll be back," Connally said.

"It'll be a few minutes."

He went out and got into the car, looking around at all the windows, feeling exposed, and sick. He bent down and put the Beretta under the seat, then straightened and tried to seem interested in the inside of the car, as though he were looking through the several pieces of paper on the dashboard — old bank notices Carol had put there, and here was her signature with its flourish on the last letter of his name.

Inside, the older police officer was sitting alone with a magazine open before him. He looked up when Connally came in, but said nothing. Connally went to the chairs along the wall and took a seat. The light poured down in the open space of the lobby, and from somewhere came the sound of a radio voice — someone, a woman, talking about farm commodities and markets. Hog futures. He picked up a magazine and began turning the pages. There were ads for movies, pictures of movie war, blazing rifles and explosions. He closed the magazine and watched as four people came in and walked over to the counter to ask for the form. They were apparently from the same family, two men and two women, and one of the women held a baby. They all went to the other side of the lobby while one of them worked to fill out the form. He was the oldest, and he wrote with a stiff, arthritic effort, holding the pencil so tightly that his knuckles turned white.

"Connally?"

The younger officer had come down, and was standing behind the counter again. He still held the form Connally had filled out. "No luck," he said as Connally approached.

"I'm sorry?"

"You're out of luck today."

"I don't understand."

"He doesn't want to see anybody."

"Did you say who I was?"

"I did."

"And that's all he said?"

The younger policeman nodded.

"Did he remember me?"

"He asked if you were another doctor, and I told him who you were, and that's what he said. He said he doesn't want to see anybody today."

•

In the little fenced yard behind the building, a group of prisoners in heavy jackets were playing basketball while some stood around and smoked. Pulling the car around to head back into the city, Connally saw that at the edge of the basketball court in the shade, someone sat in a wheelchair, a blanket over his knees. He stopped the car. It was difficult to distinguish the features of the face from this distance, but then, as the man put one hand to his mouth and wiped across his lips, Connally knew it was Hughes. He knew it without reason and certainly, with a chilly, tidal rushing in his blood. The men playing basketball were a blur moving across his field of vision, and there was the calm, interested, opaque countenance of the killer, the young, quite ordinary face, the face of a boy watching a basketball game. Connally sat staring, and the wind moved the skeletal shade of the street, changed the quality of the light on the tussling and struggling shapes on the court, and some part of him was wondering at the simple, awful fact of the thing: a person starts out to complete an ordinary daily task, worried about money, worried about a sour stomach, worried about babies and work and growing children and all the vague dissatisfactions, looking forward to some pleasure or peace and entertaining all the expectations and requirements, all the longing for love, for a little beauty, for the acts of kindness, the caresses and kisses — and in ten terrible minutes someone else, for no discernible reason, or for reasons too specific to understand — politics or ideology or the old terrible repetition of what was remembered or coveted or hated — someone, a stranger, canceled everything out, stopped it all with a gunshot to the base of the skull.

He parked the car, reached under the seat for the Beretta, put it in his coat, and got out. It was colder. The wind stung his face. He crossed the street and climbed the small grassy incline to the tall fence, clutching the Beretta in his coat pocket, feeling himself drawn to the use of it. When he came to the fence the basketball players paused to stare at him. Some of the smokers moved aside to watch him, and a guard, a heavyset man in uniform, called from the door of the building.

"Move on, sir. You, there."

Hughes was now wheeling along the edge of the court, toward the fence, but he wasn't looking at Connally.

"No trespassing, there."

And now Hughes did look.

"Excuse me," Connally said, gripping the pistol in his pocket.

The face registered something like recognition.

"I got your letter," Connally said.

The guard had stepped out and was coming along the fence. "Hey!"

"I'm leaving," Connally told him, bringing his hands, empty, out of the coat pockets.

And then Hughes spoke. "Listen, man, I didn't know it was going to happen, okay? I wish none of it happened."

Connally had started down the hill, and he stopped and turned. The guard reached the fence. "Sir, you keep going or I'm going to put you under arrest."

Hughes called to him. "The answer's in Jesus, man. I'm trying to ask his forgiveness. I didn't mean to hurt anybody. It just got away from me, man." The voice gave way. There was tremendous suffering in it.

Connally went back to the car and got in, drove up to the end of the block, waited a few moments, then turned around and came back. In the yard everything had returned to normal. The men were tossing the basketball around, some with cigarettes in their mouths. A couple of them had taken off their coats. Others were leaning against the red brick wall whose windows were barred and thickly glassed. A sign near the corner said COMMUNICATION WITH PRISONERS STRICTLY PROHIBITED.

In the shade of the detention center yard, Mark Hughes put one trembling hand to his mouth and took something off the tip of his tongue. Then he ran the hand along the thigh of his blanketed left leg, and looked off at the windows of the building. In that instant, his eyes seemed to be searching for where the harm might come from. There was something frightened and helpless in the look, the eyes brimming, and perhaps when he was a child, someone beat him with a cane or put a boot in his groin, perhaps someone dragged him around a little room with blinding windows, pulling his arm out of the socket, someone big, shouting for him to shut up, shut up, stop the crying, and the crying forcing its way out of him as if from another source, even as the blows kept falling.

Connally watched as two policemen came out and wheeled Mark Hughes back into the building. He had brought the Beretta out of his coat and set it on the seat beside him, and now he put it back, tucking a fold of the coat over it and beginning to cry. He wanted to go home now, and he had no idea where that might be.

He drove to an empty field north of the city — a fallow black expanse — and headed out into the middle of it. Walking was difficult for the unevenness of the ground, with its clods of earth and its stones. He came to a relatively smooth place and halted. Carol would have the baby, and if Connally was there, wouldn't the awful pattern be repeated? It seemed to him now that everything had already been set in motion, before he was old enough to remember it clearly. High up, crows wheeled and turned. The sky was bright blue. The wind sent small spirals of dust up and made him shiver. This was all there was now, this field. He looked around himself. In the distance was the roof of a house, small as a toy. He brought the Beretta out and took the safety off and waited.

•

Carol watched from the passenger window of the new pickup truck as her father and mother walked up the sunny sidewalk to the doorway of Grace's apartment. They looked like a couple. He had his hand in the middle of her back, as if to guide her. Grace had wanted to spend some time in the apartment, cleaning and straightening things, watering her plants. Carol and her father were going to spend the day together. He wanted to take her for a drive in the new truck. Neither of the women felt quite right about the level of his enthusiasm, though they had only hinted at it with each other. Theodore was too confident and glad, like a little boy with a new gadget to play with, Carol said, meaning to tease.

Now she watched her mother lean up and kiss him on the cheek, and she thought of herself and Charles in the mornings, making love, taking a long time getting started, murmuring to each other about their days and about various people they knew; it was difficult to imagine that they could ever work their way back to some middle ground between intimacy and distance, as Grace and Theodore so obviously had.

Grace called her name, waved, then stepped inside and closed the door, as final as shutting off a light. Theodore turned and walked briskly back.

"So," he said, getting into the truck. "What'll it be?" He was already shifting gears. He raced the engine a little, gazed with an appreciative grin at the polished wood-grain look of the dashboard.

"Dad," she said.

"See the way the light makes the wood color come out, honey? Just the way it was when you were small."

"I think I remember," she said.

"It's going to be a lovely morning," he said.

"I hope so."

It was clear that her parents were quite used to the situation: Charles gone, Carol depending on them again.

"Well," Theodore said, easing into traffic, leaning out the window and looking back. He had been driving for forty years, and he still used hand signals whenever he could, still refused to trust the rearview mirror; and, driving, he sat hunched far forward in the seat, both hands gripping the wheel. He looked like what he was: an older man doing a very cautious job of driving a pickup truck. They went on in the morning's traffic, toward the Potomac.

Carol had a memory of sitting next to him in the big blue pickup like this one, a sunny day in 1973 when she was nine years old. They were riding through the crowded streets of the middle of town, and he was talking too fast, a stream of words she couldn't quite get, about the destruction of the government. A lot of people in high places were going to jail. Her mother was somewhere waiting for them both. They were late. Theodore talked on and on, his hands holding the wheel tight, his body hunched in that way he had of always seeming to be straining to keep himself seated there. He went on about the fall of kings, and she heard a familiar urgency in his voice. All her young life, she'd had the feeling that she was being prepared for something: there had been times when everything felt like school, except that there was something faintly elegiac about it, too. Carol, in her early teens, suspected that her parents might be harboring some serious medical fact about her.

Now, riding in the truck, she said, "Was the first truck new, too?"

"Nineteen sixty," he said.

"I remember it as brand-new, somehow."

"It had a hundred seventy-two thousand miles on it."

A moment later, he said, "You know, you might give Martin a call."

"Why would I want to do that? I did my time in the Marines."

"Aren't you still friendly?"

"Unlike you and Grace, we haven't kept up a good post-marital relationship."

"I know you still hear from him now and then."

"No," Carol said. "Not in months."

"Well, maybe he's waiting for you to call him or something."

"This is ridiculous," she said. "I'm not going to call Martin. I can't believe you could suggest such a thing."

They were quiet for a minute.

"Where're we going?" she said.

"Well, I thought we might go to the Corcoran Gallery and look around."

"I can't do a lot of walking."

"Right," he said.

She sat back in the seat, feeling obscurely satisfied, as if the prospect of an hour or so in the orderly halls of a museum were a solution of a kind. With a little pulse of exhaustion, she thought of Charles in Chicago, and then was trying to clear her mind, resolving to get on with her life, to make all the preparations for the arrival of the baby, and to do so with the assumption that Charles would not return. Her father hummed softly, needy in his own way.

Now he said, "I guess they'll just flunk Charles out."

"They'll give him withdrawals. But he has to sign the forms."

"In my day, they flunked you if you didn't go to class."

"Let's not go into it," Carol said, "okay?"

"I got fired once while I was hospitalized. There never has been much patience for psychological difficulty."

During his several stays in the psychiatric ward, he had refused to allow any name for his illness but fatigue. And even the doctors — the only ones with whom he would speak in the deeps of his hysteria — were careful around him, since in fact he always did show improvement with rest, with time away from the stream of things in the life he lived every day: a retired liquor salesman living on interest from an inheritance emanating from the death of his father thirty-one years ago. For the past two years he had been maintaining himself with small daily doses of Librium. His spirits were generally good, though he was often prone to bouts of hypochondria and anxiety — products, he would bravely and good-naturedly point out, of a morbid imagination and old age: after all, he was almost a decade past the age at which his own father had died of heart failure.

"So what do you think?" he said now.

"You said we'd go to the gallery."

"So I did."

She had the feeling he'd meant something else. But he was simply staring out, concentrating on the traffic in front of them. The highway wound to the east and north, through quiet residential neighborhoods, and then gave way to an open expanse of shops and gas stations and fast-food joints. They crested a hill, and for a moment, in the distance, Washington was visible through a blue haze.

"Pretty," her father said.

It seemed to her that he had always had an uncomplicated way of appreciating things, and of assuming others appreciated them, too. For all his illnesses, he possessed an aspect of simple acceptance about so many things: love of country, of one's heritage; the necessity of certain kinds of sacrifice in public matters, matters of duty; he never complained about taxes or tried to cut corners in any civic circumstance; he was active in local politics, sat on several city boards and planning committees. He was a thirty-five-year working Democrat, and he believed in things. His mental troubles had stopped him from being more engaged — his services were often more than people wanted from him, given what they knew of his history — but he enjoyed the respect and affection of those who really knew him. There was a child-like gentleness about him, and it appeared to come out of a sort of peacefulness, a well of patient, quiet thought, as if he spent all his time thinking about how much he loved the beautiful and abundant world. He seemed to work at rightly savoring it all, but then gradually things would begin to slip toward mania; and even so, his collapses had always seemed to his daughter to have been an aberration of the moment: injuries, accidental trip-wires igniting somewhere in his soul.

"This difficulty Charles is having —"

"Yes," she said.

"Is it because people made so much of him?"

"No."

"He seemed bothered by it."

"It's something else," Carol said. "He's afraid of himself, some way."

"You mean he's afraid of his mind."

Her father, more than anyone she knew, understood what that fear was like. "Yes," she said, "but there's more."

"I'm listening," her father said.

"He doesn't want this baby." She managed to get this out without breaking down.

"Did he tell you that?"

She turned to look at him. "As a matter of fact, yes, he did."

"I'm sorry, I don't mean to pry."

"No," she said. "I didn't mean to sound short."

"Well," he said, "this other thing — does it have to do with his idea that he didn't do anything heroic?"

"We really haven't talked about this. I mean, there wasn't much I could ever get from him about it." Speaking these words, she had a rueful moment of perceiving all the ways in which they were true. And the sense of him as being in the past, as being someone about whom she was speaking in the past tense, sent a chill through her.

"You get to feeling different from everybody," her father said.

"Dad."

"It's odd, I know. But you get to feeling like a stranger. Everybody else appears to be so happy, you know, and satisfied with everything. It's like everybody knows some secret you can't know. They've all got it figured except you. And that isn't exactly it, either. You just find yourself wishing you could be as calm as the whole rest of the world seems to be, and then you get to wondering about yourself a little, and that's all it takes. A little window of doubt opens up and everything comes rushing through it, sort of. I'd like to talk to Charles about this."

"He's in Chicago," Carol said without inflection.

Her father left a pause. Then cleared his throat.

"I'm sorry," she said.

He sighed. "I guess I didn't think enough about how all this might be troubling *you*."

"That's not it," she said. "I just don't know anymore. I know he went through something terrible and all that — and he went through things as a child. Awful things. But it was like he didn't want to get over it — the way he kept dwelling on it."

"Maybe he couldn't help it."

"Oh, let's stop talking about him like this. He's just — he's with his mother in Chicago. It's not like he's — I don't want to talk about this anymore."

"With me," Theodore said, "it was always something a little like, well, dreaming. I'd get the willies first, see. And of course your mother would see it coming. I'd get sleepless and things would get kind of . . . blissful. I had all this power and enthusiasm."

It occurred to Carol that in her memory some of these times, times when he was flying, had been filled with excitement and things to do. Her own strongest recollection of him was of a boyish energy and a willingness to indulge her in anything she wished.

"It was false enthusiasm, of course," Theodore said.

"I don't remember it as false."

"Sweet," he said.

They were quiet for a time. For Carol, it was pleasant just to sit still with him.

"Well," he said finally, "things'll come around."

"I'm not so hopeful," she said. The words surprised her.

"Do you think you might move back home?"

"Oh, Dad, I don't know. I don't know what's going to happen. Please, let's talk about something else."

"I'm sorry," he said.

"And don't apologize. I'm tired of apologies."

After a little pause, he said, "Of course you're right."

"I'd like to get through the day without another mention of Charles and his trouble," Carol said.

At the art gallery, it was her father who grew tired, and had to rest on a stone bench in the atrium, near the fountain. He said, "I'll just sit here and watch the colors in the water." She sat with him, holding a paper bag of postcards she had bought in the gallery bookstore. The water seemed alive in its lovely cascading shapes, and for the moment, staring at it, she felt quiet inside. But then she saw that her father was turning pale, the bones of his face showing whiter, the veins in his forehead standing out. He was breathing through his mouth, his hands tight on his knees. "Little out of breath," he said. "You must be tired, too."

She wasn't. They hadn't walked that far.

He took her hand. "You know, this baby will have no memory of me at all."

"Stop it," she said.

"It's true."

"You don't know that."

"Well, honey — of course I do."

She gazed at the fountain. There were only a few patrons this morning — women mostly, strolling through on their way to the rooms. Beyond the fountain, several people were seated at the circular white tables of a café, sipping coffee and reading pamphlets describing the various exhibits. Carol had picked up a few of them from a stand in the long hallway leading to the atrium, and she opened one of them now, pretending an interest in it while her father sighed and seemed to grow more breathless. She looked at him with his bony, blue-veined hands tight in his lap. There was so much to worry about. In the bookstore she'd seen a postcard reproduction of Goya's *The Third of May* — men falling under the rifle fire of soldiers, the one man in the center of the painting's light holding his arms up not in surrender but in horror and questioning — and gazing at it had caused a stirring under her heart: she saw her husband as he must have been with the gun held to his face. Everything seemed connected somehow to the little portrayal on the card.

Her father leaned forward slightly.

"Are you all right?" she asked.

"I don't think I can get up," he said.

She stood before him. "Dad?"

"I can't get up." He was trying. And now he lay down on the bench. "Better call someone," he said. "Something's happening." He closed his eyes.

"Daddy," she said. "Please."

"Don't be afraid," he said.

She turned and called for help. Perhaps she had screamed, she didn't know. A pair of nuns had come through the atrium and they rushed to her. One of them took Theodore's hand.

"Sir, can you hear me?"

"He's breathing," said the other. "I'll call an ambulance."

Carol lifted her father's head and held it in her lap. "Daddy?"

"I don't think he can hear you," the first nun said. "I think he's had a stroke."

They waited together for the ambulance to arrive. Several people walked through, and some hesitated. It was just the nun holding the man's limp hand, the woman sitting with his head in her lap. The man could be sleeping. He seemed quite at peace. And then he was partially conscious.

"Grace?" he said.

"It's me," said Carol.

But he had gone under again.

The ambulance men arrived. Carol recognized one of them as the kind young man who had spoken so gently to her in Dr. Wilder's office. He was a picture of concentration, working on her father, checking his vital signs, getting him on oxygen, then lifting him onto the gurney.

"You with him?" he said to the nun. Then he looked at Carol.

"He's my father."

They went out into the cold sun, where the ambulance was parked with its strobe flashing. The two men put him inside, then turned and helped Carol climb in.

"You all right?" the young man said.

"Please," Carol said, "is he going to be all right?"

"We'll do everything we can."

In the rushing and swaying of the ambulance, she held his hand. It seemed to her now that regarding her private life he had always been almost tentative with her, as if he were doubtful about what was called for, how to proceed. She remembered being in her room and hearing him knock, quite shyly, on her door. There had been times when she found it hard to respect him for his diffidence with her, his lack of command of her mother; he seemed always worried about the consequences of everything, where intimacy was concerned.

"Is he worse?" she said to the medic.

"Seems stable," he said.

"I have to call my mother."

He nodded.

Carefully, she caressed her father's forehead. "Please be all right," she said.

At the hospital the news was slow in coming. Theodore was in surgery, and it would take some time. Grace had driven over, and had already argued with one of the nurses about the lack of information. They stayed through the afternoon, watching the sky cloud up and begin to rain, the windows of the emergency room waiting area running with rivulets of water, and Carol began to know her father was dead. It felt like knowledge, like a logical progression of trouble, one thing following on another, emanating somehow — in the weird turning of the last few weeks — from the awful incident in Chicago. She sat in a chair by the rainy windows and thought about this, and believed it, even as she knew intellectually that it could not be so. It *felt* so. She tried to think of other things, and tried to pray, and then she was standing at the windows looking out at the sheets of rain, believing him dead, her father, all his strife over, and she remembered — it felt exactly like memory, as if the fact of it were far away in time — that she was, however precariously, bearing another life. The idea exhausted her. She turned and looked at the walls of the waiting room, with its stretched-canvas appearance and its bad paintings.

Here was Grace, staring distractedly at the waiting room television, the chatter and jangle of quiz shows and soap operas, waiting for news of her ex-husband's death. "You know," she said, without taking her eyes from the television, "we were actually talking about getting back together."

Carol waited for her to go on.

"I wasn't so averse to the idea, either."

"Oh, Mama," Carol said, going to her, beginning to cry.

Grace put her arms around her. "Poor baby, you've had a bad time of it."

They remained that way for a while.

"Do you think you ought to call Charles?"

After a moment, Carol sat straight, wiping her eyes with the backs of her hands. "No."

"Honey," Grace said, "you know I don't like to meddle

in things. But no matter how scared and confused you two are, I wish you could both step back and see how much you love each other. It's obvious to anyone. And you ought to be able to overcome other things."

"I don't want to talk about Charles now," Carol told her.

Finally a pair of doctors came through the double doors at the end of the hall, talking in low tones together. They parted, and one of them approached Carol and her mother.

"He's resting. He's going to do fine."

"Was it a stroke?"

The doctor nodded. Apparently he'd had bad skin as an adolescent; his face was pocked under the cheekbones. "We were lucky. It's relatively mild. But he's going to need therapy for some motor functions."

"But he's going to be okay?"

"The prognosis is very good," the doctor said. He took Grace by the elbow and the two of them moved off toward the doors. Carol followed a couple of steps behind, feeling strangely on the outside of it all, an onlooker.

"Can we see him?" her mother asked.

"Very briefly."

Grace began to cry. "I know, we have to let him rest," she said. At the end of this hall was a crossing hall, with light in it from the double doorways out of the hospital, and as they came past the opening, Carol saw her husband at the admissions window, talking with the woman there.

"Charles?" she said.

He turned and came forward, looking from one to the other of them, his face registering surprise and consternation. "No one was at home anywhere, and I thought maybe you'd had another spotting episode," he said.

"It's Theodore," said Carol, and walked into his arms. He smelled of the outside; he hadn't shaved, and his eyes were red and glazed-looking.

Grace was telling him. ". . . going to need help. We've been here since this morning."

They all went in and looked at Theodore in the intensive care unit. He lay very still; the hollows of his face seemed deeper. The doctors had put him in an oxygen tent. His hands, lying alongside his body, were the wrong color, and there were tubes running out of the backs of them.

"Oh, God," Grace murmured.

Outside, they stood in the chilly wind and were awkward. Grace decided to go alone back to the house and collect some things for him, and Carol found herself protesting, wanting her to accompany them home first.

"What about *your* stuff?" she said.

Grace frowned and seemed puzzled. "I can get that anytime." She looked over Carol's shoulder at Charles, who had gone to wait in the parking lot. The Honda had dried mud splattered along its sides, and twin arcs of it on the windshield. "Go on," Grace said. "I'll be fine."

"The pickup is still at the gallery."

"I'll take care of everything."

Carol hesitated.

"Go on."

Charles opened the car door for her, then carefully closed it when she had settled inside. She watched him through the smears of dirt on the windshield as he walked around and then stopped to wave at Grace, who tapped her horn twice, pulling away.

He had opened the door and got in, was starting the car. It made its usual hesitation and complaint. He tried again. Carol was gazing at the side of his face.

Finally she said, "Tell me."

"I don't know where to start," he said, backing out. "I was standing alone in the middle of this field, and my mind was made up about everything. I had a gun, and I'd seen

Mrs. Wu and I'd even talked to Mark Hughes and I was as bad as ever —"

"You had a gun!"

"This old Beretta of Lee Southworth's. I was carrying it to feel safe, and then I was going to just — get out altogether."

She stared at him.

He took a breath. "I was afraid I'd hurt you. And — what was done to me — I — it all came loose inside. I was afraid for what I might do to the baby when it was here. And I was going to make sure it never happened."

"Oh, God, Charles."

"I was. I was going to stop it right there."

She waited.

"I want the baby now. I'll go see doctors if I have to. I'll be a good father, I swear it. I swear it. When I was a kid, I'd see other kids and their families, and I was so envious of them all the time, and I swore that one day, somehow, I'd make that for myself. I'd do whatever I had to do to make it happen."

She moved over a little on the seat, and he put his arm around her. "Oh, God," she said. "I hate this."

His arm tightened on her shoulder. "The gun wouldn't fire." There was a kind of hysterical disbelief in his voice. "This old thing Southworth's been carrying around to protect himself with. Completely useless."

"You actually tried to do it?"

"I tried to fire it into the ground first. I don't think I could've used it. I don't know what I would've done."

"But you were thinking of it?"

He looked at her.

"Oh, God. Can't we ever get past this?"

"Don't," he said. "Don't cry."

He drove back to the house. She stayed at his side, and she thought of all the times she had been like this with him, held by him while he drove with one hand. She wanted to believe things would begin to get better now, but there was the shadow of what he had told her. In front of the house he hesitated a moment, staring at it.

"Charles?" she said.

"It's okay," he told her, and got out of the car. As they went up the walk, he was inwardly searching for the sense of relief he had felt, discovering that she was all right. He had driven most of the night and all morning to get back, and the whole way home he had gone over the thing: he couldn't quite identify what brought about the change, yet he felt obscurely less afraid inside. It was only a little increment, the smallest shift. But he was holding on to it.

"I'd better lie down," Carol said when they were inside. "I think I'm bleeding again."

He helped her into the bedroom, which smelled like a sickroom. The bed was rumpled where she'd only partly made it. "I have to use the bathroom," she said.

He waited outside, standing in the hallway between the rooms. On the wall here were pictures of the two of them taken in the first summer of their marriage; he gazed at the faces and thought of being somewhere out of the shadow of violence. She opened the door and supported herself on the frame. "I'm not bleeding."

"Good," he said, thinking carefully of the pictures on the wall. That uncomplicated summer, so far away.

"I still better stay down. It doesn't feel all that steady, and it's been a scary day."

He helped her into bed. "Do you want the TV?"

"No."

"Warm?"

"Don't go anywhere."

"No." He sat at the foot of the bed, facing the doorway and the hallway, with its discouraging wall of photographs of their once happy lives, and he had a sudden sense of recognition, that even with everything he had suffered through since the shootings, he was only at the beginning — he had only just now reached the borderline of the changed life he would lead. It filled him with dread, and he reached over and took her hand.

"I thought I might not see you again," she said.

Her voice startled him a little. "I didn't know what I'd find," he said. "I was just running — running."

"I thought you were leaving me."

"No," he said. "I love you."

"I love you too."

Presently she said, "Doesn't that count for anything?"

"Oh, honey," he said. "It's got to."

"I'm afraid," she told him.

"Me too." He tried to smile.

"Are you very tired?"

"I stopped and rested a little."

"You look tired."

"I've been through it."

"Tell me," she said.

•

He had gone to Holy Gate, to the little cemetery just east of Chicago where his father was buried. An acre of stones on the other side of a hedge. The entryway was an arc of ivy on a trellis. His father's grave was a few paces from a family vault. Connally stood over it. He had been here once before, with his mother, during one of his visits from the Air Force — he had asked to see it. This time, alone, he knelt at the stone and read the name and the dates: CONNALLY 1900–1981. The ground here was almost bare; the sparse grass had been matted down by rain and snow and wind.

"All right," Connally said aloud. "It was done to you,

too. I don't care about it. I hope you can hear me. I don't care. You could've tried. You could've worked at it a little. And I hate you for not being better than you were given. I hate you for it. I hope you can hear me, goddam you. I hope you're suffering somewhere and you can hear me."

He stood. He was crying again. The wind blew, carrying with it the smell of the city, the feel of grit and coming rain. He felt empty, and for what seemed the first time in months he could breathe out fully, like a sigh of relief.

He returned to his mother's apartment to find Lee Southworth sitting at the table again, this time with a pitcher of martinis. They had been celebrating their decision not to change anything, according to Southworth. "Marriage is out the window, as it should be for an old guy like me," he said. Then he held up his glass. "Young man, I detest the patina of virtue on you today. I demand that you have a drink with us."

"Where's my mother?"

"I believe she's using the facilities."

He walked over and handed Southworth the Beretta. "It doesn't work."

"Doesn't work?" The old man held the thing up and looked down the barrel. "Seems okay."

"Well, try to pull the trigger, Lee."

"Not in here." The other man's expression was full of alarm.

"I took the clip out."

Lee checked the empty chamber, then held the gun to the floor and pulled the trigger. The gun clicked. "It works."

"Then it's the clip," Connally told him. "It wouldn't fire."

The old man took the clip and stared at it. "Damn. Clip's empty."

"You didn't know it?"

"Who or what did you try to fire it at?"

"I tried to fire it into the ground."

"I'm getting old," Mr. Southworth said. "I can't keep up with things like I used to."

Connally's mother came out of the bathroom, and let out a little scream. "Where'd you get that?"

Southworth put the Beretta away. "Pay no attention."

"I saw it. I'm not going to pretend I didn't see it."

"I'll take it upstairs, Tina."

She waited, and finally he rose, moving slowly out of the room. He turned and waved, and then was gone.

"I'm going home," Connally said to her.

"Then you found what you were looking for?"

"Not exactly."

"Well?" she said.

"It'll have to do." He couldn't return her gaze.

She walked over and put her arms around him. "You know, when I started out — when you were born — I was never happier. Before or since. I wanted to be perfect. Perfect. I wanted to make a family."

"I went out to his grave," Connally said.

She waited.

"Drove right to it."

"I never go there anymore."

"You loved him, didn't you?"

She took a moment to answer. "I wanted a family. I didn't know how to go about it. He'd beg me not to leave him."

"I want a family, too," he said, trying not to break down.

"Well, and you'll have one now."

"And you're a hero," Lee Southworth said, coming into the apartment.

"Lee, for God's sake."

"It's all right," Connally said. "Maybe I'm going to have to be."

"Just remember," said Mr. Southworth in that stentorian

tone, as though he were holding up a drink, beginning to make a toast — "I forgot what I was going to ask you to remember."

"Lee, please go home for a while."

"Oh, I have it — remember that there can be more sheer bravery in just simply pausing to pet a cat, or in changing a baby's diaper, than in all the wars and car chases and foiling the bank robbery. Who was it said that?" He smiled, then put one finger to his forehead. "Well, it's all in here."

"Lee."

"I'm on my way," Mr. Southworth said, turning drunkenly in the doorway. He closed it with a bang, and then knocked twice and opened it. "I hope you'll overlook my clumsiness."

Then he closed it again, this time with the care of someone worried about any noise at all.

"Well?" Mrs. Connally said after a pause.

"Goodbye," he told her.

"Come and see us?"

"Yes," he said.

"Don't say it so casually. Because I understand you, son."

"All right," he said. "We will come and see you."

"Forgive me?"

He kissed her forehead. "Don't."

"No. Please. Say you forgive me?"

"For what?" he said.

"Oh." She seemed about to cry again. "You know, for everything."

He kissed her cheek. They had come back, then, to the old relation; and he had learned, he knew, all he was ever to learn about her and the strange man who had been his father. And then he gathered his things and walked away from her, out into the afternoon sun, already making up his mind that when enough time had passed, when he had learned the way to say it precisely enough, he would tell Carol how it happened that he was standing in that black field in the bright sun, waiting for the resolve to go through with killing himself, and how it was as he tried to fire the Beretta into the ground, wanting to hear the report, wanting to look at the hole the bullet made, and how the thing wouldn't fire, and he checked the safety and tried twice more but was unable to budge the trigger. It might as well have been soldered tight. And he would tell her that it was then that he started to laugh — a bitter laugh at first, a laugh crazy with bitterness, and yet this feeling that he had done something so stupid rose in him, the idiotic gyration he must've performed, aiming the thing at the ground and wincing, a timid man expecting an explosion, and nothing at all happening. He would tell her how he even thought of working on it, looking around himself for anything he might use as a makeshift tool, something to pry the jammed trigger loose, growing angrier and angrier, feeling the desperation rise in him, stopping thought, stopping everything but the bitter sound out of his mouth, as he dropped to his knees, then lay back, stretching out among the black clods, laughing bitterly, bitterly, with a kind of immolating, macabre resentment until it was impossible to tell whether he was laughing or crying. And if he could find the words, he would say that, even so, in the next moment something in that paroxysm shook through his soul, that it was as if he were in the field of the world, completely cut off from everything, with the idea occurring to him that he could work on staying alive, too — that he had wanted to stay alive so badly in the convenience store — and how, remembering this, the full weight of the incident came down on him all over again as though it were just happening, the blood and the confusion and the terror, even the sounds, rushing over him with a surprising, almost random-feeling exhilaration, and the small hope that he could strive to be free, could try to stand up to it and to his own past, and he said aloud, "I'm one of the ones it was done to," crying, hearing it said, sending it off into the air like a kind of testimony, thinking of his father and his father's father — how far back it went, the brutal chain of beaten sons — lying there on his back, still holding the useless pistol in his hand, his own voice seeming to come from somewhere far, far away, sputtering the words, repeating them, the whole wide blue sky stretching above him with its smudge of a daymoon and its faint ribbony patches of cirrus, incorporeal as thoughts. "I'm one of the ones it was done to."

He would tell her that when the crying died down, he was just lying there among the clods of black earth in the middle of that field, which was peaceful again, with only the sounds of its life going on and with the breezes blowing across it, carrying unexpected balmy currents, little pockets of sunny warmth like the faintest traces of spring.

And he would tell her how that felt, too.

October 1988–March 1991
Fairfax / Broad Run, Virginia